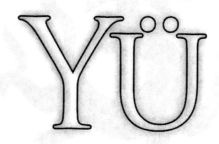

A ROSS LAMOS MYSTERY

JOY SHAYNE LAUGHTER

Open Books
PRESS

Published by Open Books Press, USA
www.openbookspress.com

An imprint of Pen & Publish, Inc.
Bloomington, Indiana
(812) 837-9226
info@PenandPublish.com

www.PenandPublish.com

ISBN: 978-0-9845751-4-5
LCCN:

This book is printed on acid free paper.

Printed in the USA

DEDICATION

To my Significant Mother, Marjorie, for all our
lifetimes of caring for one another.

CONTENTS

[The sword of the Son of Heaven] has Yen-ch'i and Shih-ch'ang for its point; Ch'i and Mount T'ai for its edge; Tsin and Wei for its back; Chou and Sung for its hilt; Han and Wei for its sheath. It is embraced by the wild tribes all around; it is wrapped up in the four seasons; it is bound round by the Sea of Po, and its girdle is the enduring hills. It is regulated by the five elements; its wielding is by means of punishments and kindness; its unsheathing is like that of the yin and yang; it is held fast in the spring and summer; it is put in action in the autumn and winter. When it is thrust forward, there is nothing in front of it; when lifted up, there is nothing above it; when laid down, there is nothing below it; when wheeled round, there is nothing left on any side of it; above, it cleaves the floating clouds; and below, it penetrates to every division of the earth. Let this sword be used once, and the princes are all reformed; the whole kingdom submits. This is the sword of the Son of Heaven.

—Chuang Tzu, 369-286? BC

BOOK I:

THE EMPEROR AND THE CONCUBINE

Someone, Somebody

Every passion borders on chaos, that of the collector on the chaos of memory.

—Walter Benjamin,
"Ich pack meine Bibliothek aus"

In some countries and among certain classes, talk of beauty is shocking unless the speaker is homosexual: then concessions are made.

—Denis Donohue,
Speaking of Beauty

1.
FAKES

The stones wanted to speak.

Three jades gleamed on the black velvet-backed tray. They were not carved by machines. My lens showed gentle irregularities, like waves on calm water. Power tools and sanders would have created perfectly sharp edges and perfectly flat surfaces. I had examined hundreds of such quickly-shaped jades, mass-produced droppings that were as bland as TV listings. These, adrift on the velvet, were literature—dense, delicious, rare. They had submitted to their designs slowly, only gradually giving in to the human hand rubbing with sand and a bamboo stick.

They wanted to *speak*.

But they had no business being here. They should never have come in to a gallery at all, not even a gallery as respected as Albert Jarro's.

When they first spilled out of the woman's scruffy, mismatched boxes onto the velvet, I had felt the room begin to spin. *It can't be, it can't be … they're Han, Han Dynasty —*

Albert Jarro himself had whirled away from the table in disgust as soon as the jades lay revealed. "Those are fakes!" he had spat in an instant fury. I had bent over to get my lens and loupe from their drawer, a fast way to get my head down low and take a few deep breaths. *Did I see right? Are they really? Han Dynasty?*

Albert Jarro had snarled "Fakes!" on his way out through the heavy curtain, into the back room, as if the jades' carrier, the woman, had vanished, and this was all my fault. "Expensive fakes! You'll see, Ross. You will see!" The backwash of his exit left me embarrassed and vulnerable in front of the woman, as the curtain billowed and settled. The judgment had come too suddenly, too violently, even for Albert's finely tuned senses. From the smile she just barely suppressed, I could tell the woman knew it as well as I did.

I set my loupe aside and laid my hands flat on the counter, so the woman wouldn't see them shaking. I didn't want to speak, not yet. Did this woman *know*? What she had casually taken from her shapeless cloth shoulder bag, then from a cheap silk drawstring purse, and then from mismatched jewelry boxes, should have gone right into a museum's guarded store-room. Not spread upon a velvet-lined tray, in a room just off a renowned gallery, within sight of a busy street. I beat down the urge to grab the tray and run after Albert—*Quick, hide them!*

The woman didn't look like a grave robber, or an interna-tional antiquities thief. She looked like somebody's artistic aunt, with forthright green eyes full of cool curiosity. Her clothes were colorful and shapeless, like her shoulder bag. She was tall, with long, heavy, honey-gold hair frosting to silver at the crown and flying about in untidy wisps. Her straight back made her seem even taller, which irritated me. I always stand straight, myself, to gain some extra height. She had no need to.

And oh, the way she was *watching* me. Hands folded, head tilted slightly to one side, like a big tall bird. A blue heron, look-ing down her beak at me. She was not dazzled by the gallery, or Albert, or me, or any of it, especially not me. The whole post-modern urban enchantment I had worked into my profession-al persona felt ridiculous in front of her. Ordinarily, someone who has no idea of an object's worth is dismissive, or anxious, ashamed of their ignorance, and for some reason my golden skin, puppyish black eyes, prematurely-gray hair, hip glasses and impeccable suits are comforting. I am a storybook charac-ter, a guide in the shadowlands, full of reliable wisdom. This woman in front of me had a fully functioning internal compass, thank you very much, so she just stood there and waited. Look-ing at me, not the jades.

This was a test, I told myself. I had been Albert Jarro's right hand for four years, and Albert Jarro had left the room.

I flexed my fingers, which always helps me relax. I tapped the stones lightly, shifting them just so across the black velvet, revealing their every angle. They were nephrite, with its unmis-takable fibrous texture, which fit the ancient style of carving. The colors were soft and liquid, as lambent as celebrities' eyes, and each stone had been carved to wear its variegated shades as naturally as skin. There was a thumb ring, mutton-fat white with a spattering of oxide red like a trail of blood. It was archer's thumb-ring, with the extended edge that hooked the bowstring and pulled it back. The smallest jade, lying next to it, was a pendant strung with a scarlet cord. Its rich sunset-gold color glowed in the simple, almost abstract form of a turtle.

The large jade, cut in clear celery-green stone, seemed a different personality altogether. It flowered with curls and points, resolving into two pale dragons writhing around empty space. This jade was the slide piece of a sword's scabbard—a very important sword's scabbard. It had fit over the top of the sheath and the blade had slid home between the dragons, which chased one another, fangs bared, in an eternal tangling coil.

This piece, of the three, was the masterwork. The impeccable quality of the stone and the extravagant design roared *Imperial Workshops* like a trumpet call. It had—almost arrogantly—what Albert Jarro liked to call the *greatness*. This was Albert's term for the charisma that moved exquisite objects from collector to collector, personal vault to personal vault, buoyed by enormous sums of money and confidential arrangements. Only in strict exception would the *greatness* be exposed to the carnival of a public auction.

I slowed my pattering taps and peered at the stones again. Each stone had traces of the powdery white degradation that said these jades were lifted out of a tomb. The similarity of the degradations on each piece suggested that they all came from the same tomb. But none of the three—ring, pendant, scabbard slide—was a standard funerary jade, intended to preserve the deceased's life-force. They had been created for the living.

The sensation charged through my nerves again—*the stones wanted to speak*.

And the golden turtle pendant—it had not always been a pendant. Two rough patches on the back suggested that it had once been a ring. Shaving off bits of a large jade for re-cutting into beads or smaller ornaments had been a money-making tactic for centuries, so this alteration was not surprising. But my personal secret weapon was working. It knew the jades had something to tell; about the pendant it whispered, *No. No. That's not what happened. That's not it at all.*

My hands trembled, now, not from shock, but from the buzzing energy that filled my fingertips and warmed my flesh up to my elbows. If the woman hadn't been standing there, if Albert hadn't been waiting in the back room, I would have cradled each jade in my hands and let the shades of their previous owners fill me with their gossip and folly. I would eavesdrop across time. They could speak all they wanted. If the woman—

"Han Dynasty, right?" she asked.

I started, jerking my hands away from the jade. *She did know.*

She shifted the weight of her shoulder bag, without taking her eyes off me or wiping that little smile from her mouth. The loose ease of her outfit was as coolly practical as it was exotic, for her smallest movements were crisp, efficient, and sourced in a still core that was ready for anything. *I could move fast if I needed. I could kill you if I needed. I could fly.*

Her question hung in the air. Her eyes still glimmered with amusement over the uproar she had caused.

"I have to talk to Mr. Jarro," was all I could think to say. She shrugged. I picked up the tray of jades and went into the back room.

This was the office I shared with Albert Jarro. It also held the business library and a large table for shipping and receiving. Within arm's reach of Albert's desk was the room's real center of power: a floor-to-ceiling steel door with a wheel-shaped lock. The building had once been a bank. The vault was now Albert Jarro's vault. Not even his junior dealer, me, was allowed inside. In there, Albert kept the items of exalted beauty, worth millions altogether, the *greatness*, securely crated up in a kind of way-station between collectors and museums. The door caught my eye every time I entered the room, stirring a delicious mix of humility and desire.

Albert himself was up on a stepstool at the library wall beside the entry, rearranging auction catalogs as high as his plump arms could reach in his snug, dapper suit. This was his standard activity when he wanted to eavesdrop on conversation in the middle room.

"Ah-ch-ch!" Albert choked when he saw the tray, and nearly dropped his armload of catalogs. "Take those things away!" For some reason emotion always managed to dishevel what was left of his hair. I put on my best disobedient-servant-for-your-own-good expression and placed the tray on the shipping table.

"They show no signs of machine tooling," I told him. Behind my matter-of-fact tone was—what? Something chaotic, unformed. I wanted Albert to back me up on this identification. I wanted to be *positive*.

"You haven't put them under the microscope." Albert tilted his head at the hooded contraption on one end of the shipping table. Under the hood was a neat gemology microscope, tiny gripping clamps outstretched like dinosaur claws, perfect for studying the minute details of small objects. Albert had affixed a little plaque to its side: TRUST, BUT VERIFY.

"My lenses have spotted drill marks dozens of times. You've used them yourself for that."

"I doubt the new sonic drills leave marks," Albert sniffed. I shook my head and raised my hand, palm out, and waved my fingers. Albert had guessed my gift of the Touch early on; this was all I had to do to tell him that I had information the lens couldn't give.

It was the worst argument we had ever had.

Albert fell into a silence that lasted a full two minutes. First he stood on the stepstool clutching the catalogs, looking like a well-baked French pastry having a personal crisis. Then he shrugged slightly. I took the jumble of catalogs from him, and Albert stepped down to the shipping table. He inclined his head towards the jades, but that was as close as he got. Finally he ended it with a violent wave of his hand. He turned his back on me and opened an out-of-date auction catalog. I hesitated a moment, to make sure Albert had actually done it—turned his back. Yes, he was studiously flipping the catalog's pages. I picked up the tray quickly, then hesitated. Usually Albert swept past me and gently took control when someone came in holding something of real worth. I had expected him—*wanted* him— to do so again. That desire gaped sudden and cold, a hole in the solid world. I *wanted* Albert to take these stones and their story—whatever it was—away from me. And Albert was not going to do it, even though we were agreed on what the tray held: ancient treasures more than two thousand years old, one of them a masterpiece. Surely Albert had noted the scabbard slide's *greatness*. The workmanship and stone quality alone could drive the set's value up into six figures at auction. But he had turned away. He had given his junior dealer a green light to work the woman: I was to find out what she wanted, then do what was necessary to acquire the stones.

I barely felt the floor under my feet as I slowly paced across the room, the tray riding lightly in my hands.

� ✘ ✘ ✘ ✘ ✘ ✘

The stones on the tray were *yü*.

Yü means "jade" in Chinese, but to me it is more, so much more. *Yü* is an extraordinary presence—a charisma, a persona—embodied in stone. The wild mineral, changed by a human design, merges nature, history and aesthetics with a fine potency that can only be called spiritual. When I am near it, *yü* stands beside me like the parent of my true self.

Yü awakened me to beauty when I was a child. Jades filled my Filipino grandmother's earrings and necklaces and its greenish glow fascinated me. When I held them I heard a murmur in my inner ear—stories told in my grandmother's voice, and in images like a pale, remembered dream. It was several years before I realized that the young woman who looked like my father in these images was actually Ga'Ma, the gentle old woman who dried my body and hair with such tenderness after a bath. When I worked up the courage to ask her about the green stones, she smiled and taught me the Chinese word, *yü*. Even as I grew older I would still sneak into her room and open her jewel box to hold the earrings, the necklace, the bracelet, because the voice and the images sharpened and multiplied: Young Ga'Ma's romance, circa 1930s Manila. A formal party where the jewels, a gift from the beloved, were worn for the first time, making her (and me) feel grown-up and elegant, beautiful, loved. Weddings and funerals in a new country, as the girl grew old. I didn't dare tell Ga'Ma of my travels through her life. But I sat and held her hand for hours as she faded, blind and frail. I tried to make my silence tell her I knew she had been someone else, once. I tried to thank her for a gift I didn't understand.

When she was gone, all her jewelry—smuggled from Manila on her crossing, sewn into her clothes—was sold to pay down debts at the restaurants my Dad owned with his three brothers. I swallowed my teenage fury and hated all of them, hated the grease, onion, tobacco and whisky smell that clung to them, even to my melancholy, affable, non-smoking father. They knew nothing of *yü*, and I couldn't say a word. It was another layer of the silence that was already pushing me out of their world.

Silence pushed me, and *yü* led me, from Ga'Ma's bedroom into the great intermingled labyrinths of art and history. There, a riot of voices from the past rushed at me from all the objects left behind. I adapted, focused, learned to adjust the volume. I told no one about the inward voice. In private, it became a friend and a navigation device. And *yü* came to me again, in forms that were simple and extraordinary; it let me explore its complex nature in stone after stone, warming to my touch. *Yü*, the Stone of Heaven, craved by emperors, opened doors for my twinkling self. Doors to international study, sophisticated parties, luxurious bedrooms. Women were easily charmed by my looks, by my hair gone silvery-gray so early; charmed to learn that my mother was Irish and my father Filipino. The Queen of the Moon married the King of the Sun, two island deities in love, ah! It was a useful fairytale. Women knew they were safe with me. Men, they were the delicious, dangerous, confusing ones. Men, so many men, and me—we all reached for something in each other, but my Touch told me too much, every time. No matter how I tried to dial back the inward voice, sex subverted my control and there would come a moment when the gift would toss up a prank, a bitchy comment, a grenade that would fly out of my mouth, pin pulled, and when the smoke drifted away I was alone again.

Yü sent relief. I was traveling through southern China doing research for my thesis and writing the catalog for a museum exhibit. Both were going badly. One day I stood in the courtyard of a prominent Buddhist temple. My head hurt from the punishing summer sun; my eyes, throat and sinuses burned from the pollution. The rest of me throbbed with misery. My growing chain of romantic catastrophes had gained yet another link, the night before. Stupid mouth, again. I wondered why I had been put into this life: too indifferent to my Filipino heritage (according to my uncles), too golden-faced to be Irish, too openly homosexual to be Catholic, and now too *something* to even be homosexual. It was a dead end, evidently, to hope that someone would be able to read *me* so easily. I stood immobilized on the worn, baking flagstones, blind to everything … until someone patted me on the shoulder. An elderly monk, wrapped in yellow cloth, had materialized at my elbow. His smile was not too broad, not too sympathetic, but acknowledged me in sum. *I see where you are, little son.* He picked up my hand and pressed something into it. It was a wrist mala, a bracelet of prayer beads. The beads were unremarkable sandalwood, but the guru bead—the large bead where the elastic was knotted—was greenish-brown jade, drilled and carved into a filigree. The hardest stone in the world this side of a diamond, and it was full of holes. There were no stories in it, only a steady *omnpmhmomnpmhm*. Om mani padme hum. The inner mantra of the craftsman-monk who carved the stone, overlaid with the chanted repetitions of the monk who had given it.

My head cleared. My body cooled and lightened, as if a cloud had passed over the sun. I looked up—in fact a cloud had done just that. And the monk had disappeared, perhaps through a hole in the world. I slipped the mala onto my left wrist, and enjoyed the play of the silk tassel in my palm. I have worn it daily, ever since.

My thesis was accepted, I finished the museum catalog just under the deadline, I stopped running after men who hated being read like a magazine. At the opening reception for the museum show, I met the distinguished, the well-fed, the discreet Albert Jarro—and a month later moved to his city to work in his gallery. Albert had no interest in me romantically—and I had none in him—but we *communicated* very well.

He held open a door into his world and I dashed through.

And arrived at this day. This tray of three Han jades. These *yü*. Here.

A shuddering certainty filled me, the way a carnival ride begins to move. I had made it into the Albert Jarro Gallery four years ago because these jades needed me to be here.

As that irrational conviction spread through my blood, the old monk in the yellow cloth smiled at me again from another memory—what I had declared, as a child, to be my earliest memory. This declaration came before I had ever touched *yü* in Ga'Ma's jewel box. In that memory, I press my face into the carved balustrade of a staircase, hiding. I am a girl, not welcome at the scene below, where members of my large family are gathered in a courtyard lit by colorful lamps, around an elderly man wrapped in yellow, who is going to tell them something important. The old man looks up and smiles at the girl, me. No one follows his gaze—they think he is sipping from divine inspiration. But he sees me, the girl, and smiles—the same smile (I realized, mid-step, in the gallery's back room, after more than four years) that he had smiled in southern China.

A hole in the world.

Albert behind me; the woman out there; these *yü* in the tray—ring, pendant, scabbard slide, archer, turtle, dragons. All of them waiting.

I shifted the velvet curtain aside and stepped through.

𝕏 𝕏 𝕏 𝕏 𝕏 𝕏 𝕏 𝕏

At one end of the middle room were two replica Tang Dynasty armchairs and a low table. From the deep aubergine color of the walls to the subtle lighting and velvety rug, the room was my design, a lullaby of luxury. The woman was settled in one chair, at ease, just a Western American female of high natural intelligence and nothing to prove. Legs crossed, hands clasped around her knee.

Get out of my house!

I almost looked around to see who had followed me into the room. Then I caught myself—it was my inward voice, my secret weapon, speaking in an unfamiliar tone. All at once I was seized by a chill of dread.

Fortunately, four years beside Albert Jarro had given me strength for such emotional moments. With an indrawn breath and an inward shove I locked that dread in a cupboard somewhere in my soul, to be examined later. There was business to conduct here.

"I'm sorry, could you tell me your name again?" I asked the woman, with a faint smile. I set the tray down on the low table and took the other chair.

"Valerie," she said, and a long last name that sounded like *lithium* or *Lithuania*, but that couldn't be right. So I thought of her as Valerie L.

"Ross Lamos." I offered my hand. She shook it briefly, never breaking eye contact. A mild jolt shot up my arm and across my shoulders. I blinked; the room trembled. *Uh-oh,* was all the secret inward voice would say. Something Big pressed through the room—a vibration, a current, a tingling electricity—too big for any internal cupboard—and it noticed our clasped hands. I withdrew mine and smiled blandly. The room settled down, but reality still felt stretched.

I leaned back in the chair and laced my fingers over my stomach, one of Albert's gestures. Valerie L glanced at the gesture, then at me. "Han Dynasty," she said. Not even a question.

"You know what that means, I take it?" *You know they're two millennia old? You know the how desperately Chinese government wants to keep hold of national treasures like this? You know what it costs to placate lawyers and avoid an international incident?*

Valerie L nodded vigorously, uncrossed her legs and leaned over the jades. She picked up the entwined dragons and turned them over. "Early Han, though I don't know which Emperor. God, such a terrible time." She slouched back in the chair, re-crossed her legs casually, and traced the lines of the celery-green dragons as if fingering a family photo. Corruption, power grabs, brutality twenty-four-seven. And the history! Lost, of course, books burned, the scholars murdered, back under the Qin Emperor. Two thousand years of shared memory, gone. Oh, the Qin Emperor, the *First* Emperor, he built the Great Wall, he had a terra-cotta army! Nobody mentions him wiping out history and all memory of the dynasties that came before Qin. Can you imagine having to reconstruct your country's history? That's what the Han emperors inherited. You've read Sima Qian, right? The Grand Historian? Boy, what a job *he* had!"

A private anger boiled up in my chest. Sima Qian was one of my favorite people in the far, far past. So few of the living could bring the Grand Historian up into casual conversation, Sima Qian felt like a treasured possession, my childhood teddy bear, and this woman had just grabbed him and tossed him in the air.

"How do you know they're early Han?" I asked, as though pleasantly curious. "Have they been appraised? Have you had them dated at a lab?" *Or did you come here just to watch us go apeshit?*

Valerie L shook her head. "You're the first professionals to see these. It seemed like a good idea to show them to somebody. I looked in the Yellow Pages for an Asian art gallery, and Albert Jarro Gallery was the first name to come up." She glanced back into the main showroom. "Albert Jarro is definitely somebody."

"Ah, you *do* have provenance documents on these, don't you?" *Somewhere in that horrible shoulder bag, please, please let there be documents. I don't care if they're creased and coffee-stained.* But Valerie L just waved hair out of her face.

"Nope," she said. "In fact, I wouldn't know what provenance documents looked like if they walked up and stole my purse."

The pit of my stomach went ice-cold underneath my burning chest. No documents. For the gallery's safety—hell, for *her* safety—there *had* to be documents. Transfer of ownership; country of origin; a customs stamp: the paper trail that proved Valerie L's possession of such *yü* was completely legal. A new thought lanced though me, and a pang of shame that I had not thought of it earlier. *A set-up. Somebody could be out to con us into accepting, and then selling, stolen antiquities. Send in an operative acting like a naïf. That must have been why Albert didn't want to come near them. Get her out of here. Get* them *out of here. Do it now.*

… But the jades need me.

"May I ask," I said carefully, "just how you came to have these in that shoulder bag of yours?"

She looked at me with that birdlike tilt to her head. A smile played into her mouth, an expression that could only be called mischievous. "Do objects speak to you?" she asked.

I sucked in a sharp breath, re-crossed my legs and adjusted my shirt cuffs. Something had betrayed me. I would rather face a team of lawyers from the Chinese government than talk about my gift, especially with this woman, who assumed she could just walk in here and—I clenched my fist around the jade bead in my mala. *Ommnipmehmmm.* "Well, yes, yes, they do," I replied.

Her smile broadened. She sat up in the chair and leaned forward. "Well then, apparently I found this gallery because you can handle this." She pressed the twisting dragons between her palms, and her clear green eyes looked right at me—no, right *through* me. Her smile did not lessen, and her voice was gentle, but her gaze said, *Listen.*

"I'm one of those people," she said, "who, when I hold things, I know what they are, what happened, and why they're with me." There was no apology in her voice.

You, too! You, too! a child's shout threatened to burst from me. My grip on the mala bead softened. Heat, anger, panic, gratitude—this roundabout of emotions was making me queasy.

She unfolded her hands and set the scabbard piece back on the tray. "The man who brought me these jades said that when he saw them, he knew I had to deal with them. And the minute *I* saw them, I knew he was right. The minute I held them ... " she blinked and sighed. Fragile, suddenly. "Well, I was shattered. That's all."

Something Big was back in the room, alive, alert. It had never left. My left hand twiddled the mala bead and tassel lightly. "How did the he—the man who passed them on—how did *he* come by them?"

At that, she averted her eyes, thinking.

Like any grownup, I have learned to live stretched between Habit and Reality, which often make little comments in my head. When Valerie L went silent, Habit sneered, *Aha, now we'll see what the scheme is*—

"They were handed to him at an antique show by a stranger who insisted that he would know what to do with them," Valerie L stated with complete sincerity, looking me in the face once more. "When he opened the boxes and saw them, he just knew I had to deal with them." She lifted her shoulders with a sigh. "Some things you just know. You know?"

Oh, great, said Reality. A brief memory of the monk pressing the mala into my hand back in China made Valerie L's testimony tolerable—but still. I wanted her and her jades out of the gallery, out of my sight.

... But the jades need me.

"And ... he said they were yours?"

Her look turned peculiar. "No, he didn't. That's not what I said. He and I both just looked at them and we both knew, *I have to deal with them.* They're my *responsibility.*" Apparently, for her that word could bulldoze high mountains.

"Ah, well. That's very interesting. And yes, sometimes this is how someone acquires an object," I said, daring a neutral smile. "Unfortunately, as much as we'd like to help you, there's not much Mr. Jarro or I can do without provenance documents on the set's origin and former owners."

She tossed her head in growing irritation and blew a few strands of hair out of her mouth. "This has nothing to *do* with documents, Mr. Lamos," she said. "I only want to hear professionals—like Albert Jarro—like you—say that these things are what I know they are. A backup. What I need --" and with abrupt speed she scooped up the dragon jade and aimed it straight at my heart—"is a *witness*."

Something flipped inside out.

The room became an infinite cavern, a road, an open space of qualities my verbose mind could not grasp. Time, provenance, lawyers, comforting purple walls and plush furniture, Albert and auctions and catalogs and vaults, all vanished from the world, from my mind, in a purge—an existential incontinence. They were unreal. They had nothing to do with this. It was only Valerie L, and me ... and the *yü*.

The cosmic silence around us was as good as a voice, echoing, as the moment opened further and further outward, like an expanding puff of dandelion silk. This woman. The jades. Han Dynasty. A mysterious arrival, and a mission. Something Big. A story, a gallery name in the phone book. An arrow, shot from somewhere far away, had driven through Valerie L's eyes, her arm and hand, the dragon jade, and found its mark in me.

It was a *presence*. It seemed to have created the room we sat in. Yet that presence could not be her responsibility alone. That was absurd.

Maybe she is a fool. Habit.

But the angels do protect us fools. Reality.

"Perhaps I should hold one," I heard myself say.

Valerie L perked up. She replaced the dragon jade on the velvet and sat back in her chair, hiding a grin behind her hand.

I let my hand float over the jades. Perversely, it settled on the archer's thumb ring. I cupped both hands around it.

I see the ring on a thumb, as the hand prepares ink and bamboo strips for writing. The hand then rests on a black-robed thigh, as the scholar—not an archer, but a scholar, a shih—kneels at his desk. The other, the right hand, lets an ink-full brush hover above a wood strip.

Then it touches the wood and a story swirls out onto the long narrow strips. ... I can read the words ...

Suddenly the wood strip is knocked askew, the writing desk is kicked over, a flash of swordsteel, the thumb-ringed hand flies up helplessly, useless because the writer's head is already rolling away. I see the face, the anxious living man superimposed over the startled twitching death like a dream. ' It was my fault ... it was my fault,' the living man tells me ....

Valerie L slapped my knee and brought me back. I was sweating; shaking; my heart raced. "Amazing stuff, huh?" Valerie L smiled with a shrewd sympathy.

"How ... how long ... was I out there?" I croaked.

"Three or four minutes. You looked like you needed to breathe."

I nodded and set the thumb ring back on the tray. I breathed. Never, with any object, no matter how exquisite, had I been swept into a full-body *moment* like that.

Details, lovely tangible business details, rescued me. "The best thing to do," I said, "would be to get provenance started on them *now*." Maybe it was my racing heart, but there was a terrible urgency in the air. "Mr. Jarro and I can send the stones off to be dated by infrared spectroscope at a laboratory—a disinterested third party, they just take a fee, no commission." A man had just been murdered. "Not that it would be the last word on their age, but it would support any opinion an appraiser like myself would write for you. It would be helpful to get signed statements from you and the man who gave you the jades, about the mysterious nature of their arrival." Blood spreading across the floor. "Then, we can hold them for you in our safe. Naturally, once they have the Albert Jarro Gallery on their provenance list, their value rises. You'll be able to ask six figures for—"

"I'm not *selling* them," she reminded me, with a hint of disbelief.

"Ah, of course," I fumbled. "Well. Of course you can bring around the people you ... ah, you can make those transfers here, in a secure setting. With the correct paperwork on hand."

"I'd rather not let anyone keep them for me."

"Good, don't ever let them out of your possession," I said heatedly, before a more businesslike response could take shape in my brain. "I mean, until the time is right." The idea of these pieces floating around, out of control, was almost more than I could stand. Something Big moved around us like a room-sized beast and settled into a new shape. My heart slowed down and I breathed normally again.

Valerie L seemed to be waiting, but I didn't know what more to say. I had wanted the *yü* gone; now I didn't want them to leave my sight. Bloody thumb ring, golden turtle ... and those dragons. Tangible stone, so hard and solid, glowed with life on the velvet, the gravitational focus of possible futures that built around us like storm clouds. Something Big.

"Hah-*hnnnh*" — A stifled sneeze burst and faded in the back room. Albert was close by, listening. Valerie L looked, not towards the sneeze, but towards the showroom. The exit. Anxious now. Her tall frame was disciplined for stillness, but needed movement. Flight. The evening light bending in from the main gallery waned and withdrew. Finally Valerie L sighed, "Well, all right," and scooped the jades into their worn boxes, and then into her cloth bag. We stood, she turned, and with one long step she transported herself into the main gallery. She could fly when she needed. I bolted after her.

"Why you?" I blurted at her back. She stopped and turned around. The room's high, arched windows seemed to lean over to hear us better. I opened my hands in a plea. "Why are these things your responsibility?"

She motioned me to come near. We were out of Albert's earshot, so she must have already spotted the security cameras discreetly positioned around the showroom. "I have these jades," she whispered, "because the people of this story are here in my life. I know one of them, I have to find the others. I have to bring the story to an end."

I felt myself choking the way Albert had earlier.

Valerie L shrugged. "After that ... maybe someone will bring one to you. I really don't know." That sorrow again in her green eyes. It made me feel unreasonably defensive.

"The man in the ring," I said. "Is he the one you know ... now?"

She shook her head. "He's close, I know that. Sometimes ... sometimes I know he's right next to me, I could touch him if I just knew where and when to put out my hand. When I held that ring, I knew he was my dearest friend in that horrible place."

"Your fr—…"

Oh.

Not long after joining Albert Jarro in his gallery, I had stepped beyond my, ahem, *eclectic* Catholic upbringing and had taken refuge as a Buddhist. Now I felt like a child seeing my first Christmas tree, loaded with gifts. What had been a wild rumor—rebirth—was no rumor, but a breathing reality.

"I'm just glad it didn't show me how he died," Valerie L said.

"Come again?" I was still adjusting to the presence of the Christmas tree.

"The man who wore the ring," she said. "When I held it—I'm sure the things I saw were my memories of him. How much he meant to me. I knew that he had died, but not how."

We must have made our goodbyes. Because all at once she was moving at full stride down the sidewalk and the gallery's big glass door had sighed shut. All the life drained out of the showroom in her wake.

The ring didn't show her how he died?! Then why did it show me?

I walked slowly around the showroom. For four years, it had been my private theater, where I could play with pools of light, angles of arrangement, to create a world of beautiful histories. I knew it better than my own kitchen counter. Usually there was a murmuring current of secret stories in my inner ear, under the room's quiet. Tonight, after Valerie L, after the jades, after a bloody murder, there was only cold silence.

It was nearly seven o'clock, so I decided to go ahead and close.

Just as I began to check the gallery's temperature settings, Albert reappeared from the back. "She's gone? You let them go with her?"

"She's not selling."

"She may not have to," he said. There was a certain arched power under his mild tone, like a padding cat. Albert's hair was smoothed down again. His smile was just a little curl of lips under his mustache. "I have a feeling she'll be back." He drummed his fingertips on the book in his hand, put it on the counter, opened at a certain page, and left through the middle room.

It was our guest book. Valerie L had signed it with her name, address and phone number when she came in, while Albert and I finished helping a garrulous, wealthy old regular add to his collection of Japanese theater masks.

Her last name did indeed begin with L, followed by mostly Ls, Ws, Ys and Ds. Welsh.

I have a feeling she'll be back. I knew the tone. Albert had an idea. Just this morning, I would have thrilled to the presence of a secret, a subtle machine shared by Albert and me alone. We would build the machine together, with murmured suggestions and quiet phone calls, working our contacts in a kind of velvet competition, until the sale was done and the gallery's bank account swelled.

That would have been this morning. There was no thrill now.

I could close and secure the Albert Jarro Gallery while lying in a coma, and that must have been how I did it that night, because I remember nothing of it. What the thumb-ring had poured into my hands came rushing back as soon as I began my nightly routine.

The thumb-ring in Valerie L's bag was definitely an archer's little treasure, rather than the plain cylinder worn by scholars to indicate that the wearer was above manual labor. But I saw what I saw, when I held the *yü*. This thumb-ring definitely belonged to a scholar, a favored servant, a *shih*, evidently one with a stylish sense of humor. Han Dynasty is one of the oldest eras in China's recorded history, and this thumb-ring, as Valerie L had said, was from *early* Han. One legend about the history of writing says that such a *shih* was often a kind of secretary to archers of high rank. Besides keeping written records on strips of bamboo wood, they kept score in archery contests. I have a hunch the cleverest became color commentators whose play-by-play banter heightened the contest's entertainment. The thumb-ring had whispered to me of the wearer's very high favor with a very high someone. Someone who was somebody.

Shutting the gallery is a 15-minute operation and the walk to my apartment is another ten. As I opened my front door, it hit me: I had taken one class on archaic Chinese pictographs during my graduate work in Beijing, and made only average marks. Yet I had been able to read clearly the *shih's* words on the wood strips in the vision. They leapt into my mind as full, fluent phrases. As if I had read them before, and knew them well.

A witness.

To a tale not yet finished.

One that began:

In the second month of a warm spring, a new Emperor rode out to see his lands ...

2.
THE FIRST JADE'S STORY

In the second month of a warm spring, a new Emperor rode out to see his lands. He had been Emperor for a year and a half, and much was still at stake in his young reign. One of his first commands had been to prepare a progress through the Ten Kingdoms so that the Emperor could subdue and lay claim to the Earth itself with his gaze. The progress would also establish the Glorious Heavenly Ruler, Son of Heaven, Eternity on Earth, Destiny of Ages, firmly in his people's minds. In turn the people could establish their fealty and worth in the heart of the Son of Heaven.

Too many months later, they were off. The Emperor was a decisive man and the bureaucracy of Empire pecked at him like a thousand tiny birds. But it was a warm spring and the land was beautiful, so the Emperor soon forgot his irritation and began to enjoy himself.

The Emperor's progress moved in a manner well befitting a Glorious Heavenly Ruler. Four legions of Imperial Guard surrounded his carriage: one riding and marching ahead, one behind, and one on each side. Dragon banners fluttered. The fluid Wu and Xiang music was played from horseback when the way was slow, the rattling Shao and Hu music when the pace quickened. Ministers were along to speak of each kingdom and province's strategic value to the new Dynasty. Scholars were on hand to comment on the customs and arts of each region. Poets and dancers were aboard to keep everyone entertained and pick up the best dirty jokes from the locals. Priests, of course, had to be included to remind everyone of their divine origin and destiny. And naturally there had to be cooks, servers, tailors, armourers, grooms, messengers, porters and slaves to look after this roaming Imperial City.

Yet in all of this crowd, the new Emperor chose to travel without his wives and concubines. Instead, he brought his nine eldest sons, all of them fine young princes preparing for marriage, and not one of them certain who would be the Emperor's heir.

This new Dynasty had no Empress. The princes' father had never declared any of his consorts to be fully divine, equal to his power, the female counterpart of the Son of Heaven. The Emperor was a decisive man, and he had decided that this heir situation needed a lot of time and study.

That was the final purpose of the progress through the Ten Kingdoms: to examine the Princes and (perhaps) choose a successor.

This open secret had half the princes bounding off their cots before dawn, looking for some impressive thing to do, while the other half drew the blankets over their heads and prayed for a dream to tell them whether they should take monastic vows or become an actor.

While four princes were bounding and four were praying, the ninth prince was not worrying much at all. His name was Jade Mountain. He was the child of the Emperor's Third Wife, and knew he was likely to wind up ruling one of these Ten Kingdoms under his elder brother, First Son, the child of the Emperor's First Wife. Jade Mountain assumed it would be his duty to be a wise and good ruler who kept in mind the benefit of the whole Empire within the affairs of one kingdom. So he studied statecraft, agriculture, calligraphy, mathematics, music, poetry and war avidly, and attended religious services with a sincere heart. When the Emperor looked at this Prince, he frequently saw the young man laughing. "Should an Emperor be capable of joy?" he wondered.

The Emperor looked at First Son, tall like his mother, whom the Emperor had once compared to a willow tree in a dawn mist. He saw First Son remove himself from a noisy dispute between two high-ranking courtiers when the words coarsened and the threats contained blood. "Should an Emperor detach himself from the petty conflicts of inferior people?" the Emperor wondered. Not long after seeing this, and wondering this, word came to the Emperor that Jade Mountain, stocky and broad-faced like his father, had engaged with the disputing courtiers and resolved matters so that all were laughing again.

As the Emperor progressed through his lands, from desert to plains to river valleys, an army of sharply trained eyes watched the nine princes and their ways. All of it was reported to their father. Every night a different prince sat next to the

Emperor at dinner, on display to the whispering regiments of eyes, ears, glances, and fans. This was another task of empire that occasionally made the Emperor break out in a rash. He suffered quietly from so much strategy. More than once he wondered how a normal father would behave, when the sum of human richness he had engendered in well-grown sons lay before him like a storehouse of treasure. Unable to admit to the emotions of an inferior person, over the course of the spring the Emperor began to see the princes as living yarrow stalks, capable of foretelling every possible future for his fragile new dynasty. He shuffled and cast their characters over and over, studying the combinations and patterns.

The progress entered a mountainous region of the Ten Kingdoms. After the desert's harshness and the farmlands' drudgery, the cheerful variety of forested bluffs, brooks, breezes and wildlife was refreshing to every soul.

"In this place is a great Temple, where hundreds of male and female acolytes study the Way of Immortality," a priest told the Emperor and his advisers. "Let us pause there awhile, and let such wisdom meet the Son of Heaven, and all his works."

"Such a visit will prompt simple minds to connect the new Emperor with fearful supernatural powers," the Ministers murmured. "More sophisticated persons, on the other hand, will understand that their ruler is a superior person of complexity and depth."

"The Temple's Library is famous," the Scholars pleaded, "for it survived the former Dynasty's dreadful book-burnings. Son of Heaven, let us visit and study the texts!"

"Defensible positions in the area"—the head of the Imperial Guard began, but the Emperor interrupted with a snap: "Let it be so! For all the good reasons, and because the weather in these foothills is becoming unbearably hot." Even before he mentioned the weather, messengers were racing out of camp to warn the Temple of its approaching good fortune.

When the Imperial encampment was comfortably situated and every conceivable preparation had been made, the temple announced a festival day celebrating the Emperor's victorious assumption of his divine destiny as Son of Heaven. There would be sacred dances and music, prayerful rites, demonstrations of the monks' physical prowess and the exercises that produced it, and of course healthful food to balance and enhance the five elements. Formal invitations were carried to the Emperor and the court. In addition, the Emperor sent individual messages to his sons, requesting their presence at this daylong event. Eight princes automatically agreed, with all gratitude and joy. But the Emperor was very surprised by the refusal sent back from Jade Mountain.

Immediately, the Emperor commanded that Jade Mountain would sit next to him at dinner that night, even though this threw the princely dinner rotation and all of its carefully engineered seating arrangements into chaos.

Between courses of Dawn Weeps Emeralds and Phoenix by the River, the Emperor swallowed a mouthful of tea, smacked his lips thoughtfully, and said, "Here is a fine riddle. When," and he paused, to enjoy how silence dropped like a rock upon the whole great dining pavilion, with chopsticks suspended halfway to open mouths. "When is the filial devotion expounded by the great teachers exemplified by withdrawal from the father's wishes? In all our travels this season, someone must have seen a demonstration of this. The wisdom of Confucius encompasses the entire earth and every heaven. Or is the answer in the verses of Lao Tzu, Xunzi, or Mo-Zi, or that rascal Chuang Tzu? Come, someone solve this riddle."

No one in the pavilion said a word. They all knew who was supposed to respond. They didn't want to miss a syllable.

Jade Mountain drew a breath. "My Emperor, as I have the incomparable good fortune to also call you Father, I will attempt a poor student's response to your riddle," he said with a calm smile.

"There are times when a general must withdraw his legions from the field, as he becomes aware of their fatigue, or need for new arrows and armor, or to refresh their mounts, or some other flaw requiring attention. The general is devoted to his cause and his Emperor at all times and keeps that good uppermost in his mind. There can be no victory if the army is not at its best. Just in this way, a son of any station must keep his father's virtue uppermost in his view, and at all times defend that honor as a general will defend the Emperor's palace upon a high promontory. A son must avoid dishonoring his father at all times, even if such an action would go unseen by the eyes of the world, or so much as the eye of a tree frog, for the eyes of the gods dwell within the very breezes and subtle vapors of the Earth. It is then that a son may face the awful choice to step aside from his father's command, to protect that precious virtue from his own weakness.

"My Emperor, as I have the incomparable good fortune to also call you Father, I confess grief at having disturbed your equanimity with my refusal to attend the temple festival. I also confess that my devotion is concealed within this refusal in a delicate manner, that is perhaps more appropriately revealed beside an altar, after purifications."

The Emperor suppressed a chuckle. He knew the audience in the pavilion would never forgive either of them if they withdrew for a private conversation. The son of his Third Wife had just created an exquisite public moment. The Emperor allowed himself to feel a glow of pride, just a small one, subtle, the pride of a superior person.

The Emperor gently waved his broad warrior's hand, the one that wore the golden Jade Turtle ring, to tell his son it was all right to continue, here in front of everybody and without purifications.

"My Emperor, whom I revere as Father, I am a young man," Jade Mountain went on. "My thoughts frequently turn to marriage, and our progress through the Ten Kingdoms has spurred me to consider the merit a well-married prince may bring to the lands under his rule. Thus, when I received the invitation to join your Glorious Person at the temple festival, I was torn with doubt. The scriptures of the Tao are precious to me and sweet to my spirit. Its disciplines have sharpened my studies in both philosophy and combat. To be near this temple is a fulfillment of many wishes. And yet as a son I must protect my father's honor and virtue in the eyes of the gods. As a prince, this duty is also a protection of the virtue and honor of the entire Dynasty and Empire."

First Son cleared his throat.

The Emperor's face drained of all emotion. So did Jade Mountain's. Someone dropped a fan. Such a sound in the throat was the way a superior person stood up and yelled, "Liar!"

The Emperor quietly took another sip of tea. Then he let his gaze slowly circle the great pavilion, which was perfectly silent and still. The purpose of this terrorizing action became clear when he stopped his gaze just before reaching First Son. At that moment the Emperor, the Son of Heaven, turned his eyes straight ahead and handed his teacup to a servant.

He might as well have shot flame from his mouth. First Son was no longer the obvious choice to inherit the Empire and Dynasty. And Jade Mountain had not yet finished his speech.

The Emperor gestured again to Jade Mountain—an even smaller, slighter hand movement - and thus insisted he continue.

Jade Mountain stared straight ahead as well, but color flooded his cheeks. "Dear Emperor my father," he said flatly, "I am a young man ready for marriage. There are female devotees lodging at the temple. They have separated themselves from the ordinary world to seek pure life, the Way, the Tao, and immortality. The gaze of such a young man as I would burden them, and their burden is your dishonor. With the same will to prevent any obstruction to your virtue, I would not obstruct their pure intentions, any more than I would put sharp stones in their path. Therefore, Generous One, I request to remain in my tent with scriptures of the Way, that I may study in the shadow of this holy event."

The Emperor nodded, a short, curt nod. "My riddle is solved," he said, without looking at Jade Mountain. A musician plucked his lute, and the pavilion relaxed.

During the music, the Emperor rose and left. Soon after, so did Jade Mountain. First Son stayed for three more courses of dinner and a dance performance. However, on the day of the temple festival he found himself stuck in the library with the scholars, counting books and copying down all their titles, at the Emperor's command.

The extraordinary refusal, the dinner and the Emperor's riddle became a favorite poem that traveled around the Ten Kingdoms for many years. But the crucial result of the incident was this: Jade Mountain did not see the brilliant young girl Water Song at the temple festival, and his father the Emperor did.

3.

REFUGE

Rapt, rapture, enraptured. The words turned over in my head as I stared at my bedroom ceiling. I decided they were all of them far too close to *rape*.

It was the morning after Valerie L tossed her jades onto our counter. I had awakened with an ache across my middle, as if something had picked me up, thrown me across a saddle and taken off at a gallop. Reality still felt stretched. I lay in bed and wondered what in hell had really happened the day before. My dreams had been turbulent, but faded out immediately, leaving me with sharpened nerves and a memory of incense.

Usually I pick up the inward voice as if listening at a door, or glimpsing images beyond gauze curtains. The words and actions belong to other people, whom I observe in a kind of cinema that co-exists with my Ross Lamos body and memory bank. The thumb-ring had erased all those safe boundaries. Ross Lamos had vanished, for three or four minutes. And the thumb-ring delivered more than just a fully-sensible body experience. That experience had its source in a different world; a different *Earth*; a different *mind*. The Earth and mind of China, long, long ago. The air was different then, the shapes of words threw a strangeling light into forest and flesh. The *shih* saw his world, he heard its sounds, in ways that disturbed Ross Lamos, me.

And yet, I *knew* that world. That mind.

I sat up in bed and looked around. Art prints and photographs on the wall; toiletries and pocket contents on the bureau. Were these things part of a real self, one unmoved by a trip backwards in time? The bed was large enough to sleep two in comfort or three snugly, but I was a smallish man, sleeping alone. Was that significant?

The closet doors were folded half-open. Without getting up to look, I knew there were a dozen designer suits in there, and twice as many shirts and ties. How important was that?

I eased out of bed and walked through the apartment, still not quite certain of reality's dimensions. Touching a wall, a table, a knickknack, I gathered up bits of myself, little memories like a pile of sticky notes.

In the living room, it all came together. A burnished-gold Buddha sat smiling on a low shelf unit, fingertips touching the ground beneath him, with little candles and water bowls, flowers and an incense pot, surrounding his knees. His seat was on a Japanese obi of brilliant multicolored silk, that draped down to the floor in front of the shelf unit and shot up the wall to the ceiling, a shower of rainbow hues from Heaven to Earth. As always, the Buddha's smile made me smile. And that smile warmed the brittle bits of memories; they softened and melted together into a living glow that suffused my body. My own living fire. Aha.

In gratitude, I touched my palms together and raised them above my head, then touched my brow, throat and heart. I dropped to my knees and touched my forehead to the creamy, deep-pile carpet. I did it three times. Fewer or none would have felt rude, even this early in the morning. My morning attentions to the shrine—fill the bowls with fresh water, light new tea candles and a stick of incense—are always offered like breakfast in bed to a cherished friend, one with whom I share secrets, our common spice. I had just lit the joss stick when I saw something that was like an unexpected hand touching my shoulder.

A book nestled in the cushions of my favorite chair, next to the shrine.

It was Sima Qian's *Records of the Grand Historian*. The single most authoritative text on the people and events of the early Han Dynasty.

The book, with its creased and frayed paper cover, was unmistakably mine. I had kept my undergraduate copy of the *Records* for the sheer pleasure of the English translation. Good old Burton Watson had taken Sima Qian's half-million words, 130 chapters, five sections, covering two thousand years of history that was mostly legend and myth, and wrestled it into a compact form that read like a house afire. The book lived on the shelf above my little kitchen desk, a homely figure in a private spot.

I did not take it down last night. I did not sit down and read around in it. At least, I had no memory of doing so.

I jammed the burning joss stick into its ceramic frog base and snatched the book off the chair as if it were about to do something animal on the upholstery. The pain across my middle returned. I felt an odd flash of shame, as though I had insulted a friend. Sima Qian had been a pathetic figure, respected at first for taking up his father's position as Grand Historian in the latter days of the Han Dynasty, then excoriated and shunned — castrated, in fact — for speaking up in defense of some nobleman who had displeased the Emperor. There was no need to treat his book like a pariah.

It wouldn't help anyway, I told myself as I slid the book back onto its shelf. Setting it firmly in place, I felt the world relax back into the reliable order of things. No, whatever I had experienced when holding the jade, it was not enough information for the Grand Historian to clarify — yet. I headed for the shower and ticked off in my mind what I did know, what I could count on as true.

As a result of my plunge into the *shih*'s fatal, aborted story, I now knew, yes, the golden turtle pendant *had* been a ring, worn by an Emperor. *Which* Emperor would be an interesting fact to investigate. The poor headless *shih* had been using a literary form, and would have fudged details for dramatic effect. Nine sons? All possible heirs to a Dynasty? I doubted that. All I could really take to the *Records* was an elder son, a younger son, and some hapless girl in a Taoist temple. I had to assume that more of Valerie L's *story* waited in the other two jades.

And how brutally would the touch of those jades deliver me there?

I stopped in my tracks, in the doorway to the bathroom. *Deliver me there.* To *them.* I shuddered; reality stretched and twisted again. Like Scarlett O'Hara guarding her land, I decided I would not think about that today, I would think about it tomorrow, or some other time. The ferocity of my decision diffused the pain across my middle, and when the hot water hit me in the shower it vanished altogether.

Let Valerie L worry about who was who. It was her responsibility. There was enough twistedness about to happen in the cold, pragmatic light of day, which would soon pour through the windows of the Albert Jarro Gallery.

Albert had a plan for those Han Dynasty jades. I had a good idea what my part in it would be: exotic mouthpiece, again. Who was Albert thinking of selling them to? It was the first question of dozens that ran through my mind as I showered and shaved. How would we proceed — no, more likely, how would Albert alone proceed with such a delicate sale, once the jades were in our keeping? Without provenance, even his most, um, *flexible* clients would be leery. And how would he convince Valerie L to sell? Why did he say, *she may not have to* sell? Following those thoughts pulled two memories up out of the past four years, memories that nagged at me all the way to the gallery.

Albert was out on business until mid-afternoon, which gave me time to go through our files and hunt down the details of those memories. By the time Albert returned, I was certain of one thing: if any of these Han Dynasty jades passed through the Albert Jarro Gallery again, I would not be allowed to touch them.

Albert had his schemes, his subtle machines. But there was a more common ritual to our work. Almost every day, Albert would hang up the phone and tell me that an item, Such-and-Such, was on its way to us. Then Albert and I would each get on the phone, calling collectors' agents, and often when the package arrived we would have a buyer waiting. I worked my own contacts seeking out pieces to display and sell in our main gallery, and I did all the appraisal work on those. If a collector simply wanted an appraisal so that she could have the Albert Jarro Gallery's name added to the provenance, that was my job. But when shipments from Albert's network came in, I was to immediately send the package out to So-and-So for a disinterested appraisal. By the time the package came back to us with the documents, a buyer was waiting—with a cozy percentage of the sale price paid to Albert, and if the buyer had been one of my leads, I got a cut. This was how we earned most of our income. The storefront gallery was mostly PR. Sales in the showroom reaped contacts, not money.

Sending items out for a disinterested appraisal, we never had to open a package or involve ourselves with the piece. When we did open a package, I was the one doing the work: cleaning it, setting up the showroom display, repacking for shipment, adding our receipt to the provenance papers. The Touch came in handy then. Few human beings dealing in artworks are pure-minded Eagle Scouts, and not every piece that blooms out of its packing material is exactly what the seller would have us believe. It's all part of the business. Albert frequently expressed his appreciation for the Touch with unexpected bonuses. The gemology microscope, for example, simply appeared one day in the arms of a UPS man. I was terribly excited by how much more detail I could see in small objects; but when Albert added the little plaque to the machine's side—TRUST, BUT VERIFY— I realized that he had guessed about my Touch. I had felt such a rush of pride that day—I even choked up a bit with gratitude that I had a man like Albert Jarro for a boss and mentor. Someone with such perception and subtlety, a sure touch of his own for the right object, the right word, the right move. My slavish attention to his every look and word was justified, I thought. I wanted to *be* Albert Jarro.

Two incidents in the past four years had given me pause, however, and cooled my ardor. Now here were their memories sitting on my shoulder.

Once, a Mongolian *cham* mask had come in for appraisal, after I had gained my American Appraiser's Association certificate. But instead of having me do the work, Albert declared the mask to be of the *greatness*, out of my league, and had me send it off to a more experienced and specialized appraiser. Again, this instruction came without Albert giving the grimacing, grotesque boar's-head so much as a glance. I never questioned Albert's ability to assess an item's potential from nothing more than a verbal description. But once the mask was sent out for appraisal, I never saw it again. When I asked Albert what had happened, he replied, "Oh, that came back while you were out. I took care of it myself, and handed it back to the owner. Look for the paperwork, you'll see."

This was the only time I had ever heard Albert speak of physically, personally, picking up an artifact. I had never seen him actually do it. He must have handled objects in his vault, but how was I to know that?

The second incident had pulled me up short and made me pay attention. A package arrived while Albert was out. It was fairly small and flat, but when I took hold of it to pull off the shipping documents, the Touch did its work. I started to shake. The shipper's manifest told me it was a painting on paper, framed. With terrific care, I opened the package to find the provenance paperwork. The object, still packed in protective Styrofoam and bubble wrap, was an original small work by Hokusai. Yes, Hokusai. Mister *Thirty-Six Views of Mount Fuji*

Hokusai. Painter of the great ocean wave with foam like curled fingers, an icon of Japanese art, *that* Hokusai. I held in my hands one of *his*. I closed my eyes and let the inward voice speak to me in the artist's own murmur: *Oh, yes, this is good. Yes, this will do. I just hope I get paid before the landlord visits.*

"Ross! What is that?" Albert's voice had cut sharply into the reverie.

"Hokusai," I whispered. I couldn't quite focus my eyes. There was no mistaking Albert's expression, however. Fury. He pointed to the felt-lined trays we kept stacked by the shipping table. I laid the precious package down on one as Albert snatched away the papers and scanned the provenance.

"Wrap it back up, it's not staying here," he announced coldly. "This is for outside appraisal, and then back where it came from." Some collector trusted only Albert to find the right appraiser for his new treasure. I obeyed, no problem, all in a day's work, and did not cosset the item again. I regretted that professionalism a month later, when the package returned from the outside appraiser. Albert was inside his vault, checking something in the shelves of treasures. I signed for the package and studied it, wondering why it was familiar. Then I saw the original shipping label underneath the crookedly-placed new one. I stared at it, baffled. That must be one busy appraiser, I thought, to need a whole month for what should have taken a day or two. Then I had no more time to think: customers had entered the showroom. I pulled out a felt-lined tray and laid the package down it. When I returned it was gone, transported to Albert's vault, surely, for safekeeping. That was when the real strangeness crept over me.

There had been no *Hokusai* in the package. No voice. No shakes, no vibe. Cold to my Touch. The thing I had held was dead.

In the files, I found that the appraisals of those two items had both been conducted by a man whose name I knew but whom I had never met. The world of fine antique objects is small, so this lapse alone was puzzling. I did know that this man worked from an unglamorous office building near the airport, although his business card was glossy.

And yes, the owners had received back the items and appraisal documents. There were the signatures. Everything was in order.

Evidently, the Touch was not an asset in all cases. Albert hadn't intended for me to hold those returned items in my hands, even when packed. The Hokusai was a fluke.

Thoughtful, I returned the files to their drawer and strolled out to the main showroom, chamois cloth in hand. Wiping down the cases and objects was often a kind of meditation. Not this time. It was a mechanical movement of the arm, nothing more. The polished glass around me only showed me myself: suit, silver hair, angular black-framed glasses. I could be mistaken for a charming antique artifact.

When Albert finally returned, I said casually, "I'll need to be away tomorrow."

Albert nodded, not even looking up from his laptop. He flicked a finger off his temple in a tiny salute. I did the same—our signal of four years: Right, pardner, I've got your back. I did it even though he was not looking at me, and would not see it. Habit. He would be expecting it, unconsciously; *not* doing it might register with him somehow. So, for the first time, I did it to deceive him. Reality.

This was another hole in the solid world I had thought I lived in. No way was I going to allow those jades to disappear into it. If Valerie L agreed to have her *yü* appraised, I would do it myself and hand them back to her personally.

That is, if she bought the logic, accepted that I was going back on my own advice, and let me take them out of her hands.

After closing up that evening, I did not walk back to my apartment. Instead, I caught a bus and rode north. I wedged my way into a window seat as soon as I could, because I had seen in the sky that it was going to be my favorite kind of evening.

The day's cloud cover did not quite make it to the horizon. The early autumn sun soon dropped into the gap and shot fierce light through the air; it heightened the bronze tones that had taken over most of the trees. The bus route turned and I was ready, face to the glass. We crested a hill, and there was spread a broad vista of the city's skyscrapers, perched on metallic tiptoe at the harbor's edge. The sun's low angle flamed those towers into proud, burning gold, backed by the slate-blue damask of the cloud-cast sky. I gasped, as I had hundreds of times before, forgetting the other people on the bus. That I should be in such a city, such a climate, such a topography of hills, crisscrossed with insane streets, all thrown together like an anarchic riot of misfits who suddenly discover an orchestral sound ... the first time I rode this bus and turned my head at exactly the right moment and saw *this*, I wept. Nothing could be more *alive* than this beauty, which thinned and disappeared in a handful of minutes; no beauty could be more generous, given absolutely free to everyone on earth, and impossible without the city built exactly as it was.

I must be here for a reason. Thinking what I was thinking now about Albert Jarro, my note fell sour; the orchestra paused. I could follow Albert's baton, or the voice of the jades, the face of a dead man. A man reborn somewhere, right here.

Being a Pacific port, the city is chock full of Buddhists, all kinds of Buddhists. There is only one Tibetan temple, with a small monastery tucked inside, but it is spectacular, even for a remodeled warehouse in a light-industrial neighborhood. Other lamas in the lineage thought our head lama had gone nuts, designing this. But Rinpoche had the last giggle. Double-thickness cement-block walls inside the outer warehouse structure created a rich silence any concert hall would envy. Devout artists from all around the Himalayas came to fill the shrine room's walls and ceilings with murals, statues, and *thangka* paintings. Back when I was still a newcomer to the city, work on the shrine room finished and there was a grand opening night. I went (and got lost, and was late) just to gape at all of it. Just to look. I stayed for the consecration ceremony, the dedication prayers, the meditation, the reception, and the informal *darshan* with the lama and his attendant monks that went on past midnight. I walked out into a silent city knowing I had found my spiritual home.

It was long ago at some family dinner that my grandparents (Mother's side—Boston Irish) had asked me about my earliest memories. I replied truthfully about being a young girl hiding on a staircase so I could listen to an old man talk about enlightenment. That put my elders in quite an uproar, since it was hardly the response they expected from a five-year-old Catholic boy.

It was another twenty years before I told my family any more truths about myself.

Walking into the shrine room that Tuesday night with too many truths in my head, the cool and spacious sense of *refuge* enfolded me again. It felt like falling in love. At least, the way I knew how to fall in love.

I take refuge in the Buddha, the Dharma, and the Sangha. My refuge is the Teacher, the Teaching, and the community of practitioners. What a relief to do three prostrations and touch my forehead to the teak inlay floor. This formal, full-body surrender unlocked me from the careful way I had to live. It allowed me to feel the strain of the exacting dance I danced at the gallery. No matter how my own network of contacts grew, I had to watch out for the moment when I must submit and hand Albert his victory. Stung, stepped-on, silenced or patted on the head, with Albert I must always be ready for a new waltz of wits.

Here in the temple, however, the atmosphere of acceptance was genuine. *Refuge.* Here, I could fall apart in calmness and be a wreck in sweet silence.

Settled on our cushions, the silence rose. I turned my attention inward, on the breath. The chant leader began intoning the principles called the Four Immeasurables. These principles brew the rich compassion at the center of the Dharma—*bodhicitta*, a vital love for all the world, just as it is. I closed my eyes and murmured along, letting the simple words become my entire reality. Well, almost entire. Some nights there's just no quashing the chitchat mind.

May I and all beings have happiness, and the causes of happiness. Yes, let's go back to the whole point of being alive, shall we? *May we be removed from sorrows, and the causes of sorrows.* Then we can stop pecking each others' eyes out. *May we never be separated from the beautiful bliss that's beyond suffering.* I felt that bliss, I'm sure of it, when in junior high I realized that the jock bullies could beat up this fairy boy all they wanted, but they would never touch the real me. And I told them so, before I puked and passed out. *May we dwell in the great equanimity, free from attachment and aversion to others far and near.* Ah, attachment and aversion, those dear neighbors, so familiar to a sensitive sucker like me. Neighbors? Are you kidding? They're my clones. My life is built on attachment and aversion. Beautiful, ugly, valuable, worthless, gimme-gimme, take it away. I've tried to root it in an attitude of service, honest I have. Is there any better, any more *fun* service to the world than to preserve magnificent beauty?

With the motivation to perform wholesome activities, we offer our devotion of body, speech, and mind. That was Dave's voice leading the meditation. He was seated off to the side with the temple's resident monks. Pale, freckled Dave, a buff little elf with fashion-model cheekbones, wrapped in his maroon and gold robes, head shaved, vows intact, not yet ordained, but on his way. Dave, now known as Trinley, previously known as "Darling."

🦋 🦋 🦋 🦋 🦋 🦋 🦋 🦋

"*What* did you say you did?" Dave set down his wine glass and stared at me wide-eyed.

"Took refuge. I became a Buddhist."

"Just now?"

"This afternoon. There was a ceremony at the temple. I signed up for it a couple of weeks ago. Didn't know if I would actually do it, but …. Couldn't stay away."

"Hmmm. Not just looking anymore."

"No. "

"What does it feel like? 'Refuge.' Sounds like you've escaped. What do you have to do? Give up stuff?"

"Not … well, yes and no. Mostly I just have to … pay attention."

Dave rested his chin on his fist and lowered his eyes, then raised them to meet my gaze, a slow flutter of his long dark lashes. He reached across the table and stroked my hand with one finger. "Don't pay it all. Save some. I don't like being lonely."

"You won't be. I'm not going to give you up."

It had seemed easy, fated, a dream. I was in a new city, a new job, with new friends, we went out to celebrate my new appraiser's certificate, and across the dance floor there had whirled this light-boned being with floppy auburn hair and a commanding grace. "Your *hair!* Silver? I am *stunned!*" he had shouted over the music. "Who *are* you? Come on, it's time to *dance!*"

"Why don't you come to the temple with me next Tuesday? You should just see this place. It's gorgeous."

"Okay," he said.

❊ ❊ ❊ ❊ ❊ ❊ ❊

We sit with the back straight and hands resting on our knees, thumb and forefingers touching, Trinley-who-was-Dave intoned. *The three fingers of the right hand represent the three realms: the desire realm, the form realm, and the formless realm.* There it was, the precept that nailed me to Buddhism, Dave or no Dave. This world we live in is the desire realm. Yum, yum. Desire leads to action leads to a brief pleasure and then a complicated mess. Take Dave, for example. Wait, I already did that. And now he's a monk. Well then, take Albert Jarro.

The three fingers of the left hand represent the three times: past, present and future. Sometimes I think I devote myself to the past at Albert's gallery—everybody else's past, that is—so that not knowing the future is less painful. Being Albert's protégé is a privilege, yes, but not a guarantee. Of anything. *The thumb and forefingers make circles, signifying emptiness.*

Somebody kicked me.

I jerked aside. Everyone has someone in their life who triggers an utterly irrational revulsion. Someone who can be avoided but not escaped, someone who must be admitted into your life for reasons beyond your control, someone who pushes every button and buttons you didn't know you had. For me, this person was Betsy. She was short—shorter than me—tubby, and coarse. She could function in the world, but with great emotional disorder and awkwardness. By some invisible assignment, Betsy was drawn to me like a cat to an asthmatic. She was also a devout Buddhist, and showed up at every single temple event. This time she was late, waddling between the seated people to the empty cushion beside me.

"Sorry I kicked you," she said in her flat, affectless voice, which was thunder in the deepening meditation. I nodded and smiled, and patted the empty cushion.

She teetered, then landed on the cushion with a thud and a fart. Wheezing, she pulled her legs into a notion of the lotus posture. Her sweatpants and t-shirt were overdue for their weekly wash.

"Sorry," she said again, still at normal volume. "Guess I'm a little clumsy." Like a bat's call into the night, apology was how Betsy steered through the darkness of people.

I concentrated on making circles with my thumbs and

forefingers. Emptiness, emptiness. Please, Buddha and bodhisattvas, help me sit here in equanimity with Betsy. Betsy is an illusion. Betsy is suffering. Betsy is clear like an image in a mirror, like the moon's reflection in water. Betsy is an emanation of a great bodhisattva, arising in my life as a teacher. Thank you, Betsy, for letting me think about something other than Albert Jarro, and those Han Dynasty jades, and Valerie L, for five minutes.

It worked. Betsy's odor and wheezing faded into the environment of silence. The sense of cool spaciousness returned. My troubles lay arranged before me like jewels on a velvet-backed tray.

The biggest jewel was Albert Jarro. Four years was plenty of time to lose all naiveté about the art and antiquities business. We were really just salesmen, after all, in a brutally competitive field, one where official regulation was elephantine and personal regulation was, well, personal. In this twilight land I had latched onto Albert as a mentor. If I could apprentice with the best, I would eventually be the best. So what did Albert *need*, that required this kind of subterfuge?

That Albert Jarro, of all people, should *need* something … there was another hole in the world. I let my thoughts step away from it.

Next on the tray was the second biggest jewel, Valerie L holding her boxes of *yü*. Tall bloody blue heron. Her acceptance of her own Touch made my discretion lame, simpering. Worse: I was a certified professional appraiser, I touched antiques all the time, I'd felt thousands of stories. Why was *this* story a nuclear blast mutating me from the inside out? Why had it changed how I saw Albert Jarro?

What had I witnessed?

The thumb ring had pushed me into another world, one more brutal and deadly than the world I shared with Albert. Had I only glimpsed that world through someone else's eyes?

Or had I witnessed it?

As a boy, when I learned what the word "Chinese" meant, I knew that the curious girl in my memory was Chinese. The Han Dynasty had lasted from 206 BC to 226 AD, which placed Valerie L's story well before Buddhism took firm root in China.

It was simple to entertain the possibility that an earlier

lifetime than the girl and the monk linked me to the story in the jades. I was a Buddhist, after all. Entertaining the possibility was a done deal. What had me in pause was what came after entertainment. That breathless moment on the threshold of chaos, decision, relationship, *responsibility*. It was already clear that Valerie L's version of the story was different from my own. The thumb ring proved that.

The jades had something of mine. They stood in front of me like cold-eyed extortionists, waiting for a decision. I couldn't call on Valerie L for help, either. She had her own mission, bringing something to an end. I was on my own.

To find what was mine, I had to hold the jades. All of them.

Valerie L knew I had the Touch. Could I just ask her? What did I have to lose?

Albert Jarro's rippling little laugh echoed in my inward ear. *Doesn't exactly make you a disinterested appraiser, does it?*

Something hardened in my gut. The *story* was nothing Albert knew about, and was none of his business anyway. But he knew what the jades were, and he was counting on my tenuous connection with Valerie L to put them in reach of his scheme, whatever it was. My job was clear, as far as he cared. Orders had been given.

Om ma ni pad me hum. The mantra chant began. I had let Albert and the *yü* distract me completely. I slipped the bracelet of beads off my wrist and counted each repetition. *Om ma ni pad me hum om ma ni pad me hum omanipadmehumomanipadme humomnipmehmomnipmhmomnipmhmomnpmhmomnpmhm …*

The wash of sound curled around that surprising inner hardness and cleansed it to reveal a trail of thought: If Valerie L still refused to allow the appraisal, I could ask to hold the other two jades, get my *story*, and that would be the end of it, goodbye. If she accepted the warning about protecting herself and the jades with authentication and provenance, I would have her sign over to me the sole right to appraise and authenticate. I would do it without Albert's knowledge. Not for the gallery, but for myself. For my name, my career, my future. He would be furious, he would fight, he might fire me. But I was ready for this fight. We would see what I had learned from Albert Jarro about subterfuge.

I coughed, sudden and hard.

BAM! Betsy's fist hammered my back. Reflex made me throw my arms up to protect my face.

Omnpmhmomnpmhmomnpmhmomnpmhmomnpmhmomnpmhm, the mantra chant continued.

"You okay?" Betsy asked.

"Fine," I whispered, lowering my arms. I breathed deeply to prove it.

"Okay," Betsy said, uncertain.

I stared down at my beads and ticked them through my fingers as if counting the mantra repetitions. But I was faking it. The shock of the cough and Betsy's fist had not made me forget my last thought. They had knocked it askew and rearranged my perspective.

Subterfuge? Competition? A calling-out of the old lion? What was I trying to do here?

I shut my eyes and clasped the guru-bead jade of my mala in my hand. I implored the inward voice: *I have tried to turn my work into a service to all beings, through the careful preservation and, yes, circulation of beauty,* I murmured to it. *Is this futile? A wrong assumption?*

Emptiness, impermanence, the inward voice whispered back. *All things fall to dust, even beautiful objects, even yü. Didn't you notice that powdery degradation that told you the yü had come from a tomb? Even yü, the Stone of Heaven, dissolves in time.*

So should I just forget about it? Let Albert have his scheme, whatever it is? Just let the stones go?

NO! came the screaming reply.

My eyes snapped open and the first thing I beheld was the horrifying face of Vajrayogini, a red-bodied, wrathful female deity with three glaring eyes, who danced in a ring of fire and drank blood from a skull. Her dancing feet stomped on a hapless man whose wispy mustache reminded me of Albert.

Okay, thanks, I get it, I thought. Vajrayogini faded back to being a *thangka* painting hanging to one side of the great golden Buddha statue's proscenium arch.

Through this virtue, may I and all beings be endowed with the accomplishments of body, speech and mind, and may all suffering be pacified, Dave-now-Trinley intoned, and the assembled *sangha* droned along.

It was a pretty full house for a Tuesday night meditation, so there was a milling crowd in the coatroom afterwards as people put on their shoes. Betsy had no trouble waddling up to me.

"I'm sorry I was so clumsy," she said. "I didn't mean to hit you so hard."

"That's okay, Betsy, really."

"A good thump on the back usually stops a cough, but I kind of overdid it."

"No problem, Betsy, thank you."

"Maybe you should see a doctor and tell me if I cracked any ribs."

"Betsy, sweetheart, reality check here." Be nice, be nice. "You didn't hurt me. I'm fine."

"I'm sorry I kicked you." Was there a medical term for this behavior? A syndrome of some kind?

"I know. It's fine to be sorry, you just don't have to be sorry all the time. Nothing's that bad."

"Am I making you mad? I'm sorry."

"*Betsy.*" I cupped her pudgy cheeks in both hands and put my face near hers. My voice rose into the danger range, the flaming queen tones. "Stop apologizing. If somebody somewhere got really mad at you one time, *nobody here knows about it*. Move on. Feel other things. Just set the shopping bag down, honey, none of that stuff is yours."

Maybe it was that last non-sequitur, or maybe something else, but she shut up and blinked. Her eyes tracked back and forth, fast. She was thinking. I squeezed her shoulder and gave her a tight smile. "Okay? Okay. See you around." And I got the hell out of the temple. Something had been set in motion. I hoped I would be forgiven.

4.
BARDO

I didn't set the alarm, and slept in. Then I made a big breakfast and read the paper, watered the plants, dusted, and generally puttered around. All to avoid looking at the sticky note where I'd copied Valerie L's address and phone number out of the guest book. I rationalized that I wanted to be fully awake and dressed before deciding whether to call ahead or just show up at her door. I was picking out a shirt when the phone rang.

"God, what are *you* doing home?" a familiar and wonderful voice caroled. "You're never home! Here I had a witty message all thought up and you ruin it by talking to me in person!"

"Mark? Jesus, Mark! How are you, for fuck's sake!" Only with the best of friends could I cuss before noon.

"Oh, I'm frazzled and cranky and so is Scottie. So we decided to blow off everything this weekend and head up to the islands for sunshine and sailing. We need a crew, and you're on it."

I couldn't help laughing. Most humans avoid houseguests when they want to relax, but Mark throws out a net and hauls them in.

"How else are we ever going to see you?" Mark shouted into my laughter.

"Aaagh, I know, I know, I'm a *bad* gym buddy. I'm paying for it, believe me." It was true. I could pinch way more than an inch of pliant flesh down at my belly button.

"Ross. You aren't still moaning around the house about the monk, are you?"

"No, no, that's long over with."

"Good. I can still hear him complaining about how his new boyfriend was going to drag him off to some weird church service. Go figure."

I chattered happily with Mark for another twenty minutes, discussing meal plans and ferry schedules. This was another world I could surrender to gratefully. Among these friends I could speak in another voice, with other rhythms, just turn away from Albert and be elsewhere. Teasing, laughter, quick and pointed conversations, tender regard. Dinners, hugs, heads laid on shoulders, the joy within men's bodies. Not that any of it could make Albert or the gallery disappear entirely. Everything I had in this city, I had because of Albert. Nor could it erase Dave, whose memory lounged on one side of me, while Trinley the monk sat in lotus posture on the other. Even while cherishing Mark's voice on the phone, I sensed all of my different lives hanging together like blind trapeze artists, sailing through the air, each trusting that from some direction, a slim bar at the same moment was swinging in their direction.

Mark and his partner Scottie were realtors who had kept their heads cool and their investments conservative while riding the crest of the long housing boom. Their island cabin could easily sleep twelve and their favorite hobby was a 45-foot two-masted wooden yacht. I met Mark when he came into the gallery to see about borrowing something lovely for a Street of Dreams open house. Mark peered down at the world from a six-foot-seven-inch height and had a blonde handlebar mustache that he actually twirled, putting a second perpetual smile on his face. Only the Pied Piper had a bigger Rolodex. Scottie, Mark's partner in life and business, was about my height (kind of short) and barrel-shaped, a profile emphasized by his shaved head and tiny black-rimmed glasses. I often think of him anchored next to Mark like a mailbox next to a telephone pole. A weekend at their island house sounded like exactly the escape I needed.

When I hung up it was nearly noon. I dialed Valerie L. Endless ringing, no call waiting, no bump into voice mail. Some people think that makes them more honest. Okay, she asked for it. I tucked her address into my pocket and left.

Valerie L's neighborhood was full of sturdy, close-hugging cottages that had come out of the millennial rehab frenzy with fussy paint jobs and proud gardens. Valerie L's address did not have the best lawn care on the block. Moss was winning occupation of the roof. In fact, it looked like a rental. I found a parking spot on the street in a lineup of Subaru Outbacks. As I took the key out of the ignition I glanced into the rearview mirror and saw Valerie L come out of the house, followed by a man.

Instantly I scrunched down below the headrest and watched in the mirror as they got in one of the Outbacks. What a stupid, marvelous thrill! Exactly what I had felt playing "Stakeout" as a kid. Still scrunched, I turned on the ignition again and shifted into drive. The Outback pulled into the street and passed my car. I popped up and pulled out to follow.

I tailed the Outback according to the standards in every *Rockford Files* and *Simon & Simon* re-run I had ever seen. Keep them in sight but one or two cars in between. It's harder than you'd think.

We wound up at a modish strip mall, one that had been refashioned into a pseudo-village with courtyards and covered walkways. I was walking well behind them when it occurred to me that I had no idea what I would say if Valerie L saw and recognized me. I had been having too much dirty fun just looking at them to stop and think about it.

Valerie L was still straight-backed and clad in loose layers that flowed around her long stride and precise moves. Still cutting her way through the air like a razor blade from Mars. Still scraping my senses, for some maddening, unknown reason.

The man, now … the *man*. There was a severe disconnect here. Four years of ultra-high-end retail sales had taught me body language, especially between couples. The man walked with that virile sway to his shoulders and swing to his beefy arms that bound the territory, announcing that he and this woman were together. But Valerie L's body language said, Just looking, not buying. The man's said, Sold, bought, paid for, comfortable with the mortgage. The somewhat more minor disconnect was what she could possibly see in him.

There was one thing everybody could see in him, and that was his hair. His hair was born from a race of gods. Thick, red-gold, curly, it jutted proudly from his brow and flowed back in a bountiful leonine mane. It was deftly shaped into a mullet that didn't actually look like a mullet, an admirable achievement all by itself. award all by itself. Somehow this hair had made a triumphant descent from Apollo's chariot … and landed on a baked potato. The barrel-chested, frog-eyed, bow-legged, acne-scarred guy underneath that glory walked confidently beside his woman, but with denied anger loaded into his tense back muscles and bristling red mustache. He knew the rest of him would never live up to what sat on his head.

My inward voice whispered, *he worships her.*

For some reason, Betsy flitted through my mind and I felt a glimmering of kinship with Valerie L.

They got in line at the multiplex cinema. So did I, with some trepidation. How was I going to know what movie they were seeing? Fortunately the speaker from the ticket window was loud. It squawked their choice, the amount of their change, and advised them to have a good day.

I bought a ticket for the same movie and followed them in, staying out of Valerie L's peripheral sightline. They sat in the middle of the house. I stayed in the back. They bought a tub of popcorn. I made do with a bottle of soda water.

The movie was Chinese. It was a historical epic, frantic with kung-fu action. There were fight scenes spun out like arias and most of the character development lay in how the opponents handled their weapons. I was swept away. Hooked in the delicious heart, lured by the dream of an immense past where anything could happen.

The end credits rolled and I had just noticed that the composer and music soundtrack were identical to that *other* blockbuster Chinese historical kung-fu fantasy adventure, when I felt a tap on my shoulder.

Valerie L smiled and waved at me, as she walked past with her man in the crowd's exodus.

I went rigid. Number one, I was mortified. Caught. No wonder I had never made it onto a TV detective series.

Number two, Valerie L was wearing *yü*. The golden turtle pendant, suspended on its red silk cord, glowed against her pale skin. A two-thousand-year-old national treasure dangled from her neck *in a movie theater*.

I banged my knee rocketing out of my seat, and so limped painfully up to the lobby.

They were still in the lobby when I hobbled out. Royal Hair was saying something to her, leaning in close to whisper into her ear. She looked surprised and happy; they both smiled; her arm circled his waist with affection. His hand went to her hip and rested there. His back had not relaxed, but there was a softening in his eyes, the beginnings of happiness in his scarred face. They gazed at each other, satisfaction having caught them by surprise.

It suddenly struck me that Royal Hair was younger than Valerie L. By how much? I couldn't even tell *her* age. But all speculation froze as another figure glided towards them.

He was tall, he was Black, he was bald, his body came from the same race of gods that had forged the other fellow's hair; and he made a beeline for Valerie L. He spoke her name - not quite a greeting, closer to a command. Valerie L spun around; I could actually see the color leave her face. Royal Hair stepped away, to get a better look at this guy. His hand stayed on Valerie L's hip, holding her in place, staking his claim. I ducked behind a life-size cardboard cutout of Bruce Willis cuddling assault weapons, and watched.

Their voices were just audible through the chatter and clang of the multiplex lobby. The words were trivial. Nothing. But the crowd parted around them, leaving them in a clear circle where Something Big flexed and snorted.

Did you see the Chinese movie, Valerie? That must have been what you were seeing. Uh, yes, we did. I hope it was good, you've been looking forward to it so much. Why does he want to know if we saw the Chinese movie, Val? Greg, this is my friend Del —I'm her friend. An old friend. Greg, he met my son in—What does it matter if we saw the Chinese movie? Lots of people want to see this movie. I hope we can still see this movie together, Valerie, if you don't mind seeing it again. Del, this is Greg, he's a—I think I can take Valerie out to a movie without being interrogated by a stranger. I said I'm her friend, an old friend. Greg, he met my son in—We can go out in public without the third degree.

Bald God would not look at Royal Hair, even when he was addressing the man. He stared at Valerie L with a calm, stone-cold countenance. Bald God was even younger than Royal Hair. I was watching two virile men fighting for possession of a woman who could be old enough to be their mother.

Valerie L lowered her eyes and took a deep breath. Her hands lifted like silks on the wind. One touched Royal Hair's sternum, the other touched Bald God's cheek. They shut up.

"Del, it was great to see you, please call me. Greg and I have to be somewhere, we have to run, but please, *call me.*" Maybe she gave Royal Hair the lightest shove imaginable. He turned, she turned with him, and they sped out the door.

Bald God watched them go. He lifted his hand in a desultory farewell, then turned away, shaking his head, as if trying to clear it. Maybe he wondered what all that had really been about. I certainly wondered. Something Big dissipated, but clung to Bald God as a glowing charisma that sharpened his elegantly cut features.

The man was eight feet away from the Bruce Willis cutout as he moved back into the lobby's crowd. Nothing suggested he had seen me, but I would swear I felt a fleeting brush of attention as the beautiful man passed by.

5.
MISSION

On my third call, around dinnertime, I finally got Valerie L on the phone. She sounded very tired, under her busy voice. "Thank God you called. This fixes everything. I'd forgotten you were there at the theater. He saw you, when I waved. Yikes. I'm so embarrassed you saw that scene today," she said. Good grief. Bruce Willis had been no help at all. "But at the same time it was perfect, because it'll make this easier," she went on. "Can you come over? As soon as possible? I have to ask you a favor."

Twenty minutes later, I rang her bell. I was relieved to see, when she opened the door, that she had taken off the *yü*. Her energy level was about eight notches above what she'd projected on the phone, but maybe that was just tension.

Valerie L's living room enveloped me in a blanket of earthy colors, handcrafted objects, chenille throws and pillows, and the smell of spicy cooking. She waved me onto the sofa and sailed around the kitchen making tea. Her vocal bursts from the kitchen—"Herbal? Black? Green? Lemon? Milk? Sugar? Mug? Glass? Cat, get *off* the counter!"—were blasts of sunlight that forcibly swept a miasma of sadness off of the furniture and into the corners, where it huddled in sour shadows. Usually I don't like spending much time in strangers' houses, because the quality of their most frequent visitors tends to cling like an odor. I couldn't help noticing the two ornate wooden music stands and a tall bookcase full of sheet music crowding up against the sofa. The instrument itself was carefully stowed on an upper shelf. It might be a violin, but the case was kind of big. A viola? If she were a teacher in this house as well as a performer outside of it, her students were a gloomy lot. Still, on top of the bookcase, in the spare inches between it and the ceiling, a small stone Buddha sat smiling down on us. Hello there, Mr. B. Lucky you, perched way up there, just watching.

I had just taken the tea mug in my hands when she said, as if there had been no break in the conversation, "I should have stopped there in the aisle and introduced you to Greg. But there were so many people, we had to keep going." She folded herself into the deep overstuffed armchair with her tea mug. "It was so damned clear that you were supposed to come out with us and start talking to Greg about the jade, the pendant. He's old-fashioned, but he does pay attention to synchronicities. Whatever *you* said about this little jade would have meant something to him. And then Del showed up. God, that shook me." She paused to brush straying hair out of her face.

I set my mug down and held up both hands, to slow her. "Before we get into this, whatever it is, there's a reason I called you," I said. "It's about the jades. I'm afraid I was a little too casual about letting them go yesterday. There are other factors to consider, that we didn't discuss."

"*I* had no problem with you, Ross. Did Albert Jarro slap your wrists? *He* thought I had fakes."

"Actually, the trouble is that they *are* real, they *are* Han Dynasty. Valerie, have you ever had to defend yourself against Chinese government lawyers in an international lawsuit?"

She was sipping her tea; she stopped, staring at me over the mug. She lowered it calmly. "Oh. You're trying to scare me."

"I'm trying to get you to protect yourself and whoever you're giving these jades to. The story you wanted me to witness, well, that's all rainbows to a judge. The Chinese government is very committed to gathering and protecting its cultural treasures—especially ancient ones like these."

"And they would know for sure where these jades came from? Which court, which Emperor? Because I don't."

"That's where I can begin to be of help. If you allow me to study the jades, get them dated at a lab, I can put together basic due diligence documents. The point is, Valerie"—and here I dropped my voice to a whisper, just as if Albert were still listening to us—"these objects are treasures. There are a lot of very, very wealthy people willing to pay a lot of money to own these, even in secret." One of Albert's taboos forbade ever speaking of the special market for the *greatness*. But I was making my own rules now.

Valerie L was unimpressed. She brought the mug to her face and swallowed more tea, then wiped her mouth with the back of her hand.

"Sounds like the best thing to do is nothing at all," she said. "Taking them to a lab would put the word out. If we just let all that drop, nobody knows anything. They don't exist. Wouldn't that be better?"

I sighed heavily and rubbed my face. I heard her chuckle. I kept my hands over my eyes; I wasn't interested in watching her laugh at me.

"Cheer up, Ross, you're preaching to the wrong choir anyway," she said. "Pretty soon I won't be holding these jades at all. I'm giving them back to their rightful owners, remember? They'll be the ones to make this decision."

"Well then, just do me a favor and don't wear that turtle in public again, all right?" I said, exasperated. "Unless you're winning a Grammy or something."

She *was* grinning. "No problem," she replied. "The turtle pendant is Greg's. I need you to give it to him as soon as possible. Like tonight."

I had to swallow and clear my throat twice, then gulp some tea.

"You asked me to come over here, so *I* can give it to him? Why? He doesn't even know me." That chill of dread, still unexamined in its cupboard in my soul since I shoved it there on Monday, escaped through my joints and raced along my nerves.

"Like I said," Valerie L rattled on, "Greg is old-fashioned. You're a man, and you're a professional in Chinese art. Greg accepts that I'm an intuitive, and I've gotten him to trust more of his own intuition. But he needs the extra boost from outside. You've got an edge here, because you know the *story* in the jade. Plus," her voice and gaze wavered, "we had a fight on the way home from the movie. Rather, *he* had a fight. I was trying to calm him down and figure out what had happened. So it didn't end well when he dropped me off." She lapsed into a worried reverie, looking drained.

I let the silence sit for just a moment. "Who's Del?" I asked neutrally.

"Prince," Valerie L muttered, distracted.

"Who is Del Prince?" I asked again.

Valerie L looked up at me. "Del is *the* Prince," she said irritably. "The Prince in the *story*, in that lifetime."

Oh.

There was that Christmas tree again. Wild rumor made flesh.

Buddhist practice had evolved the notion of rebirth, for me, from an excuse for fanciful gossip to a source of serious reflection on how actions and relationships reverberate across time and throughout the fluidity of matter. This fluidity, this emptiness, had come, for me, to be the accepted "reason" for the stories I could feel and see in the antiques filling the Albert Jarro Gallery. Now that fluidity extended to faces, bodies, names, responsibilities, a hand wearing a thumb ring, writing a forbidden story.

"I've known Del for years, and I've never run into him in public like that, *never*," Valerie L went on. "Today, I'm with Greg and there he is. And he has never, ever behaved like that or spoken like that around me. He is truly a prince of a man."

"They were fighting over you," I blurted. *Oops*, said Habit, and prepared me to be thrown out of the house. Instead, Valerie L sighed and nodded.

"It didn't hit me until Greg had left," she said. "When we were getting ready to go out this afternoon, well, out of the blue, Greg asked to see the jade turtle. He insisted I should wear it. In*sisted*. So I was wearing the jade, Del showed up, and they were ready to kill each other." She smacked her forehead theatrically. "Duh! It's obvious, right?"

"Erm … ?"

"*Greg is the Emperor*. The turtle was his jade, in that life. I was wearing it. Here comes the Prince from that life. And there I am wearing the Emperor's jade."

There was that vertigo again. How lucky I was, always to be sitting down when the wall of time that separated me from wonderful, terrible old China was breached, gaped wide, air and sounds and sights rushed through, and there was no distinguishing this life from that. What had played out in the movie lobby was the story that had cost a man his head two thousand years ago.

"You're … you were the girl in the temple," I whispered.

"So I am," Valerie L said. Her voice was quiet, her face sad. "So I was."

Now I could see that she was in her fifties. Little sags and lines lapped over her face and down her throat. Still, in the lightness of her presence, and the gravity, there was the acolyte of the Tao, the seeker of immortality, who had drawn the gaze of the Emperor himself.

"I've told Del the story," Valerie L was saying, as I dragged my focus back to the more-or-less here-and-now. "He was concerned that he didn't remember it. I told him, he didn't have to. So he accepts it on my word … on his faith in me."

"On his love for you?" I barely murmured it, but Valerie L nodded vigorously. Melodrama didn't stand a chance in her energy field.

"The way he put it, it was the only way his feelings for me made any sense," she said. "I had to agree, because that's exactly how it is for me." She looked even sadder, like a grave priestess. "You see, the first time I laid eyes on Del, and every time I'm with him, I feel like I'm cut open and bleeding."

Oh. A preview of coming attractions.

"He's a lot younger than you," I said.

She smiled. "As a matter of fact, he's my son's age. They met on the University's fencing team." The thought of Valerie L with a son was a little more information than I wanted. "The first time my son brought him over, he would not come into the house. Would not. Would *not*. I finally had to go out to the car with a cup of tea and invite him in. That's how strong it was. On a very deep level, he remembers. He remembers everything."

Maybe he did, but I felt like I was tangled in gossamer veils of amnesia. "Do you suppose I was there?" I asked Valerie L.

"You've come along this far, so possibly yes. I can't really tell." She arched an amused eyebrow at me. "Do you mind?"

"No! No. But, really, why does Greg need to get his jade tonight?" Things were moving too fast. I'd have to negotiate a whole new exclusivity agreement with this Greg person, Mr. Royal Hair.

"He was very upset by Del, the whole thing in the theater lobby. Of course he doesn't know the story, so he doesn't know why he's reacting like this. That makes it worse for him, and all he can think is that it's something *I'm* doing. So we get in the car and he demands to know if I'm having an affair with this bald Black guy." Her look at me sharpened. "And no, I am not. We are not, not this time. That's why meeting Del again has been

so hard. We both have the passion, but we don't dare go there."
Again, I added silently.

"So Greg goes into feeling betrayed, wanting to trust me completely, he thought he knew me and thought we were very close friends, yadda yadda. I'm trying to stay clear inside all my emotions, so I can figure out what's going on. Whenever Del walks into the room, something's going *on*. And Greg could feel that." Another woman would have been up pacing the floor by this time. Valerie L simply sat up straighter and tucked her long legs up in a full lotus posture, origami'd in the comfy armchair. The emotion crackled off of her like electricity.

"Finally we pull up to my house and Greg turns to me. 'Valerie,' he says, 'you can figure that I care about you beyond friendship. Way beyond.' You can see where he's headed, right?"

"Oh, yeah."

"Oh, yeah. Wants to go to the next level, the whole nine yards. Now, Greg is a good man, believe me. But, you and I know now, he was the Emperor. And he's *still* the Emperor! He thought he was doing me a favor by offering me a choice! Bless his heart, he hardly knows what a choice *is*."

She had finished her rant, or at least come to a significant rest. "So, why tonight?" I asked. "Why not tomorrow or next week?"

"He said something to me in the lobby that showed his viewpoint is changing," Valerie L answered. "We walked into the lobby and he said, 'You know, I'm sure I lived back then.' That made me so happy. I damn near kissed him. Remember, I didn't fully realize his role right then. I was just happy that he had opened up to feeling a truth that couldn't be proven. Then Del arrived and that shit hit the fan. And when I said 'No, thank you' to Greg, he said he would leave the door open until I was ready. He drove off, and I realized that he was the Emperor. He, the Prince and I had all played our parts today in the same way we had back then. Do you understand how dangerous that is?"

"Well, as long as they're unarmed …" I began, lamely.

Her hand shot forward and her index finger touched—so gently!—the bracelet of beads on my wrist, that had crept out from under my sleeve. "You know the Dharma," she said, with a firmness that pinned me like a butterfly. "You *know* what I'm talking about. Greg and Del won't harm each other physically—

but their souls have been crippled by this fight and it is *my responsibility* to end it. You know the story in the jades. You know what has to be *dropped*. Once and for all. Gone, done. We have struggled long enough, all of us. The moment for change is *now*."

She rose from the chair and went to the back bedrooms. I still felt the ring of that *we, us,* and resented being dragged into the fight that was theirs, not mine. My story was different.

She returned with a small wrapped package and a sealed envelope bearing a sticky note. When she put the package in my hands I felt the familiar dimensions of a gem box, and the tingling rush of the *yü*'s presence.

"His address is on the sticky note," Valerie L said. "He goes to bed at eleven o'clock on the dot, so you've got time to get there tonight, while all this stuff is still fresh for him."

I got up, too. Valerie handed me another sticky note. "There's Del's phone number," she said. "You'll want to talk to him next. I gave him the scabbard piece yesterday. For his birthday."

Breathe, I told myself sternly. In, out. Just because it's gone from her possession doesn't mean it's *gone*. "Oh. Could you perhaps call him first, as a kind of introduction for me?"

"Sure. Don't worry, I know he can be kind of intimidating. But really, he's a prince. Just treat him like one and you'll get along fine."

Intimidation didn't concern me. I just didn't want to melt at his feet like a burning Skipper doll.

The thumb-ring! Habit interrupted, fidgeting like a child. *What about the thumb-ring? If I'm in this fight with you, tell me who I was! Am I the* shih? *Can I have the thumb ring, can I have it now, can I?*

But she was still talking. "Will you call me, when you've given it to Greg?"

"Will I reach you? You don't have voice mail."

"Of course I have voice mail. But it's like wearing watches. You like my watch?" She held up her wrist. It was bare. "Watches don't work on me. I stop time. Same with the phone. Nothing gets through unless I really need to hear it."

That actually sounded kind of wonderful. I agreed to keep trying until we connected. As I stepped onto the porch, Valerie

L touched my arm. Again, that little electric jolt. The *uh-oh* that silenced both Habit and Reality.

"This is a good work you're doing," she said quietly, with an extra force under her words, and an intimacy that made me blush.

"May it be for the benefit of all," was all I could think of to say.

Valerie L grinned, like the sun breaking through cloud cover. She reached over and tapped the bracelet of beads again. "The Dharma helps, doesn't it?"

"Yes, it does. It … well, it clarifies, it gives perspective. On things like passion." Now why did that embarrassing word pop out of my mouth? Was it the imminent introduction to Del, the Great Bald God? Valerie L opened her mouth to say something, then shut it. She just smiled and nodded, and closed the door.

I shut my car door and welcomed the cocoon of silence. I touched the little package in my coat pocket. *Tingle*. Passion? I had a perspective on passion?

What I had was a two-thousand-and-more-year-old jade in my pocket. Did I really have to reach Mr. Greg Royal Hair tonight? I could zip over to the gallery and fire up the gemology microscope for a deeper look into the little turtle's nephrite body. Tiny mineral deposits called "inclusions" could tell me where the jade was mined. That would direct my historical research into China's regional jade mines, which could determine the turtle's real age, and connect it to other jade works in collections and museums. Would it really hurt anyone so much to give Greg his treasure tomorrow, rather than tonight?

A traffic light switched to yellow, and I realized with a jolt that I had been driving in a complete trance. Under the influence of jade. I pulled into a convenience store lot to get my bearings, and think.

I was hot all over, I wanted so much to get started on this line of detective work. It could become an article, published in *National Geographic*. What a project, what a career boost, what …. Ah, shit. What if Albert was at the gallery, making international phone calls as he often did late at night, when I walked in with the turtle pendant? Just the thought made my shoulders feel weak and I saw myself handing over the little gem box. My body heat faded. It would happen. He would just glance at me and know. With Albert in the room I would submit, and continue the dance of antique beauty, on and on.

I got out of the car and went into the convenience store, where I bought razorblades and Scotch tape. In Greg's neighborhood, I parked on the street a block away from his house, in the shadow under a generous old cedar tree. I just hoped nobody would call 911, thinking some crusty, silver-haired old guy had stopped under the tree to masturbate.

I clamped my key ring's tiny flashlight between my teeth to illuminate the package. My new razor blade carefully slit the tape and I unfolded the wrappings. There was the musty gem box. In it, the golden jade turtle. In my hands, the rushing buzz of the *story*. I cupped it in my hands around it and closed my eyes.

Water Song

The reason I experience great evil is
That I have a persona.
If I have no persona:
What evil could I experience?

—Lao Tzu,
Tao Te Ching

German tr. Richard Wilhelm,
English tr. H. G. Ostwald

6.
THE SECOND JADE'S STORY
PART I

My son is angry with me because I have taken a new concubine.

He has given me his ring.

There is merit in his anger; I have caused him to lose face.

The golden turtle, a jade the color of firelight. The turtle signifies longevity. Not immortality, understand.

It will have to be so. The girl shines too brightly to leave her on this mountain.

He means it as a protection for me.

I look at her; I listen to her discourses, her poetry and recitations; in my presence she performs the lightly dancing movements that cultivate immortality; I can feel immortality growing in me as I watch; a precious gift the Son of Heaven did not expect.

He wore it on a finger, I wear it on a thumb. I have never worn jade as an ornament except in my hair, even after more than a year in the Imperial Palace. Strange how the stone grows warm on my flesh.

Her name is Water Song.

Protection. Another shell to cover me in this dead world of endless walls and gardens. Endless rooms, endless screens. Endless servants piercing me with their dead eyes.

After the temple's festival day, I lie in my pavilion and speak that name to the softly billowing tent roof: Water Song.

But when I wear this turtle, the whispers will stop. The cruel comments and pranks, the pokes and pinches, the murmured threats and rumors of poison will stop. Must stop. Because this jade is a sign of the Emperor's regard. His affection. His protection.

The next day I sit in a hall with the girl and her Masters, and debate with her—with a fourteen-year-old girl! And we make each other laugh!

I have been two people ever since putting on the Emperor's silks and stepping into his palanquin.

The second night, I lie in my pavilion and think of the great Imperial Palace, the seat of the Son of Heaven. It seems a very dark place, without Water Song in its halls and courtyards.

An absurd tale says that the Emperor's gaze created the whole world as he looked down from heaven, before taking birth in the human realm. I do know that the Emperor's gaze created a second Water Song.

How can I explain this to my son?

Water Song, the concubine. A girl from no family, raised to unheard-of status and carried off to the Imperial Palace! A character in a poem, now sung everywhere in the Ten Kingdoms.

The others hardly matter. My son Jade Mountain has lost face and I have a duty to his honor as much as he has a duty to mine.

My Temple Masters forbade me to think of this as a cruel fate. Everything is the Way, the Tao, they said. Do not resist, let the Tao's movements guide you, become one with their current.

Here is how it shall be done: The choice to become a bright jewel of the Imperial Household shall belong to the girl.

But I am not one. I am two. I am myself, she who dances the movements of immortality, who unites with life itself. And I am Water Song the Imperial Concubine ... dressed, painted, beaded, bathed, perfumed, paraded, instructed, protected ... and despised because I have not yet entered the Emperor's bed.

If she enters the life of a concubine of her own accord, who has been harmed? My son can be pacified by this, and so can those pestering voices around us.

I am still a virgin.

And she has no family! Is it possible to describe the freedom in this? She is an open door, a clear sky. Not even my First Wife can accuse me of having a political purpose in elevating this girl. Surely my son will understand this.

To the other concubines and the many Wives, to their eunuchs and maids, I am a monster.

Water Song is angry with me, too.

I have a friend.

I remind her that coming with me was her choice. She retorts: "Whatever it pleases the Emperor to offer is a blessing from heaven and cannot be refused." Another proper sting, given fearlessly ... yet with eyes cast down and a quiet demeanor—which is not the air of the quick debate mistress who made me laugh.

In the first week of my new life as an Imperial concubine, I joined the entire group of Wives and concubines for a dinner. After the meal, a musician appointed to our Court told humorous stories and sang poems, all of his own invention. He was young, only a few years older than myself, with dimples like two extra smiles on his moon-round face. His nickname, I learned, was Cookpot, because he bubbled with surprises. It was true—he wove his anecdotes and jokes into designs that revealed the Way's teachings. I laughed with delight! It echoed in the room. No one else even chuckled.

There are shadows in this situation. If the Son of Heaven cannot bestow the gift of free choice, what is his true power?

The Emperor's Wives and concubines seem as varied as a quick-fry dinner, but underneath their robes they are all vegetables from the same patch. At that moment they looked at me with one expression: contempt. I was a bumpkin from nowhere, to laugh so. I was ignorant, to feel so much pleasure. I was a fool, to show what I felt.

Here is how it shall be done: Water Song is a gift of freedom to me because she has no family. I shall gift her with as much freedom as can be granted to a concubine. I shall invent such freedom for her that Emperors a thousand years from now will honor their favored women in the same way.

There was one who did not look at me. That was First Wife.

The first and greatest freedom is this: The Silence of a Hundred Paces, no listeners or watchers for that distance around us, so that Water Song and I may speak as man and woman.

Her cushion raised her higher than the other Wives, for she is not only the first woman taken to consort with He who ascended the Dragon Throne, she is the mother of the Emperor's first-born son. The other mothers of the Emperor's children sat on cushions that raised them higher than the still-childless concubines. First Wife does not need a cushion in any case. She is long of limb and waist, with an extended neck like a swan's, and her face sweeps up from a pointed little chin to a wide forehead perfect for carrying elaborate swirls of hair and jewelry. It is evident that she considers herself an Empress, even though the Emperor has not named his First Son, her child, as his heir, which would officially elevate her to the rank and title.

The second freedom is this: Water Song shall enter my bed only as her own desire dictates. I shall not force her. But I shall win her. It shall be a campaign the great scholars of war never imagined!

This Jade Crane of Heaven did not look at me when I laughed. Instead, she slowly lifted her fan and wafted it back and forth. As if dispersing a stink.

She asks for the use of the large garden, the Sunrise Garden, for her exercises. Well, why not? The other conditions, though—they are somewhat more complicated. No guards visible. And one blind, mute music master to accompany her movements. Well, if the Son of Heaven can create the Silence of a Hundred Paces, he can create a garden where no one watches a girl exercise.

The other Wives and concubines looked away from me and did exactly the same. It wasn't another breath before the many eunuchs in attendance had their fans out as well. Waft, waft, waft. What a breeze.

She is less angry than before. Perhaps she is getting used to life in the Palace. A good bed and good food—who wouldn't prefer that?

My face flooded hot with shame. I knew what this meant for me from now on.

But my mind tingled—the feeling that someone was looking at me.

It was Cookpot. Holding my gaze, he lifted one eyebrow and one corner of his mouth, so that one dimple winked just for me.

"Why bother with them?" was his message.

I gave Cookpot a smile of gratitude. A small one. I had learned that much in one day.

We have been friends ever since, in the small ways that are the only ways possible in this world of protective shells and peeping eyes. Although he is not a eunuch, Cookpot is permitted to enter the Women's Palace for entertainments due to his artistry. Fortunately this same artistry makes him unfit to wield power in the Emperor's government. Music has un-manned him in the eyes of the law. Everyone in the Women's

Palace knows what punishment our funny poet would suffer if he were caught in a liaison with one of the Emperor's women; some of the concubines find this exciting, but I am content to observe the customs of this matter, to preserve his life.

Yet when he made a simple gesture of kindness to me, a suffering concubine, I felt such a suffusion of emotion throughout my flesh that I wondered at it, before remembering— such sweetness is the welcome of friendship.

"A poor poet, long building a shaky tower of inkstrokes, seeks the sure foundation stone of your understanding," he wrote to introduce a roll of poems sent for my commentary.

"What does the nightingale remember of flight among the stars? Fill your ears with stars, and listen," read one of them.

Small things like this landed like drops of rain on a drought-sickened earth.

I have often stood in the woods, or on the stones of the mountain, and lifted my face to receive the rain. I would make my mind unite with its downward-blessing rush, until I could feel myself rise into the air with the dew and ride the wind like a cloud. Then, when my mind came to my body again, I looked out upon a new, clean world.

In this way I closed my eyes in the gentle rain of friendship with Cookpot. And when I opened them again I found a different world, where I had no more wisdom, nor any ground under my feet.

Rebellion has broken out in one of the Kingdoms.

If I were a cruel Son of Heaven, straightaway I would harness hunger and desperation as my Generals. These two masters drive the most ragged and untrained peasants to a ferocity that overwhelms even Imperial soldiers.

Once again, the peasants of a poor farming region have rallied behind a self-appointed savior who will liberate them from the heartless Emperor. My father dealt with many uprisings like this, and I saw such rebels first hand in my military youth.

This time, it seems that no one knows who the rebel General is. He rides masked, and goes by several code names. His peasant army has already liberated seven granaries and redistributed thousands of head of cattle. Some rustic poet has even composed a bawdy song about him and his army.

This is no ordinary country hero, then. He does not boast of his name for local glory. He understands the uses of drama and mystery.

I went to an archery contest. Cookpot invited me.

His special place in the Imperial Court, in addition to being the foremost student of the Emperor's best musicians, is as shih to Third Wife's child, one of the Emperor's sons. This prince had challenged some of his brothers and other young men of the Court to best him in archery. It was all a matter of fun, a chance to gamble and enjoy being outdoors. I wanted to see Cookpot match wits with the other shihs, improvising poetry as they counted the hits and misses.

I must send an army to crush this rebellion, even as my ministers and their deputies scurry to gather reports from the region on the conditions that inspired it.

I sat in a pavilion with the other concubines. They tolerated me in public but could be vicious in our private apartments. Needles in my food, for instance. Mice in my bedding. "Oh, look, your country cousin has come to visit!" they would laugh. In public they merely joked about me behind their fans. It was easy to ignore them and watch the contest.

Even as I enjoyed the action and antics, sadness misted the edges of my mind to see that the Imperial Court considered this to be "outdoors." Really it was a large garden, surrounded by high walls wide enough for guards to stroll on the top. My mountain temple and its forests seemed to be a heaven on the other side of the sky.

Here is another chance to test a son's character. First Son is already away suppressing barbarian incursions on the Southern border, so this rebellion will be Jade Mountain's task.

By his own merit and effort, he has regained the honor my new concubine cost him. He defeated all challengers in a recent archery contest. An industrious Prince, indeed! We shall see what lessons he teaches to the masked General.

My mind tingled. Someone was looking at me.

It was the Prince, Jade Mountain. The son of Third Wife; the Prince who had mounted the contest. All day his happy smile and natural way with the Court made the competition a relaxed, festive affair.

He was definitely looking at me. One hand on his hip.

I will never forget this memory of him. It was like a break in the clouds, for someone to look at me in a clean way, without contempt. It could only mean he had no idea who I was.

This memory is still as sharp as sunlight. The blue and black of his tunic, the tight topknot of his raven-black hair, the red cords on his boots. The sweeping black wings of his eyebrows. His face, pale gold and shining slightly in the late summer heat, had an afternoon's beard shading his smooth, broad cheeks. He was not exactly smiling, but rather puzzled and held by the sight of me.

The Prince called Cookpot to his side. Cookpot knelt with happy obedience. The Prince posed a question. Cookpot glanced at me, then answered. The Prince dropped his hand from his hip, but he kept looking at me. The serious curiosity in his face changed to something else, something that shifted like a bright river. What was it?

Then I remembered that this was the Prince who refused to come to the temple festival, so as not to burden the female Seekers with the gaze of a young man looking for a wife. He had lost much face when the Emperor walked out of the temple with a new concubine.

No wonder his expression was full of unreadable emotions, seeing me.

I had learned some of the messages that could be passed back and forth by movements of a fan. I rarely used them, since no one would talk to me and I talked to no one besides the Emperor and Cookpot. But I drew my fan from my sleeve and touched it to my left shoulder, for the Prince. I had no hope of going unobserved, but at least I would not disgrace him. My fan movement meant, "I honor one of true heart."

He blushed. He blushed! I could control the shape of my mouth by this time, but I know a smile of delight filled my eyes.

Then the Prince was called away to the archery contest, with his shih attending. I was left alone with the concubines. But something wonderful had happened.

I felt like one person again.

🌾🌾🌾🌾🌾🌾🌾

A few days after the archery contest, another roll of writings came from Cookpot for my commentary and suggestions. Folded in with the bamboo wood strips of poems and funny anecdotes was a piece of silk. One of the most exquisite passages from Lao Tzu was written on it in delicate inkstrokes. At the bottom was a line of characters in a different hand. It read, "If the Way could be foretold, it would not be the Way. With great respect — " and the red stamp of the Prince Jade Mountain.

I stared at the silk for I don't know how long. The light in the room had changed by the time my mind came back to my body. I heard the heavy padding of an exceptionally fat eunuch coming down the corridor. It was time for one of my private visits with the Emperor.

For the first time in my life, I had something to hide — in a room where servants and enemies were always poking around! I stuffed the silk into my robe, under my breast. The eunuch opened the screen to find me going over Cookpot's poems.

The march to the room set aside for my visits with the Emperor follows a strict order, to protect us both. First the Exceptionally Fat Eunuch retrieves me from my quarters and escorts me to the edge of the concubines' compound. There we pick up three more eunuchs for a trip across a courtyard. In the next compound we are joined by two guards, fully armed. This group trots along a shortcut through two more compounds — I have never known what they house — to a very large gate where we are met by more guards, two of whom take their places in our group. Now we are in the Emperor's private household. Four guards striding foursquare, four eunuchs in diamond formation, and in the middle, me.

I am always glad of the thick bodies around me in the Emperor's household. Somewhere in these halls lives First Wife. Her ability to spy on and torment her rivals is legendary. The stupider concubines whisper that she is the daughter of a spider, so that all the spiders in the walls and rafters must bring her news of the entire court and even the entire Empire.

The Emperor has arranged that our visits are within the Silence of a Hundred Paces. That means no watchers, no guards, no spies, no servants at all for a hundred paces all around.

I enter the room first, and kneel on a cushion in the center. Painted silk screens are placed around me. There is a short wait, and then the screens are whisked away. There before me sits *the Emperor. The servants carrying the screens disappear fast. Thus we have something like privacy.*

It would be false to say I do not enjoy these visits. Cookpot is a privileged servant in the Court, but he is still a servant, and I have to be very careful in my communications with him. The Emperor, on the other hand ... well, he is the Emperor, but he is also a man of intelligence and spirit, with an interesting character. We were at ease with each other from our first debate in the temple. We made each other laugh! I remember thinking that night that I would not mind debating the Emperor again, should he decide to visit again.

Now here I am his concubine, isolated inside a maze of palaces and spies, and he is the only human being I can really talk to.

With that scrap of silk tucked under my breast, I knew I was betraying him.

I was two people again.

Once back in my rooms, I hid the letter in the little box that holds my clean monthly bloodrags. Not even the eunuchs like to poke in there.

🏵 🏵 🏵 🏵 🏵 🏵 🏵

The Emperor gave me use of the large garden, called the Sunrise Garden, for my exercises, the movements that cultivate immortality. To accompany me, Cookpot chose a blind musician who seemed to see with the strings of his instrument. For a while, I could forget that I was in a walled garden with armed guards posted just out of sight.

And then, one day ... tingle.

Someone was looking at me.

My eyes could not see anyone concealed in the bushes or lying on top of the wall. I returned to my exercise, and sent a question to the bushes, trees and sky.

They replied, and showed me a tree. Someone was hiding in it among the thick golden leaves. I couldn't see him with my eyes, but he was there. Like a rock in the flow of a brook.

A guard? No, it did not feel like a guard. The flow of the brook said this rock was not a guard.

There is always a point of choosing. You can resist, or flow. You can open a gate and step through, or lock it shut. I could have called for a guard. I could have walked up to the tree and shouted, "Hello, who's that?"

Instead, I focused my light, dancing movements on the person in the tree. As if I were dancing for him, or as if we were in a kind of friendly combat.

I wanted this person to join me in my dance, whoever it was.

This was a game I used to play with my Masters and the brother and sister Seekers in the Temple. A screen would be set between us. The game was to dance together and respond to each others' movements, without being able to see each other. Later on, we progressed to blindfolds in a room, or a courtyard, or a snowstorm. Always we would dance together, sometimes touching, sometimes not, but always feeling and responding to each other's movements.

Many people think this exercise is intended to improve combat skills. What a misunderstanding. The exercise is not possible if your intent is to kill or harm the other person. The movements are destructive to both body and spirit if their source is anger.

The exercise is an increase in lightness and joy. To be done properly, you expand your welcome and embrace of all life, refining each perception and response to the most subtle levels. It is teasing play, where two minds learn to meet, speak together in silence, and then have a witty debate in movement.

That was how I embraced and teased the person in the tree. To make a quicker journey to the subtle lights, I wrapped my scarf over my eyes. The Sunrise Garden was a place of waving colors and light behind my blindfold, as if all the trees and plants were made from illuminated silks paddling in a breeze.

First I met the awareness of the person in the tree, then embraced it—as if gently picking up that rock in the brook. I danced with that awareness until the rock softened and wriggled, and became a small dragon in my hands. I let it run up my arm and then across my shoulders, down my back, around my waist, circling my legs. The musician heard the extra fire in my movements, and added flame to the peppering melody plucked on his instrument.

Thus I danced with a dragon in that garden of lights.

I ended the exercise resting on one foot, with the other leg and arm extended. I released the dragon back to the air, and to the tree, so he would reunite with the body of the person who had been watching me. The musician sensed my completion, and brought his melody to an end.

In the garden's sudden quiet, I removed my blindfold and turned to the tree that I knew held the watcher. I still could see nothing there with my eyes.

But I bowed deeply to the tree, and then left the garden, touching the musician on the arm so he would follow me. My watcher should have as safe a passage out of his tree as he had getting there.

It was not even a full day before I found out who had been watching me.

I received another silk, tucked into a roll of bamboo strips from Cookpot.

"Forgive me," it read, in Jade Mountain's hand. "I heard such stories of your immortality dance at the temple festival, I convinced Cookpot to help me hide in the garden to see you for myself. Please have no anger towards Cookpot. I had to win a bet with him before he would consent to expose his friend in obedience to his lord."

And then, his stamp.

Nothing more than that.

Irrational anger rose up in me. Nothing more than that?

I found my own set of brushes and inks. I turned the silk over and prepared to write, "I hereby give Cookpot permission to hide you anywhere you would command. I understand the Imperial Stables are well-guarded and full of secrets. Please tell me what you find there." Fortunately I stopped my hand.

Probably he did not want to speak of his experience in the tree, or perhaps he couldn't find the words to speak of it.

Finally I wrote, "The Tao that can be spoken of is not the Tao." I hesitated, wanting to write more but not daring. Did I need to ask the Emperor's permission to correspond with one of his sons? "I am grateful in excess for Cookpot's friendship," I added, and set my own red stamp on the letter to end it.

I re-rolled the silk into the bamboo strips and reached for the door to call a servant—then stopped myself again. Why would I send back Cookpot's writings, when I had just received them? That would raise all kinds of gossip among the servants.

I hugged the bamboo roll tight and just sat there. I didn't even want to read Cookpot's poems.

Suddenly I unwrapped the bamboo strips, shook out the silk and picked up my brush again.

Beneath the line, "I am grateful in excess for Cookpot's friendship," I added in very small characters, "And yours."

The next day I sent the bamboo strips back to Cookpot. I still had not read his poems.

That night we concubines sat with the Emperor at dinner. Some of the Emperor's Sons were also in attendance, along with much of the Court. The air among the men was that some important matter had been settled, and festivities were in order to raise a screen around their already buzzing plans.

Jade Mountain was there, beside the Emperor. At closer range, I could see that his eyes were not entirely black, but lightened with green.

I could not rest my gaze on him for very long, because of course the concubines were on display. To signal with my fan was impossible, in this setting. Yet the heat of Jade Mountain's gaze was palpable.

My hand surrendered to that heat. It rose and caressed my hair, as if checking the balance of my pins and ornaments. Slowly, it circled my ear and traced the line of my jaw. Slowly, it lowered across my body, touching my robes, and finally came to rest in my lap.

He blushed again.

Someone spoke to him and he turned away ... but the heat diminished only slightly. Food arrived. Jade Mountain carefully lifted a morsel of meat to his mouth and ate it. Slowly. Staring at me with that heat. Even without looking directly at him, I could feel the strength of his jaw and melting of the meat. I took a morsel of the same meat from the same dish at the concubines' table, and ate it, slowly.

We spent the evening like that: eating, talking lightly with others, attending to the Emperor's remarks, but always in that subtle communion. Savoring each other. The room's width between us was nothing. The Imperial Court nodded around us like flowers in a breezy garden.

My next roll of bamboo strips from Cookpot bore this note from that dear shih: "Dear Fragrance (his name for me since my laughter was fanned away), I have gratitude as high as the Yishan mountains that you should desire ever more invention from my ragged brush. It is with some panic, then, that I advise you of my increased duties in service to my lord the Prince. Thus if my poem-rolls are to remain the same size, I must include some old works. I hope you will forgive me, and perhaps find a familiar pleasure in these tales re-told."

I untied the bamboo strip rolls and saw that not only were these old works, they were drafts of poems I hadn't liked much. Puzzled and disappointed, I unrolled one more layer of strips … and stopped.

The middle of the roll had been cut out, so that the whole of it was fashioned into a secret box. It held a narrow roll of silk, and a cloth belt.

The belt was embroidered with a garden's worth of flowers. Twining in the midst of them, a dragon held the moon in its mouth.

I turned the belt over and over in my hands and fingered its entire length. It was fine quality stitching from the Imperial workshops. And, oh – the backing opened up. In fact, this was a long, secret pocket disguised as a belt.

Did I hear a shifting outside my door? I may have imagined it, but fear stabbed my ribs. It would be so easy to be caught, in this spiders' nest! I made myself laugh, and begin singing one of Cookpot's poems, as if I were reading an old favorite.

I had an idea what the belt was for. The rolled silk confirmed it. It was a letter from Jade Mountain.

*"**Bright Maiden**," it began, and my heart leapt – then sank as he revealed that the matter underlying last night's dinner was the peasant rebellion going on in a remote Kingdom. It had been decided that Jade Mountain would lead the army to crush it. In three days he would leave the Imperial Palace. "I never thought that presenting an archery contest made a man fit to command Imperial soldiers, but apparently my father holds these things differently," he wrote.*

"I will not tempt the gods by saying when I hope to return," he continued. "Until then, Cookpot remains behind at the palace to take care of my affairs here, and—most importantly—

to receive and post my correspondence with my mother. You can imagine there may be a letter not addressed to her! To maintain your safety, the belt enclosed here can hide the silks. If you examine my livery as I ride out, you will see that I have taken similar measures for my silks from you. I have grown to manhood in this Imperial puzzle-box, and will keep us both safe from its intrigues.

"I must take my leave of you now, dear Maiden, in haste, but with this final confession: I envy Cookpot. He, and not I, once heard you laugh."

And his red stamp.

I had fallen silent while reading. I began to sing another one of Cookpot's older poems. At the same time I hurriedly stuffed the letter into the belt. I added the first silk letter from its hiding place among my bloodrags, and tied the belt around my waist. I then removed the roll of blank silk and tucked it among the bloodrags. Then I re-rolled and tied the bamboo strip bundle and laid it beside my writing desk, where I always kept Cookpot's works.

I finished singing the poem, stretched out on the floor and stared at the ceiling. I wondered if I could die just by willing myself to float through the dark-stained wood.

I had never given up my hope that the Emperor would tire of me and send me back to the Temple. That somehow, some year, I would return to my Seeker's robes, and once again live stripped down to essential Life. Like a stubborn child I silently vowed to never, ever fall in love with the Emperor.

It never occurred to me that I might fall in love with his son.

Three days later I sat with the concubines to watch the army depart through the main Palace gates. The autumn sun was unusually warm and the crowd's fans fluttered like a field of butterflies. I sat still and waited.

I am surprised to see Water Song join the concubines at the grand departure of Jade Mountain and his army. There she is, the youngest in my box of pearls. Her hairstyle and ornaments are less elaborate than the other concubines, and far less so than the Wives. As always, it is her eyes, her gaze, that captures me. The other pearls, I can almost taste the warming spices of their mouths and smell their individual perfumes, hear echoes of their various love-cries. When I see Water Song, I wonder what she is thinking.

Jade Mountain rode past. He saluted the Wives' pavilion, where his mother sat. He did not salute the concubines.

A colorful embroidered belt peeked between the layers of his armor.

Jade Mountain passes my seat and salutes me. I think, "I hope he returns."

Please let him return, I prayed to the gods. Please, please let him return.

🦎 🦎 🦎 🦎 🦎 🦎 🦎

Autumn has turned to midwinter, and still Jade Mountain stalks the rebel General.

The weeks have dragged on through the autumn and into winter, with no letter from Jade Mountain. I have dared send off only two to him—both were short. It seems my heart has begun speaking a language I don't understand. I have scoured the scriptures seeking the wisdom that can translate myself to myself. To Jade Mountain I could only send scraps of scriptures and poems, with brief remarks of my own.

I have begun to hunger for the hours with Water Song.

There are times in our empty room that we do not speak, and barely move. I simply need the silence, and her presence. It is not entirely freedom, but it is close enough to give me ease.

Yet her gaze searches me intently now, and her face is more open. Could it be that she is warming towards me?

The Emperor, too, is worn down and silent. I search his face for the beginnings of Jade Mountain's face. If the Prince does not return, the Emperor will be all I have of him. Then, Cookpot sends the roll of "old poems." Inside the hidden compartment is a bundle of silk rolls from Jade Mountain. Cookpot can only shrug – a large delivery of letters and messages came all at once through the winter snows.

There are several short notes, each beginning, "Written in haste -," and saying merely, "I think of you often," and describe some phenomenon of the weather or landscape that brought me to mind. There is one long scroll.

Bright Maiden, *it begins, and my heart leaps as if no time had passed since autumn. But again it sinks, for the leisure to write comes at the price of a battle wound.*

My account of the hardships and horrors we have seen, endured, and caused (worst of all!) would be a standard tale of war, he writes. I have asked Cookpot never to write of a campaign's glory, for there is none. At best it is a world fully opposite the sedentary frivolity of the Imperial Court. Your two notes (why no more?) lifted my heart with their reminder of a third world, a peaceful way of Natural Life.

Again I will not tempt the gods, but will say that when I return, I will ask my father for a formal introduction to you, and request to be allowed some hours in your presence. I have seen and done things that I would discuss with you, as a Seeker who is also a Prince.

If this purpose is agreeable to the gods, I will indeed return and we may indeed develop a friendship, with my father's approval. Some days this hope is all the brightness I possess.

I spend the next three days praying feverishly that such a purpose would indeed please the gods.

I cannot help but compare the feeling of peace in Water Song's presence, with the feelings when I courted my First Wife … nearly twenty years ago! Such an extraordinary beauty! I called her my willow tree. I craved the sight of her, arching her neck, raising her face to the sky to reveal her endless white throat. She knew her throat could mesmerize. She knew I was caught. She knew I dreamed of possessing her. She knew I was determined to have her in my house, as my consort, and Wife when she became the mother of magnificent sons.

That was only the first step towards her ambition. I am not the great passion of her life. But I am necessary to achieve it.

She wants to be Empress. She has thought of nothing else since feeling my eyes upon her throat. This was long before I assumed the burden of Son of Heaven, but no matter. When she gave me my First Son, her desire only burned hotter. Even so, I did not immediately name First Son as my heir when the Kings and Lords proclaimed me Emperor. Had I done so, she would have been assured of becoming Dowager Empress upon my death. Perhaps I relished holding her great desire just out of her reach. Let her be mesmerized for a change.

Frankly, by the time I had maneuvered my way to the Seat of the Son of Heaven, I had seen enough of First Wife's family. In fact, some years after First Son's birth, while I was still a Lord of three Regions, I realized with shock that most of my ministers and their deputies were First Wife's uncles and cousins. They were competent and diligent, but I cursed myself for allowing such nepotism to grow like a mold as I slept in the luxury of my First Wife's body. Her voice had caressed each name with the same intoxicating murmur that she murmured on our pillow; I looked no further than that name for many of my highest-ranking officials. I was happy to shuffle most of them out to new duties in remote regions when I moved to the Imperial Palace.

Perhaps I can speak of all this one day to Water Song, in the Silence of a Hundred Paces. I would have her know what a treasure she is to me, because when we are together we are somewhere outside the tangled walls of family.

First Son has returned from the South, successful in his campaign against the barbarous tribes. Privately he confesses to me that the barbarians were easily routed this time—it wasn't much of a campaign. Nor was it a demonstration of the skill an Emperor should hone in battle.

"No matter," I sigh. "Your mother still polishes the throne."

His response is surprising. He smiles sadly, and says, "Father, it gives me a pain, too." We look at each other, suddenly understanding that we are two men yoked to a blind woman. And we laugh together.

In our laughter is a kind of freedom. So many things become possible.

One possibility is this: First Son might deserve a certain pearl as a gift ... if that pearl will not choose an old man for her consort.

A messenger arrives from Jade Mountain. Prisoners have divulged the name of the rebel General. It is an odd name: Bird Bird.

I receive this information in the company of several of my ministers. One of them makes a silly little hiccup that sharply annoys me. I turn to rebuke him—and see that his hiccup was actually a gasp. His elderly face is ashen. He tries to suppress his reaction, but it's even more evident in his watery eyes.

Immediately I demand to know why this name "Bird Bird" should cause such emotion. The minister falls to the floor and launches a volley of pleas, praises and wheedling babble that infuriates me. I practiced this kind of diplomatic word-stampede when I was securing my place as heir to the Dynasty, but now I have no patience for it. I bark a demand for the truth, in a single word.

The minister rises shakily to his knees and whispers one word—the family name of my First Wife.

"Bird Bird" is the childhood nickname my First Wife gave to a distant cousin, the minister explains. I blink and remember that this aging minister is one of those kin my First Wife murmured of in our private chambers. He had proven enough skill and intelligence in government to follow me to the Imperial Palace. But as he implicates First Wife in this rebellion, he implicates himself and his whole family.

My bones turn to ice. It is the cold of knowing one is surrounded by enemies with drawn bows.

I say quietly to my ministers that this news will not go beyond us for now. Word will be sent back to Jade Mountain that the prisoners who provided this name are to be brought back to the Imperial Palace alive. And Bird Bird is to be brought back dead.

I dismiss the old minister who revealed Bird Bird's identity, with this reward: that he may immediately begin a quiet retirement in a far kingdom, studying in a hermitage. The old man crawls backwards out of the room, mewling gratitude.

When he is gone, I command my Minister of Internal Affairs to make a secret investigation into all of First Wife's kin who hold government positions, no matter where they are. I am especially interested in how easily they are bribed.

I speak all of this in a whisper. My ministers are utterly still. They make obeisance and leave me, in silence. I am left in the empty room, the Son of Heaven turned to ice.

I can say nothing of this to Water Song.

Instead, I ask her to teach me the dancing movements that cultivate immortality.

She points out to me that it is spring, and we can practice in the Sunrise Garden where she exercises. Has it really been a whole year since I first saw her brilliant face?

If only the springtime sun would warm these icy bones of mine. Lift hands, turn, shift weight, lift foot, follow Water

Song's impeccable form. "These are the motions of combat," I tell her, "only too slow to be of any use."

Without warning Water Song's tiny form, a silhouette in the simple tunic and trousers of her temple, explodes upwards into the air. Her foot extends and kicks a deadfall branch off of a tree limb five feet above ground. She lands with barely a sound.

"Ask the gardener to decide its use," she says, smiling.

Challenged, a fire rises in me. My gaze picks out a thick, healthy branch the same height from the ground. I shriek and leap with a fury like a dragon breaking free of a stone prison. My foot lashes out. The branch and its limb shatter, down to the trunk.

Water Song is somber. The dragon's fury has spoken to her.

"The tree has lost half of itself, and may have to be cut down completely," she says. "Again, I would ask the gardener to decide the victory."

I stand shaking, full of heat. The ice is gone. "Enough poetry," I say hoarsely. "Take this—" I point at the shattered branch, "—and make it immortal. It will be cut down, another tree planted in its place. No one will know the difference! The new tree will blossom and shed just like the old one. No one will remember the old tree! Where there is no memory, there is no immortality!" My voice has become a shout.

Water Song's silence is her response. Her silence, and her unbroken gaze.

The gentleness of it is both a rebuke and a caring hand on my hot, hurting soul.

Water Song walks to the shattered tree and lightly touches its white ripped flesh. "One day you will not see an enemy," she says.

Maybe she can hear my muscles stiffen in readiness, and my eyes narrow. Like a great warrior or a foolish child, she turns and looks me full in the face. "You will not see an enemy," she says again. "Instead, you will know that there is no difference between you and any person or thing around you. You will not see an enemy, even when weapons are flying. You will see only the Way. Only the life that never ends."

The Son of Heaven can create the Silence of a Hundred Paces, but Water Song has created a silence that truly is silence. It is a silence within all things … even within an Emperor.

"Tell me if it is possible to be both a deadly warrior and a Master of the Way," I say at last.

Still her gaze upon my face is unbroken. But she smiles the tiniest of smiles.

"That is a very good question," she says.

After a moment, I bow to her like I bowed to my Masters when I was a boy. And I leave the Sunrise Garden.

No enemy, only the life that never ends.

The silence Water Song created lasts until I step through the garden's doors back into the Imperial palace, and I am engulfed again in ministers, advisors, generals and diplomats. Perhaps my next question to Water Song will be whether there is more than one life that never ends.

🌞 🌞 🌞 🌞 🌞 🌞 🌞

Jade Mountain sends word: he is coming home, successful in his task.

All spring my Minister of Internal Affairs has been setting snares for the little mice in this plot. "To understand the large disturbance, study the small ones," is his motto. And oh, what a number of little mice he has found! Most of them are relations of my First Wife, or clerks working under her kin.

The real cause of the rebellion is price manipulations coming out of the local Agriculture office. Farmers have been forced to sell their harvests for next to nothing, while the transport fees have been raised. First Wife's cousin, the regional Governor, helped the Agriculture deputy carry this out by looking the other way. He then shared in the profit skimmed from the grain sales on the open market.

In this situation, the region's local Public Works Ministry has been flooded with hungry farmers looking for work—a road, a bridge, a swamp draining, anything! But the local Deputy has been undermining projects in that region for years with delays, canceled projects, or inadequate tools and planning. Or he just didn't pay the workers. Of course it was all blamed on the Emperor's policies, while the Deputy pocketed the unspent Imperial funds.

How easily Bird Bird raised a rebel army from such a desperate population! Only the gods know what the Deputy expected to gain from rebellion. His name is hated throughout the region.

And then there's the Department of Accounts! There, the Deputy is one of First Wife's most ineffectual kinsmen, a figurehead for his clever Clerk. That Clerk has been short-counting the region's food production, and sending the difference to Bird Bird's troops. Apparently he aimed to be a Senior Minister in Bird Bird's power structure.

As Jade Mountain's campaign encircled Bird Bird, the snares snapped and the little mice ran to their holes—to no avail. The Public Works Deputy hung himself, which saddened no one except a few in his immediate family. The regional governor drank poisoned tea, which is being reported as a sudden fatal illness.

These news items have been kept from circulation as much as possible. I know my lovely First Wife has her own spies swarming the Imperial Palace and the surrounding city. I don't expect to keep much from her, but I am saving the choicest revelations for a private audience.

The army returns home as spring swells into summer. Jade Mountain rides at the head, alive but changed. It's in his back, his face, his eyes gone shining and full of purpose. It's in the still-red scar high on his left cheek. It's in the soldiers, who instantly fall to one knee when Jade Mountain dismounts his stallion. The Prince with the happy smile has vanished.

Jade Mountain's triumphant entry through the Imperial Palace gates is a stunning spectacle. Returns usually are. Departures for war are all hopeful agitation, an excitement that has the horses dancing and the infantry marching in sharp unison. Returns are quieter, slow with fatigue and the memory of what has been done. The welcoming crowds search the ranks of the returning army for the faces that are missing.

I am seated under the great canopy at the top of the grand stairclimb in the Palace's most impressive courtyard. I know my little Imperial City is small when compared to the deserts and river valleys of my empire, but when all the Imperial Court is gathered in this courtyard, their glory invites the very gods to admire and praise.

Yet, for all of this … it is Jade Mountain who captures my gaze. He is no longer just a prince – he is a man, transformed by battle. A fresh scar high on his face says he has earned his breath and heartbeat. His once easy smile comes more slowly, after watchful consideration. His eyes are open. His back is straight and his seat on the black stallion is assured.

There are two baskets hanging off his saddle, one on each side. Each is just big enough for … oh, but I will have such a surprise for First Wife very soon!

And the soldiers—I almost forgot to observe them. They take their every cue from Jade Mountain: the pace of their march, their reserved demeanor. Grooms appear at his horse's side even before he raises his hand for the halt and dismount. As his foot lands on the courtyard paving, the whole army as one drops to one knee, landing on the paving at the same moment. It is thrilling.

Now Jade Mountain holds out his hands and the grooms give him the handles of those baskets. Jade Mountain will carry those baskets to me himself, up the steep stairclimb. This is perfect – his instinct couldn't be better. He is doing this menial yet symbolic task himself, and his soldiers love him for it.

And all this time, since entering the courtyard, Jade Mountain's gaze has never left my face. It is a bold challenge, and exhilarating. With each step I am convinced that my young prince is now a man to be respected. But I keep my face stern and blank, and let him play out the scene.

Jade Mountain reaches my seat, breathing deeply but evenly from the climb. He sets one basket before me. "My Emperor, Son of Heaven, here is the rebel general," he says. He sets the other basket before me. "And here is the rebel general's second in command. May you be pleased with the efforts of your devoted sons, these soldiers, and your son, this prince."

With all my heart I want to clasp his shoulders and at this moment proclaim him my heir. Shout it to the court, and to hell with anyone who would lose face. To hell with First Wife and her damned ambition.

Instead I simply lower my eyelids. It is as much as a nod, an affirmative. Well done. No one loses face. My selection is made in my heart. The tests and preparations, from now until the elevation, are nothing but pageant.

To begin, there is a certain question I would like to ask Jade Mountain. I will invite him to sit with me at a small dinner.

I hear nothing from Jade Mountain for days. Cookpot is rushed with new business for his lord, and has no time for more than a note saying that the Prince is well and will contact me soon.

My First Wife arrives in the private audience room. I have a basket beside me, hidden behind a screen.

I ask after her health, her mood, her satisfaction in general. Excellent, thinking of me every day, in general feeling blessed. I ask after her family. We never meet one another outside of the business of running an empire. She replies that as far as she knows, everyone is content, but as a Wife she doesn't get out much.

No, you command the whole world to come to you, I think. "You received word of your cousin the governor's fatal illness?" I inquire.

"Oh, yes, and I sent the funeral gifts straightaway," she replies. "It was terrible to come in the middle of an uprising. It must have been the emotion, it was too much for him to see his people so brutal and foolish!"

"Perhaps so."

"I would like to give Jade Mountain a special gift at his birthday celebration this year," she says, "in gratitude for his bravery."

"That would be appropriate," I say. "And speaking of gifts, an extraordinary message came back with Jade Mountain. A greeting from one of your kinsmen, one we haven't heard from in a long time. Odd that he'd be out that way, in such a remote kingdom. But there he was, and he gave something to Jade Mountain, which I'll pass on to you ...."

I reach behind the screen, into the basket, and bring forth Bird Bird's head. It is well-preserved in honey, so that its features are still quite moist and natural.

First Wife stares, mouth slowly opening wide, then wider.

"Oh yes, his name was Bird Bird!" I say. "Same name as the rebel general, strangely enough!"

First Wife's eyes roll back in her head and she faints dead away on the floor.

I put Bird Bird's head back in its basket and wonder if the woman has been lying to me this whole time.

I do not see First Wife again, but for the next several days every hour brings a new message from her: she denounces Bird Bird, she denounces every member of her family who helped him or profited from the rebellion. She calls for executions and exiles. She offers her own suicide to protect First Son. And on and on.

Suddenly, for some reason, the constant harassment and teasing I endure increases. Dead spiders float in my teapot, or sprinkle my food. A minor concubine sends her eunuch to me to tell my fortune; I have nightmares over it for days. Finally, one evening I hurry alone down a darkening corridor, returning to my rooms from the toilet—and I am grabbled from behind by the hair. A hand claps over my mouth before I can scream. I am turned around—it's First Wife. But I hardly recognize her. Is she drunk? Her hair is coming undone and her face is halfway to oblivion with hate.

"Your plan will fail," she hisses. "Your Temple of demons—they sent you to poison him. Tantalize him with a virgin … it will fail, you evil scorpion, it will fail!" And she slaps me across the face. She has to let me go to do it, and I scramble madly down the corridor back to my room.

I have just set my seal on the orders for three executions in the rebel region: two from the Accounts department, and one from Agriculture. Besides the Grand Controller of Agriculture, who alerted me to Bird Bird's real identity, First Wife's uncle is also retiring, from the Office of the Imperial Family Records.

The rest of First Wife's family will cower behind closed doors. After all, it is the custom of long standing that the families of traitors should be executed, to three levels beyond the criminal. I have not ordered these conventional executions, because they would include both First Wife and First Son. Let First Wife and her family quiver in fear, then, while I sort out what action is best.

I send an urgent message to Cookpot, begging for advice—is it possible she knows about Jade Mountain's letters? No, Cookpot replies, her actions were too wild. When she is sure, her moves are quiet and elegant, like her contemptuous fan wave over my laughter. But Cookpot is shaken by the tale. There is something happening in this court that is not reaching this monster virgin's ears.

There is a mountain of work to do to set things right in the rebel region. New Deputy Ministers to appoint, new work projects that will employ the farmers until the next planting.

I smell smoke.

A servant rushes in to tell me First Wife is burning every family memento in her possession.

I send the servant back with a command that she will stop this blasphemy at once and take control of herself. She is still my First Wife and her child is still my firstborn son.

I stop short of reassuring her that the heir is yet to be named—I don't want to feed that hope.

My head hurts. I send servants to bring Water Song to the Silence of a Hundred Paces.

And still Jade Mountain does not contact me. We concubines continue to practice our dances, our stitchery, our makeup and hairstyles.

This dream comes:

Jade Mountain snaps the reins on a team of black horses, and drives away from me in a large wagon. The wagon's wheels are huge and flash like rainbow lights. I run after the wagon. Cookpot is beside me, running as hard as he can. We are on a country road. Jade Mountain isn't driving any more, he stands in a box in the back of the wagon. No, he stands in a coffin. No, it's a puzzle box, boxes folded into boxes. I trip and fall into a field beside the road, a field full of smelly fresh cow dung.

I awaken … and find that someone has entered my room and enjoyed their midnight bowel movement on my bed.

The next day I am called to the Silence of a Hundred Paces. The Emperor looks as wrung out as I feel. I confess my sufferings—but only tell of the harassment—and plead for some kind of rescue.

Water Song has dark circles under her eyes. What now?

"Is your beloved First Wife ill?" she asks. "Her opinion of me has always been low, but in the past few days I have begun to fear for my life."

She tells me a tale of an ambush in the corridors, where First Wife pulled Water Song's hair and slapped her face, accusing her of plotting to kill me. Then there are the dead insects in her teacups, and a fortune-telling eunuch with chilling, detailed predictions. And then, last night, someone entered her room and emptied their bowels on her bed as she slept.

That is it. I stand, and bellow to be heard a hundred paces away: "Let it be known that the concubine Water Song has my favor! She will be respected and honored as a favored concubine, and now wears my ring as a sign of this protection, by the will of the Son of Heaven!"

And so he gives me his ring.

I take the golden Jade Turtle from my finger, and hold it out to Water Song. She gives me her left hand. Her fingers are too small for the ring so I slide it onto her thumb.

A jade turtle the color of firelight, to wear on my thumb. I am now a favored concubine, protected.

I bury her hand in both of mine, and hold it to my forehead.

There is anguish in him as he does it. He folds my little hand into his broad soldier's hands, and shudders with emotion. I pull his head down to touch mine, brow to brow, as friends do.

I break into a sob. Just one.

He carries so many more secrets than I. We both need so much comfort.

It seems we stand on an island, friends for no particular reason, while dark waters rise around us.

7.
THE SECOND JADE'S STORY
PART II

The golden jade turtle warms to my thumb. It is a comfort to fondle, when my hands are folded together inside my sleeves.

The harassment has stopped. I am so relieved, it takes me most of a day to realize that the entire Court has something else on their tongues in any case: an outbreak of fatal illness, suicides and retirements in First Wife's family! As we women stitch our embroidery, I open my ears and bite my lips to keep from asking questions. I piece out the conspiracy aimed at toppling the Emperor and shifting the Dynasty's full power to First Wife's family.

Most of the women's gossip makes no sense. Was First Wife planning this overthrow? I doubt it, simply because having her entire family (including First Son) executed, or cast out of the Imperial House completely, would be far more catastrophic than never becoming Empress.

The gossip revolves around First Son's chances for the succession. He seems to have regained the Emperor's favor since repelling the barbarians in the South, which could be the reason why the Emperor has not ordered the usual storm of executions. Then talk turns to Jade Mountain. I stare fixedly at my needle and silk thread. Nearly a fortnight and still no note from him. But his birthday celebration is approaching. I stitch it into my memory: choose a gift. Choose a gift.

"… so Jade Mountain should have at least four marriage proposals by the New Year!" a plump concubine brays. I jab my thumb viciously with the needle. Rather than cry out, I shove my thumb in my mouth. Nobody notices this until a moment later, when Third Wife says, "It's not lunch time yet, Water Song."

A wave of giggles goes through the room—then somebody coughs, elbows nudge ribs, and a resentful silence falls. The thumb I'm sucking wears the jade turtle. Perhaps I'm the only one who doesn't see it in grand terms: the Jade Turtle. Perhaps

I should. Third Wife merely harrumphs her disdain for the whole arrangement.

The Emperor invites me to sit with him at a small dinner—with Jade Mountain.

I prepare myself more carefully than for any other event with the Emperor. Jade hairpins. Layers of silk robes. Perfume, face paint. And a detail I could not forget: the belt with the dragon and moon.

They are both there when I enter the room. I wait, with hands folded inside my sleeves, because this is the formal introduction that Jade Mountain has requested. "This is the rainbow pearl of my precious garland," the Emperor says to his son. I prostrate to the Emperor and then to Jade Mountain. I settle myself on cushions at the low table set between them, that holds the tea-service. Only then do I dare look at the Prince.

The scar changes his face in a subtle way. It is as if a hidden part of himself peeks out from beside his eye.

His eyes soften when they meet mine. He inclines his head in acknowledgement, and smiles a little.

Then I reach for the teapot to pour for the Emperor … and Jade Mountain's eyes go hard. Color rises in his cheeks. Anger? Why? I follow his glance down to my hands.

It's the ring. He sees the Emperor's ring on my hand. He thinks it means I have given myself to the Emperor.

I nearly drop the teapot. I don't even notice the food being brought in on platters. Tea is all I can put in my mouth. I barely hear the Emperor's conversation. He's talking about how he and I have debated the Tao together in our Silence of a Hundred Paces.

"Like a good Master, she has made me ask questions that have no answer—at least, none that appear easily. So, Son, I will pose this to you, and hope that you can help an old man. Is it possible to be both a deadly warrior and a Master of the Tao?"

Jade Mountain's eyes flick to the Emperor and back to me. The Emperor is enjoying this immensely. I think if he were facing Jade Mountain's expression on a battlefield, that would change quickly.

"I will say what I have learned," Jade Mountain says, "but I do not know if I will satisfy your Master."

I am shocked by the jealousy in his voice.

I wonder if I'm going to faint. The room seems unreal, fading in and out. Breathe, please breathe. Regulate the taking in and letting out. What is Jade Mountain saying?

"According to my understanding, to master the Way, the Tao, is to disappear into the flow of Life Itself," he says. He looks at me. A cold challenge in his eyes. I say nothing, letting that silence be my agreement. "In combat," the Prince continues, "to disappear is impossible. It is desertion. One must accept that one is visible, a target. Because one is a target every day, every moment, every breath, death surrounds the warrior. Life is only as broad as the sole of one's foot, or the spread of one's hand on the sword-hilt."

Jade Mountain's focus returns to the Emperor ... who leans forward, completely alert, ready for battle himself. He can hear the young wolf calling out the aging pack chief.

"Therefore the warrior in combat must *become* Life—to be as alive as it is possible for that man to be," the Prince continues. "He does not disappear into Life; he pulls Life into himself to the point of bursting." Jade Mountain's eyes narrow as I have seen the Emperor's do when he readies for a fight. "The warrior who is most fully and completely alive in combat," Jade Mountain finishes in a tone of deadly quiet, "is the one who causes the enemy to slip ... out of life, into death. It is the enemy who disappears."

The Emperor's eyes, too, have narrowed. The son and the father are locked gaze to gaze. They could leap up and disembowel each other at any moment in an ecstasy of rage. The emotion holds me at the point of a triangle. I may be held there forever if I do not speak.

"The single error," I say, "is to assume there is a Master of the Way in this room who can teach the correct answer. We are three seekers, each on our own path. The Prince has a task to fulfill at the head of an army, so his is one kind of combat. The Emperor is the Center of the World, the bridge between the Earthly and the Divine. His combat is far different." I hesitate a fraction of a moment. I have not broken the triangle, but the rage has trembled and thinned to a mist. "The concubine is also a visible target, in her own way," I continue. "She is grateful for her allies, who shield her in grace and kindness"—here I touch the Jade Turtle ring reverently—"in the midst of those who do not understand why she remains a maiden." And I bow deeply to the Emperor.

I lift my head again, and give the Emperor a lingering look of tender respect. Then I look Jade Mountain full in the face, feeling naked.

His face has opened. He understands.

There is a breath of silence, then the Emperor chuckles. "I should make this concubine my senior minister," he says. "What do you think, Son? Shall I seat her at our councils?"

"I think if she were beside the Emperor at every dinner, the Ten Kingdoms would know harmony," Jade Mountain replies.

I sigh with relief, and touch my belt. Jade Mountain touches his.

Yet the triangle remains. And the mist of that father-son rage does not evaporate. It clings to me, long after the dinner is over and we have gone our ways; I am surrounded like a tall pine on a mountainside; the mist swirls around me daily, restless. In such a refined place as this, we never look into each others' eyes, yet the gaze of the Emperor, watching through his spies, sits heavily in the sultry summer air. Mixed within it must be the gaze of Prince Jade Mountain, but I do not know which servants are his loyalists, except Cookpot. Behind all of them is the manyeyed gaze of First Wife.

The only clear-sky understanding is that I must make a choice. I can wither and vanish in the maze of this Imperial puzzle-box, burdened by everything around me. Or I can begin my freedom by making a choice.

I have chosen the Prince's birthday gift.

A sword, beautiful enough for ceremony yet sharp enough for battle. The scabbard slide is extraordinary, a pale green jade carved as two dragons bound together, embracing the sword as it slides into its holding-place. The other jade fittings are masterful, too, but it was the dragons that stole my breath when I saw them in the Imperial craftsman's display room. I requested the entire sword, scabbard, and belt at once.

These dragons are the message I wish to send to Jade Mountain. I pray he understands it. I arrange to send the sword to Jade Mountain early on his birthday, before the official celebration. I add a poem, written on a length of silk:

The sole of your foot, the entire earth.

The palm of your hand, life itself.
All others slip away,
Returned to the stars.
Then my red-ink stamp, my signature.

I send it off, in a box tied up with silk cords, delivered by a servant. Sliding my door shut, I begin to shake terribly.

I have made my choice. My freedom has begun. I can never leave this Palace again.

🦎 🦎 🦎 🦎 🦎 🦎 🦎

He understands the message of the jade dragons.

We write to one another on silks. Many little scraps flutter back and forth between us.

Bright Lady,
I must confess shock at my powerful emotions when I saw you wearing the Emperor's Jade Turtle at our dinner. How fortunate that you have such wit to read my jealousy's source, and then engineer its remedy!

My Dear Prince,
Why do you call me wise? At our dinner, my desperate wit scrambled to defend the only truth I see clearly anymore: that your regard is more precious to me than anything else in these walls. Beyond these walls, I have forgotten everything.

Bright Lady,
After reading your silk, I had to run to the stables and mount my favorite stallion with only a bridle, as I was too rushed to put on a saddle. I needed to ride fast and far into the countryside, to shout my happiness to the wind—I am precious to the beautiful Water Song!

My Dearest Prince,
I think of you every moment. With every stitch I put into the concubines' tapestry project today, I chanted your name in my mind. Wherever that tapestry hangs, it will be a hall I shall love to visit.

Bright Lady,

*Forgive my silence! I beg you to be kind! Although my
father has left for a state visit in the East, his ministers
pester me with questions and demands. These are called
"extraordinary lessons"-- tests, I know, to determine
the Emperor's successor. They have me in a race with the
accomplished First Son, but beyond a certain point I no
longer care—I desire only to picture you on my inward eye.
How often I return to that garden treetop in my thoughts!*

Cookpot complains of exhaustion, running back and forth
bearing the weight of our silk. I tuck each silk into my belt and
wear it even while asleep. The little jade turtle wards off my old
tormentors, but I am still alert to the whisperings of eunuchs
and maids. Only Cookpot has my full trust.

❈ ❈ ❈ ❈ ❈ ❈ ❈

I am pulled from my bed.

It is the still hour of the night, long before dawn. Six soldiers
enter my room, sweep off my coverings and throw a robe over
me. Two lift me up and two more jam shoes onto my feet. Then
we march, me stumbling and shaking, my hair falling in my
face. Not a word has been said, no shout given. Just, come.

I clutch both the jade turtle ring and the embroidered belt,
both of which I wear even in sleep; both are with me now.

Our march enters a stone barracks and then goes down,
down a staircase lit by torches. The air is close and fetid.

The stone corridor is full of groans. We pass a room—where
we pause, and a soldier forcibly turns my face to look in. The
torchlit room holds a dozen men, some with head and hands
locked in thick planks of wood, some chained to the wall, their
bodies twisted and broken. One of these broken men looks me
in the eye. His pain and suffering clutch at my heart, pull at my
spirit; his spirit writhes in a frenzy trying to trade places with
mine, to escape, escape ….

The soldier pushes me ahead and we march on.

A torchlit stone room, with a table made of rough boards.
Behind it, a Minister I recognize from the endless Court dinners.
I have danced for this man, along with the other concubines.
Whenever he smiled he seemed to have too many teeth for his
mouth. He's not smiling now. My mind and spirit cool, rising
above the fear-stain of the broken man's spirit.

I bring my hands out of my sleeves and cross them over my breast, making sure the Emperor's Jade Turtle ring is in front. Let it be grand. Let them always remember that I am a favored concubine. I silently call on my Temple masters and their lineage of masters for help: please calm my mind and breath; please help me say the right words.

"Water Song, the maiden," the Minister says with that sheen of contempt so familiar to me. "Your plot against the Emperor's life has been discovered. Confess your evil plans now and we will show mercy. Rather than torture or execution, you will be exiled to a prison in the Western desert, with scorpions for company and thorns for food!"

"What has been discovered is a path for your own advancement, that treads on the back of an humble concubine," I reply. "I shall not confess to such a plot, because there is none. You show no evidence of such a plot, so why should I confess to what has not happened and does not exist, either in my mind or in evidence?"

"*Confess!*" He screams at me, nearly leaping over the table. I stand utterly still and do not blink.

"The burden of this debate is upon you, Minister," I finally reply, quietly.

I think I have startled him, because he does not move. Then he slams his hand flat on the rough wood of the table. At the sound the soldiers rush me out of the room. We pass once more through the corridor full of groans, and I fleetingly hope that the Minister has to spend the rest of the night picking splinters out of his palm.

I am in a filthy, lightless room for what might be a full day, or more, or less. I focus my mind and call on all my training for calm, for breath that doesn't flinch at the stink, and subtle nourishment for my flesh. Then the door flies open and I am rushed back into the room with the table and the Minister. Again I press the hand wearing the Jade Turtle to my breast, so the Minister can see it at all times.

"Here is the evidence," the Minister says, smiling in the way that pushes his jumbled teeth out at me. He reads a servant's statement from a bamboo strip—a statement that not only says I sent a package to the Prince outside of the scheduled birthday celebrations, but includes the poem I added to the gift.

"The sole of your foot, the entire earth," the Minister reads with a leering pleasure. "The palm of your hand, life itself. All others slip away, returned to the stars." He waves the bamboo strip at me. "This is your plan to remove the Emperor from his throne and place Jade Mountain there! Confess now, you little whore!"

This is a narrow path, indeed. "It is well known that the Emperor loves to pose riddles," I said. "Jade Mountain has given beautiful answers to his riddles. I think you yourself can say whether this is true or false, since you were present at the dinner where the Emperor asked Jade Mountain about a son's duty to his father's wishes. It was a dinner held not far from my Temple, a little less than two years ago. I am sure the people of that region still sing the song one of our poets composed about it. Well, there was another dinner not long ago, after Jade Mountain's return. The Emperor dined with Jade Mountain and myself. You were not invited, but the conversation was not for your ears, as odd as that may strike you. The Emperor posed another riddle to his son, one that sprang from his private conversations with me about the Tao. Jade Mountain's reply, once again, was beautiful and full of wisdom." Indeed, recalling my Prince's words, I am in union with him again—the world at this moment is only as broad as the sole of my foot, and all of life is in the thumb that bears the Jade Turtle ring. I take a breath, to pull as much Life as possible into myself, that this Minister might slip off into obscurity. "My poem and my gift were intended to celebrate that wisdom," I go on. "If you don't believe me, ask the Emperor himself about his question and Jade Mountain's answer."

"You still will not confess this terrible plot?"

"I have said all I will say today. For more, you have to ask the Emperor."

I am taken back to the dark, filthy room. The wait is longer this time. I breathe and focus, but a doubt creeps in with the wretched stinking air. What is Jade Mountain doing? If they are accusing me of this, what are they doing to him? Does he know where I am?

A third time, I am brought into the stone room with the table and the Minister. My robes are filthy, my hair hangs in strings, my skin feels like mold. I place the hand with the Jade Turtle ring on my breast, and wait.

The Minister is smiling again. There is a wide, flat serving bowl on the table, with a cloth over it. "Today you will confess, little whore," he says. "Today I have what you desired—the burden of the debate. Jade Mountain's confession sits before me ... here!" He whips the cloth off the bowl.

A severed hand, ghastly grey and blackened with blood, lies in the bowl.

It wears Cookpot's thumb ring.

I shriek and scuttle backwards, ramming into the soldiers standing there. They pull me forward by the arms so my face is almost touching the hand. I crush my eyes shut, screaming. Cookpot always wore an archer's thumb ring, not a scholar's, as a private joke. And oh, I know the hand, the shape of the stiff fingers and curling thumb, that could pluck a lute, twirl a brush, flutter a fan as he told some tale.

The soldiers drop me onto the floor. I sob violently. "Cookpot ... not Cookpot ... please, not Cookpot ..."

"The Prince's most trusted servant," the Minister sighed, "was known to be your errand boy as well. Rushing messages back and forth. And more. We have signed statements from three eunuchs that you and he were lovers."

"*No,*" I scream.

"Now confess!" the Minister roars, standing over me. "You and this dung-heap *shih* conspired with the Prince Jade Mountain to usurp the throne! Confess! The *shih's* blood is already on you, how much more do you want to spill? Confess!"

"I love Jade Mountain!" I shriek. "Cookpot carried our letters, but that's all! There is no plot, there is only our love! Two foolish children speaking to each other through a wall, that is all of our crime! You have murdered a poet for nothing!"

The Minister snorts like someone who has thought of an obscene joke. My own rage rises then, and I stand up on my feet.

"By all that we owe the dead," I say, shaking with wrath, "how will Cookpot be buried? Like me, he has no family. What will be his shroud and his tomb?"

"He'll wear the clothes he died in, and be thrown in a potter's field," the Minister says lightly. "Better than the gutter, where you'll find most other dead poets."

"Then let me at least wash those clothes clean for his spirit," I plead. "This *shih* was a true friend and the best of servants. And if you had ever let a poem touch you deeply, you would never have consented to murder him."

The Minister looks away, bored. I throw myself on him. The soldiers grab me and pull, but I clutch at the Minister's brocade robes with my soiled hands. "Where are your orders from the Emperor to murder a Prince's servant, and arrest a favored concubine?"

"In the Emperor's absence, I am his voice!" the Minister barks, tearing his robes to get me away from his scented perfection. "You have committed treason upon his person, you slut!"

"The Prince and I have never touched! " I scream at him. "There is no plot, no intention to harm the Son of Heaven! It is a matter of private affection! Can you speak for the Emperor's heart where a favored concubine is concerned?" The soldiers succeed in dragging me off of him.

"Betrayal is betrayal, whether in the bedroom, the battlefield, or the mind," the Minister sneers. He fusses with his robes to hide the rips.

"Yet the Emperor was merciful to his First Wife," I counter forcefully. The Minister looks up at me sharply, eyes narrowed. The soldiers pause, waiting for his next word.

"Take this filthy thing back to her slutty room," he says to the soldiers at last. They assemble around me and we start for the door. "Maiden," the Minister calls to me—still sliding contempt through the word—"be sure you *stay* in your room. Assassins don't debate." He turns away, and I am escorted out of his presence.

Back in my room, I bathe myself, and can't stop weeping. How did this happen? The servant who delivered the birthday gift must have opened the gift box, read the poem and reported it to someone. As much as the women and eunuchs of this palace hate me, it makes no sense for any of them to concoct this lie. The only conclusion is that it is directed at Jade Mountain, to prevent his elevation to Crown Prince … above First Son, above First Wife. I rack my memory to discover whether this Minister is part of First Wife's family, but I can no longer think in long threads. I break down and weep again. *Oh, Cookpot!* I struggle to bring his sweet dimpled happy face to mind, so I will not see that gruesome hand with the archer's thumb ring.

My door slides open, and I cower in a corner. A servant pushes a bundle past the door and shuts it again swiftly. It's Cookpot's clothing, which he was wearing when he died. The outer robe is stiff with dried blood, mostly around the neck. His throat must have been cut, or worse. I use the bathwater I have left, and my best salts and perfumes, to clean the garments. I sing prayers to the gods, and to Cookpot's spirit, pleading for his safe passage to the other world. I sing his poems, frequently sobbing them out. Finally I spread the wet garments on my verandah to dry. The afternoon sun hurts my eyes, after all those days in that lightless hole.

Without Cookpot, I am truly lost. There is no other servant, eunuch or maid, whom I can trust to take a message to Jade Mountain, or to the Emperor on his journey. I have a slim notion of the layout of the Palace grounds, but how to escape from it is beyond my imagination. At my wildest despair, I pray for a dragon to materialize from the air and carry me back to my Temple.

My door slides open again. It is a servant carrying a package. He sets it down just inside the door, saying nothing, staying outside. He has delivered the box holding the gift sword, tied up in its silk cords. Two breaths later the Minister glides in past him—is he perhaps panting a bit, as if having run to the door? I have no time to study this thought. "The Prince has renounced you," the Minister declares with a brazenly fake sympathy, his eyes bright and face flushed. "He sends back your birthday present, you see. Whether that will save either of you your heads remains to be seen." The Minister then glances around, takes out his fan and stirs the air as he leaves. To these people I am nothing but a bad smell.

I collapse to my knees, press my brow to the box and wail, hopeless. This news has to be a lie, but I do not know what to believe anymore. I claw at the knotted cords on the box. With the sword, at least, I can end my life.

But the box shifts too easily under my hands. I pick it up. It's far too light to hold a sword and scabbard.

Off come the cords, and I open the box.

A dragon is inside.

It is Jade Mountain's belt—embroidered with a dragon holding the sun in his mouth. The setting sun's light glints off the circle of gold thread. My mind goes completely still. I turn the belt over and pry open the folded backing. One silk note is inside.

My Beloved Water Song,

If you are alive, I will see you tonight. If they have already taken you as they took Cookpot, I may see you soon in the other world. Your beautiful birthday note to me reached First Wife, who has been desperate for a way to regain her honor in the Court. Under her tutelage, one vile Minister has spent the entire season raising talk against me, hinting that I am too eager to assume the name Son of Heaven and have created a new plot against my own father's life! Although it is absurd, it is believed, for the plot within First Wife's family has the whole Court looking for conspiracies. I have tried to send word to my father, or First Son, but faithless servants have taken those messages straight to First Wife, while trusted runners have been murdered on the road to the East. The murder of Cookpot has also murdered my faith in any of this Court, save you, precious Water Song. If I am to be assassinated at dawn by First Wife's soldiers, my only wish is to have you close to me tonight. If you can find the means, disguise yourself in some way and go to the gate of the concubines' compound. Your blind musician waits on the other side—he knows not for whom!—and he will bring you to my quarters. He alone of all this Court's servants is still faithful to me above all others. I remain in hope of seeing your face –

And his red ink stamp.

Carefully, I tuck the note back into the belt. Then I step onto my verandah to watch the evening light fade from the air. The possibility that I might not see the dawn makes the dimming of the garden all the more magical.

The cleaned garments are reasonably dry, and I carry them inside with me. I shut my screens, light a small lamp, and prepare.

I tie my hair up in a young man's topknot. I mix my writing ink and draw myself a new hairline. I also thicken my eyebrows and add a small mustache. Then I blow out the lamp and change my clothes in the dark. I whisper apologetic prayers to Cookpot's spirit, for he will have to go naked to his potters' field.

Clad in Cookpot's robes, I sit in my dark room for several hours, so that any watchers will assume I am asleep. In my mind I see my path to the gate: slipping off my verandah I will creep to the toilet-house, where there is a low fence I can climb into the tiny courtyard. From there I know the quick route to the gate. I practice this route over and over in my mind.

Finally it is time to go. I take the last roll of wood strips Cookpot sent me, to carry as a sign of a *shih* on late business. I have both my belt and Jade Mountain's around my waist. I reach out to open my verandah screen—then stop.

The Emperor's ring is still on my thumb.

There is no question, no second thought. This golden turtle has no more protection for me. My life will not be long.

I remove it, and set it in the center of my bed.

Man Country

Thus also spoke the Man of Calling:
"Whosoever takes upon himself the filth of
the realm,
he is the lord at the earth's sacrifices.
Whosoever takes upon himself the misfortune
of the realm,
he is the king of the world."
True words are as if contrary.

—Lao Tzu,
Tao Te Ching

German tr. Richard Wilhelm,
English tr. H. G. Ostwald

8.
CLUELESS

"WHY DIDN'T YOU CUT OFF THAT BITCH WIFE'S HEAD WHEN YOU HAD THE CHANCE?!" was ready to jump out of my mouth when Mr. Greg Royal Hair opened his front door.

But that would not do, that would not do at all. Instead I smiled and introduced myself as being from the Albert Jarro Gallery and a friend of Valerie L. With a package from her. And a proposal.

He stood there in the doorway and assessed me. A dog barked frantically somewhere in the back of the house. "I saw you today, didn't I?" he asked.

"Um, yes, Valerie waved at me as you were leaving the movie. I, ah, happened to be there too, and she, ah, we talked later and she wanted you to have this but thought I should be the one to give it to you." I sounded exactly like the last four years of sophisticated retail experience had never happened. Amazing what a psychic tsunami can do to you.

Greg tilted his head and crossed his arms over his chest. "Valerie sent *you* to deliver something?"

Oh dear, he *was* old-fashioned. In *that* way. Well, on to the professional edge. I held out the package, carefully re-wrapped and taped shut. "It's the jade pendant she wore today. Remember, you asked her to wear it? It has some value" (Do not choke, do *not*) "and since I'm a certified antiques appraiser specializing in Chinese art, it seemed right for me to bring it to you—oh, she sent a letter, too, here—so we could talk about how you might want to handle owning an object like this."

Greg held the box and the envelope and looked glum. "This damn thing …" he muttered. "You have a card on you?"

"Ooohhh … not on me right now." Lie. Lie. I didn't want him to associate me with the gallery. Greg stepped back into the house. "C'mon in and I'll get you something to write on."

How very weird, to enter the house of the former Emperor of China! Who seemed to be, now, a construction manager, judging from the binders and blueprints spread across his dining room table. The little laptop and attendant coffee mugs were snowed under. Well, I thought, it probably feels like a vacation next to running an empire without telephones and decent plumbing. I had just taken this much in when the barking source, a black Labrador, clattered in at full speed and shoved his muzzle into my crotch. I danced up onto my tiptoes. "*Down*, Lopez!" Greg boomed from the kitchen. Lopez obeyed and sat, a good soldier, and I was released back down to the floor. The dog grinned at me and flapped his tongue. "Good Lopez, good down," I said, and turned away to wipe off my pants.

And saw Valerie L.

It was a poster, announcing a concert (last year) up in the posh islands north of our city. Valerie L was dressed in a long gauzy black gown that floated in a breeze as she walked barefoot on a wet beach, sand so shiny it seemed she was walking on water. She played her violin-or-maybe-viola as she went. The poster was framed and set above the living room couch, dominating the décor like an image of the Virgin Mary.

"Here you go." Greg came through the dining room and handed me a graph-paper notepad and pen. I scratched down my name and home phone.

"I missed that one," I nodded at the poster of Valerie L. "Lovely."

"Yeah," Greg said, glum again.

"I think I missed the CD, too," I added. "Any good?"

He just looked at me, assessing again. Time to shut up about Valerie L. Evidently there would be no invitation to sit down. "So anyway," I continued, resigned to delivering the whole spiel standing up, "I'm doing this because that little jade is something very special. I'm amazed Valerie is letting it go. But, she really wants you to have it. What I can tell you is," and here I went into my pitch for appraisal, the legal benefits of having provenance documents handy at all times. How I would be his exclusive appraiser with just a little document signed quickly, like tomorrow. Greg crossed his arms again and stared down at them where they rested on his man-belly. I felt like I was talking to his hair.

I finished. Greg sighed and raised his head. I was startled to see tears in his eyes.

"I'll let you know," he said. "I have a lot to think about right now. Thanks." And that seemed to be that. He pocketed my name and number and turned away. "Bed," he said to Lopez. The happy black beast trotted away into the kitchen.

"If you need any reference books on jade," I began, but shut up as Greg turned back to me. Yes, his look could still command.

"This is between me and Valerie right now," he said. "I'll let you know when I want to do business." I shrugged and smiled, and moved towards the door. "Wait a minute," Greg said. "C'mere." He went into the hallway, not looking to see if I followed. Of course I followed.

We went to what must have been intended as a master suite, but Greg had turned it into a woodworking shop that opened out onto the back deck and garden. It had the vibe of a holy sanctuary. Hanging from the ceiling and the wall, in pieces and whole, were guitars. Dozens of beautiful, delicate guitars. So this was his true passion. Up on the wall were framed eight-by-ten glossies of musicians holding their guitars, with penned messages thanking Greg for working his magic. One glossy showed a tuxedoed guitarist sitting in front of his classical chamber ensemble ... which included Valerie L in a tight, black velvet strapless gown. *Oh*. And, *Wow*. That loose, shapeless wardrobe I'd seen her in suddenly had significant purpose.

Greg stood at a large shelf unit holding what must have been nearly ten thousand CDs. "Here," he said, and handed me a CD with the image of Valerie L from the poster. "I got a bunch of her stuff from this promotional thing I did. *"Oh yes, I'm sure, just a promotional thing. Uh-huh.* I scanned the credits on the CD.

"Hey, you produced this," I said, surprised. "Good going, it's a beautiful set, great cover image. How's it been selling?"

Greg made a face. "Hasn't. Production and duplication, coupla concerts, ate up the marketing budget. Well, that was my education as a record producer. Construction biz is getting me back on track. I should be able to get around to it again sometime next year."

Oh, once more. Lost his shirt, did he. "I'd think your guitars would be in demand."

Greg looked even more pained, and a bit lost. "Building these sweeties don't pay near as much as building condos," he sighed. "Next year for them, too." He surveyed them longingly, hands thrust in his pockets. He pulled one hand out. It held *yü*.

The gold turtle pendant, red cord spilling between his fingers. He gazed at it, then tossed and caught it like a gambler with a coin. "So. What the hellzit worth, anyway?"

"High four figures in a private sale," I responded quickly, professionally. "Possibly mid five at auction, if we can be sure about its age and where it came from."

Greg made a half-snort, half-grunt which I half-imagined he learned from his dog. "Good luck with that. Woman who shoved 'em at me disappeared while I was looking in the bag. Gone, *phht*. Nobody around me even saw her."

Thrice, oh. "You're kidding ... you're the guy? Antiques show ... somebody handed you ...."

"Yeah, I'm the guy. Surprise, surprise. Jade from nowhere. Not the way I like to do things, but that's how the world is sometimes. Weird. I get one, huh? Guess I must be special." His voice graveled, and he stared down at the jade. I suddenly feared I was going to have to hug him. *Come on, pal, you're losing her, so lose her*, said Reality. *I would like to go now*, said Habit. Fortunately Greg manned-up and sucked in a deep breath. He glanced at me and waved his hand at the wall of CDs. "See any others you want?" he asked. "Take a few, pass 'em around."

I picked out three. The chamber ensemble, another of the solo CD, and one where she was in duet with a violin. Definitely, that was a viola on her shoulder. Points for taking the string section's road less traveled. Greg watched me make my choices. I could feel the weight of his gaze. The anger in him pressed it into me. "You listen to those," he commanded, "and then you *tell* me that lady shouldn't be a star."

Leave. Now, Habit and Reality chorused. I smiled as if I knew exactly what he was talking about. "Keep my number with that jade," I said, and edged out of the room.

Greg deflated again. "Yeah, I'll call you when I've thought it over," he said. "Who knows, those high four figures could come in handy." It was an unsentimental parting. I thanked him again and got out. No sign of Lopez around the door. Apparently, when Greg said Bed, Lopez stayed in bed. Good soldier.

So that was the Emperor of China. Still trying to buy the affection of a woman who had no interest in being his concubine. Definitely stuck in an endless fight. I wondered what Del-the-

Prince would be like, when we met. He already had his exquisite dragons, so maybe it would be easy.

When I got home, I played Valerie L's solo CD. It must have been good. It put me right to sleep.

9.
TOYS

While opening the gallery the next morning, I remembered that I had promised to call Valerie L as soon as I had given the pendant to Greg. Damn—well, poor girl. Albert was on the phone all morning and then ran out to a client lunch, so he didn't ask me whether I'd bagged any jade on my day away. As soon as he was gone I called Valerie L. It was meant to be. I got her voice mail.

"Mission accomplished," I told her. "You tell me if it was a success, because I have no idea. Wasn't for me, at least not yet, although there is hope. By the way, Greg gave me a couple of your CDs. Nice work!" As I hung up I wondered why I had to go into the *girlfriend* mode with Valerie L. She wasn't treating me like a best pal or pet faggot. It must be the addition of a man, I sighed. Why does throwing a man into it change everything?

Then I mentally kicked myself for not adding on a reminder for her to call Del and introduce me. Well, I could take the chance that she already had. I peeled the sticky note with Del's number out of my pocket, took a deep breath, and dialed.

She *had* already called him. What a relief. Yes, he wanted to meet. My knees softened to liquid under the deep velvet thrumming of his voice. Talk about throwing a man into it. He gave an address for someplace called "Mercy's," and we set an appointment for early that evening.

When Albert returned from his lunch, he glanced at a fax, which propelled him onto the phone, which occupied him for nearly an hour, and then he announced he was off to Toronto in the morning to look at some bronzes. I couldn't help smiling down at the porcelain bowl I was polishing. Albert had just solved a sticky problem. And he did not ask me about jade.

The address for "Mercy's" was in an old industrial neighborhood, home to a defunct, once-famous brewery. The brewery still dominated the area: an empty, red-brick dinosaur shoved up against the sidewalk, breathing enough industrial oppression for a Dickens novel. Tough artists and motorcycle clubs were gleefully reclaiming the sooty, dirt-cheap storefronts and warehouses around it. The resulting bars and live /

work / studio / performance / galleries had a half-finished, handmade flash. "Raw," I remembered a newspaper columnist gushing recently. Personally, I think that quality should stay in vegetables, where it belongs.

Mark and Scottie had gotten into an argument about the neighborhood at one of their dinners. Scottie saw a breeding ground for innovative art that could rearrange the city's international profile. Mark agreed but gave it another five years, maximum, to strut its beefy attitude. The usual gentrification cycle would assert itself, he insisted. Artists would pioneer the infrastructure, hard-working queers would clean it up and make it safe. When the affluent straights moved in, the artists would be priced out of the market and disappear, taking their innovation with them, and everyone else would feed on the nostalgia. Five years, and there would be an outlet mall in the creepy old brewery. Scottie called Mark disturbingly cynical. Mark called Scottie sweet as punch. They ended it by clinking wine glasses and vowing to stick to those prudent investments that were above 2000 square feet, preferably on a lakefront.

So there I was, five years ahead of the revolution, nervously looking for a place to park. Commanded there by the Prince of China with his jade dragons, and the story inside it pulling me along. *My* story was in there, palimpsest, faint and shadowy. In the thumb ring, and then the turtle pendant, I could feel the tile floors of the Imperial Palace under my feet, and see the angle of daylight in courtyards and gardens. I knew the smells of the food, the perfumes, heating braziers, the baths and toilets. As the *yü* told me their memories, they brought up memories that were *mine*.

I drove past the address. I circled the block and drove past again, just to be sure.

"Mercy's" was a gun shop. Del was meeting me in a gun shop. "LOANS" glowed neon in the window, so it was a pawn shop, too. Oh, God. I was in Man Country.

The memories *this* environment brought up were not perfumed. Wait, I take that back. Cheap deodorant and trendy cologne were always present when the jock bullies surrounded me. Okay, maybe Del was testing me. See if a hostile environment would shake loose any lies I was telling. Well, I knew how to prepare for that. Parked, I sat in the car and clicked my bead bracelet through my fingers. *OmManiPadmeHumOmMani PadmeHumOmManiPadmeHumOmManiPadmeHum* ... until my murmur was indistinguishable from the mantra that rose up from inside the big brown bead of *yü*.

I stepped inside Mercy's under the jingling doorway bell, and immediately my eyes teared from the sting of tobacco still ghosting the air. The smell overpowered the memories of Eau de Locker Room. Tobacco was the smell of all my uncles, the redheads and the golden-skinned, a smell even more jelled into their personalities than beer, whiskey, or fried onions. Reflex made me shift my weight back onto my heels and shove my hands in my pockets—assuredly masculine, enough to get through an hour or two of Easter dinner after Mass. I blinked and looked around. Rifles filled two glass cases like stacks of blue-black tree limbs. Handguns filled another glass case like nasty fists. Enormous knives and machetes crowded the last glass case. Express tickets to karmaville. A glint of color caught my eye.

I registered what it was—and dropped the Family Defensive posture; I trotted through the aisles to where it squatted just above eye level.

How did a Tibetan Buddhist heruka statue get in here? Sitting on a shelf between a Klingon spring-action dagger and the double-headed axe carried by Gimli the Dwarf?

I craned my neck to get a better view and pick out the statue's details. It wasn't a particularly expert fashioning of two multi-headed, multi-armed deities in sexual union, but it was sturdy metal and painted in bright colors. I riffled through my memorized catalogs of Asian religious objects, searching for a name and attributes.

"If you know what that thing is, you get the prize of the day," a mournful voice said. I turned around. Behind the counter was a Black guy in his 30s, wearing oversized aviator glasses that gave him a wistful look. He leaned on the counter, his meaty elbows barely reaching it over his belly. Above him a huge elk head stared down from the wall, as if checking his arithmetic. The elk had a cigarette stuck in its mouth.

"It's a Buddhist meditation deity," I answered the man. "I think the name is Chakrasamvara."

The fellow grunted. "Medi-*tay*-shun," he grumbled. "Just what I need. Looka here," and he waved at various statues around the shop. "Dancing Shiver. Mister Elephant-Head. That blue badass bitch stickin' her tongue out. And now I got Mister and Missus Shakra-samovar makin' mutant babies. Dunno whether I'm turnin' into a porn shop or a church."

I relaxed, unable to suppress a smile. Now that I was paying attention, I saw that the place was definitely more than guns. The pawn shop side of the business added musical instruments, electronics, power tools, and the odd piece of ethnic art.

"Oh, I don't know, I think you're in luck," I said. "Mister Elephant-Head, there, is the party king who invites good things to happen. Put him closer to the door so he can call in the business. Miss Badass should be sitting under your 'Shoplifters Will Be Hung By the Balls' sign. Dancing Shiver keeps things moving and changing, so he could sit above the door and make sure those who need to leave actually do. Now the mutants, here … well, look at all the weapons they're holding. Chakrasamvara is actually a protector deity. The weapons are symbols for what cuts through the bullshit."

The guy was listening, and ready to buy, if I had been selling anything. "Do they have to be doing that?" he asked, poking one index finger through the other circled thumb and forefinger, filling emptiness. "I got ladies come in here. You know they can give you some shit if they see disrespect."

They can keep rugby. This is my sport. "Here's the thing about this kind of statue," I said. "The man is about *knowing*, the woman is about *doing*. We each have those parts of us, the part that knows, and the part that does. Whatever the man is holding in all his arms is what he knows. When he's got a woman on him, what the man knows becomes *real*, because the woman brings action. So looking at the weapons, the short version of Chakrasamvara's message is, 'Cut the bullshit and *do it*.'"

The guy's face split with a generous grin and he guffawed with delight, making his blubber dance. "I *like* that, I *like* that!" he roared.

Probably my temple's head lama would disagree with that interpretation. Dave might cover his face and moan. This shopkeeper's loud joy was a nifty reward for the moment.

"All right, Vern, you *like* it," a deeper, more velvety voice thrummed from the doorway. "But are you gonna *share* it?"

"Deeeeeeeeeelll!" Vern hollered. "Get on in here and take some love, brother!"

Deeeeeeeeeelll! my insides echoed, as the Bald God himself strolled through the door. Vern shifted his wideness out from behind the counter to give Del a one-arm hug, which Del returned along with a light slap on the cheek. I blushed hot with a primitive envy. Del possessed a cool grace; he was naturally vigilant and ready for confrontation. He was the guy I had longed to have as a friend in school; a commanding figure who would step in among the bullies, come to the rescue. *My Prince. I thought I had outgrown that wish. Hah.* The Prince was twenty years late.

And yes, deep down he *did* remember a shining campaign at the head of an Imperial army. His long-sleeved thermal pullover was clear red, no logos, fit like a second skin, with the sleeves pushed up to display the cordwood strength of his forearms. You did not want to mess with his forearms. Well, maybe *you* didn't want to. And his pants were black twill, belted, svelte. Del would be the last breathing human anywhere to show up in baggy clothes. I stood baffled that Valerie L had not leapt past the age difference, to land on this man and taste every last drop of wonder. But she had not.

This man turned and looked at me, met my gaze; reached out to take my hand; a brief pump. His grip was big, warm, and muscular but with the softness that always surprises me in men's hands.

"Vern didn't make you nervous, did he?" Del asked, with a sidelong wink at his buddy. "I thought I might be late, so I asked him to keep an eye out for you."

"He's all right, Del," Vern said, back in his nest behind the counter. "He even told me what that thing is." Vern pointed at Chakrasamvara.

"Well then, share the word."

"Helps you meditate on a beautiful truth—cut the bullshit and take action."

"Hmm, that is beautiful. Now then, Mr. Lamos," he turned back to me, I who had only just begun breathing again, "I didn't ask you here just so Vern could get an education, though he's desperate in that department. I need you to take a look at something. Vern, is it still here?"

Vern put on his shopkeeper face: wary, melancholy. He reached under the counter, shifted some things around, and came up with a long, thin something wrapped in blue velvet. Vern carefully laid it on the counter and unwrapped it as if it were treasure. It was a Chinese sword.

"Take a look," Del said. "Tell me what you think."

"I'm not really a sword man," I protested.

"Just tell me what you see," Del repeated. His tone was light, but underneath … it was an order. I stepped up to the counter and let my fingers dance over the metal and fittings.

"Um, definitely some wear on the blade. I'd have to study up on the patterning in this metal—you know, metalsmith techniques. The hilt and pommel look recent, maybe replacing an older fitting. The tassel was definitely added recently, for show. It *could* have been an actual ceremonial sword refitted and used for fighting practice since the end of Imperial rule."

"Come on, Del," Vern prompted. "The last owner had black belts in six kindsa martial art. He wouldn't handle no fake, any more'n you would."

"I'm not interested in the last man who owned it," Del replied calmly. "I'm more interested in the *first* man who owned it." And he looked at me though lidded eyes.

Oh. Uh-huh. Okay. That was the test. I took in a lungful of air and blew it out. I hefted the sword lightly. The prickling rush was there in my hands, the murmur of the inward voice in my ear. I closed my eyes.

"Fat white man in a fedora, first time in Hong Kong, on business. He's in radios. Drives a Hudson back in Michigan. *Drove*," I corrected. I opened my eyes. Vern and Del were still staring, waiting. I shrugged and set the sword back on its velvet. "That's it," I said.

Del turned a long slow look to Vern, who fumed.

"Fifty," said Vern.

"Thirty," said Del. Vern chewed the inside of his lip.

"Thirty-five," said Vern. Del looked away. "Thirty-two," Vern said. "Come on, Del."

Del erupted in a laugh that seemed to come up through the floor. "Thirty-two will do!" he shouted. "That's good, brother!"

He reached for his wallet. Vern pulled out the sales book and grumbled as he wrote the ticket.

"Slick ofay mothafucka told me it was a an-*teek*. Ain't never gonna trust one a them karate mothafuckas again. Paid out a hunnert-twenny-five! *Hudson*. Shee-*it*."

"Next time call the man, Vern," Del said with a nod at me. "Call the man." He picked up the sword and checked its balance. "*Jian*, one-handed sword." He held it vertically, then slowly traced shapes in the air, gracefully twisting and turning his body in what I suspected was the Tai Ch'i sword discipline. Like I said, I'm no sword man. Suddenly he burst into a lightning-fast move—twirl, lunge—and the sword's tip stopped right where my neck met my shoulder.

Its touch—its *near* touch—sent a freezing needle of electricity through me, neck to foot. The look in Del's eye was pure fire. Warning me of what he *could* do, if he needed. Then he grinned.

"Hey, cut that out, I got merchandise in here," Vern said.

The "raw" bar Del ushered me into had a kind of Bride-of-Frankenstein charm. Its interior had obviously been stitched together from pieces of long-dead bars and restaurants. I was just happy to realize I wouldn't stick to the vinyl seat of our booth.

"Valerie said you were radar on legs," Del apologized. "Probably even better than her at the Touch. Me, I always have to check these things. Some stories are just too good to be true, you know?"

"Too well."

"In that case, it's time to talk jade. Let's hear it."

I laid my hands flat on the table. "What you have," I started, "what Valerie gave you is something extremely ... well, let me put it this way. To you and Valerie, it's priceless. But *only* to you and Valerie, hm?"

"Hm."

"Did Valerie tell you what dynasty the piece is from?"

"Han. About two thousand, two hundred years ago."

"But without a qualified appraisal, that's just speculation." I pulled my business card out of my breast pocket and handed it to him. Until eight-thirty on Monday morning, the gallery was mine, only mine. I needed it; the Prince would feel at home in a palace like the Albert Jarro Gallery. Its solid elegance would justify Del's trust in me as the exclusive representative of his Han jade. "What is of utmost professional concern to me," I continued, "is that you and Valerie possess these pieces without any kind of documentation whatsoever. They came to Valerie in a mysterious way—well, sometimes pieces do. But with possession of a treasure comes responsibility—and liability. It would definitely be in your best interest to bring this jade to our gallery where I can give it a professional appraisal, establish its age, estimate its value, and even set up an insurance plan for it."

"Why should a small object in my private possession be a liability?" Del asked. He lifted his beer in a languid way, a man with all the time in the world, and all the cool. But I already knew it was meant to tease my purpose out into the open. "It's not a weapon," he said. "It won't harm anyone. Only a specialist like you would recognize it if he saw it."

"All right, let's say life goes on," I rejoined. "And a time comes when you have to look at even the most precious personal objects in terms of their monetary value, to cover, say, a catastrophic medical bill, or some other kind of loss. If you were to take that scabbard piece to an auction house or a dealer, without any documents about its age or authenticity or vetting your ownership ... well, at best it would be assumed to be a replica, and you'd get a tiny fraction of its real value. At worst, and this has happened, you could be accused of a major art theft."

That was it, that was the trigger word, *accused*. His jaw tightened, a glint sparked in his downcast eye. *Accused. No one will accuse me*, he was thinking. *No, not again, not ever again*, I thought back at him. *So bring it down, please bring it on down. Let me hold it, please.*

"The same situation would come up for whoever inherits the piece after you," I added, for the maraschino cherry. Del shifted and considered his beer. Time to close the deal. "We open at nine," I said. He played my business card between his fingers. "Tomorrow I'm there at eight," I continued. "Or, just give me a call."

Del laid the card on the table. "I will definitely think about this," he said, and took a draw of his brew. I sat back and smiled.

He still thought he was the hard target, sitting there in royal leisure. But I knew I had him. The Prince was mine.

I got home to find three messages from Mark on my voice mail, reminding me of the Friday afternoon ferry schedule and asking me to pick up last-minute items for the island weekend, which would get underway tomorrow night. Frantic, I called Mark and said something had come up, I couldn't get away early, I had to be at the gallery all day Friday and possibly over the weekend. Mark pouted and extracted my promise to get the last possible ferry if I could manage it—and bring champagne truffles as a sign of sincere contrition.

I cussed my way around the apartment while throwing a weekend bag together. Yesterday—just *yesterday?!*—I'd been so ready to skip town and leave the *yü* behind. Now I had to hang by the gallery's phone like a teenager and put my best friendship under a cloud. Mark and Scottie were two of the few friends who knew that I was an intuitive with the Touch, but with them it was never a big deal—kind of like having an appendectomy scar or a preference for pinot gris. I didn't know if I could communicate to them the passionate need that was holding me to these *yü*. I certainly couldn't mention Del, or the political love tragedy that was tearing me apart from two thousand years away. I couldn't begin to explain the search I had to make for *myself* in that tale. It was all so strange, and I hungered for the ordinariness of their comfortable friendship.

I put on the CD of the chamber ensemble featuring Greg's guitar and Valerie L's viola. The guitar's sound was rich and clear. Greg definitely had his own touch with wood and glue. In fact, something of the Emperor seemed to emanate from the guitar's voice: the violin's twitter and the viola's reassuring warmth circled the guitar like attendants, stepping lightly, with devotion. Approaching, engaging, and then moving into a deferential position. Like wives, or concubines.

When the CD was done, I put it back in its case and tossed it into my weekend bag. The guys might like it.

Eight forty-five a.m. the next day, Friday, bright and early, I had the gallery gloriously to myself. I was in the back office going over the night's faxes when someone started rapping on the gallery's glass door. I fairly skipped out to the front—and saw a crowd of retirees gathered on the sidewalk. I stopped short and picked out the leader: a grizzled Groucho Marx lookalike. I caught his eye, grinned, made a "just a sec!" wave, and bolted back to the office.

I grabbed the big dayrunner off of Albert's desk. Good God. *Elderhostel*. Albert had never said a word. I sped out to the front, wondering what the hell Albert had been planning to say to a dozen senior citizens determined to learn something.

But Australian rules rugby is nothing to me, compared to the thrills of winging it on the sales floor. Twelve curious minds with seven hundred years of life experience between them? Bring 'em on. I let the group in and had a quick whispered exchange with Groucho Marx about my sudden substitution for Albert Jarro. He obligingly showed me the Elderhostel catalog copy for "Seeing China in a Bowl."

Sure enough, as soon as I let them lead the way with their own questions, one thing built on another and I had a dozen budding collectors on my hands.

Is it possible to show anyone China in a bowl? In my travels around China as a graduate student, I pored over antiquities in museums, shards at archaeological digs, figurines in private collections, until I was dizzy. No one was foolish enough to proclaim one object as containing the epitome, the substance, the essence, of China. But I could talk about aesthetics, the balance of qualities in objects that reflected the balance of the five universal elements in Taoist philosophy, which bled into the Buddhist philosophy that came later. Oh, I could talk. And they listened, while their eyes roved over Asian history under glass. Knotty fingers tapped creased lips as two ladies peered at a set of teacups from the 17th century. I connected their scrutiny in our classroom moment with a painting on silk, carefully framed and lit on the wall: a landowning family of the Tang Dynasty relaxing in their garden after dinner, with teacups filled by a servant girl. "What might the dinner's conversation have been about?" I prodded the students.

"Oh, probably marriage and raising children," one of the ladies said. "Politics and sports," said a smiling old fellow on a folding chair. "Money, too, I bet," added a sharp dresser with his hands his pockets.

"Most likely you're right," I said, "every one of you. Because even though China's civilization is much older than

Egypt's—no, don't look stunned, Egypt just had the luck to sit closer to Greece—it was still a civilization of human beings. Human beings seeking happiness, balance, peace, and beauty."

Oh, couldn't I talk! I could make them laugh. I could make them think. I could pick them up and swirl them through time on the pearl inlay of a storage cabinet and the craggy edges of a prehistoric axe head. It was an exaltation of Habit. All the time, the voice of Reality chuckled at the hidden irony: *And this, all this is nothing! Nothing, compared to the real greatness—the greatness in stone, metal, porcelain and jade, that no one ever touches and even museums are lucky to see. The treasures that move the money. Compared to the stores of godlike artistry behind that iron door by Albert's desk, behind a thousand iron doors all over the world, in rooms that will always be invisible to you, this gallery is a box of shabby toys.*

So I charmed them, so I teased them. I took their applause and shook Groucho Marx' hand when it was done. They scattered, murmuring, around the airy showroom, squinting into the glass cases. Del the Bald God walked out of the back office. He was smiling.

The world went silent.

What was it the Emperor described? Surrounded by enemies with drawn bows ... the bones turn to ice.

"How did you ... where did you come from?" I whispered.

"You were busy," Del explained cheerfully. "I didn't want to interrupt. So I went around looking for the back door. Jarro himself was just coming in. On his way to the airport, he said, but he took time to look at the jade and set me up. Provenance file, insurance policy—it's all in place. We're good."

Cracks in the earth. Widening. Cities fall. Dynasties vanish. All in silence. No sound.

"Where ... " I couldn't finish the question.

"He called this appraiser, found out the man had an opening in his schedule," Del said. He showed me the glossy business card I knew too well. "Jarro said he would just have time to drop it off before he caught his flight. So he wrapped the jade up, and they're off. Most professional man I've ever met. Really knows how to treat people well."

Please let a comet strike the Earth. Let dust cover the ruins. Let there be silence. Silence. Silence.

"See, I'm having a scabbard made and I want the jade slide to fit," Del said. He looked cinematic in his immaculate khakis and white shirt, open at the neck with a slim strand of gold chain just visible at the throat, topped by a navy corduroy blazer. Perfectly suited for striking a deal on an *objet d'art* worth scores of thousands of dollars. "I figure the sword I bought yesterday is good enough for a wall hanging, so ..."

There was a hole in the fabric of space, the size and shape of a pale green jade. Everything that mattered, all the greatness of art and life, sped vanishing out that hole. The concubine took the ring from her hand, set it on the bed, and that was all. This shining man was a chattering puppet, and I was a hollow doll. We gathered nothing but dust, in a box of shabby toys.

BOOK II:

THE PRINCE
AND THE POET

Spinning Wheel

Only after we are awake do we know that we have dreamed. But there comes a great awakening, and then we know that life is a great dream. But the stupid think they are awake all the time and believe they know it distinctly.

Once I, Chuang Tzu, dreamed I was a butterfly and was happy as a butterfly. I was conscious that I was quite pleased with myself, but I did not know that I was Tzu. Suddenly I awoke, and there was I, visibly Tzu. I do not know whether it was Tzu dreaming that he was a butterfly or the butterfly dreaming that he was Tzu.

Chuang Tzu, 369-286? BC

10.
EXQUISITE

Mark's mouth made an O when he saw me coming. The six other guys at the table quickly stopped talking and turned around to see what he was looking at.

I shoved a box of champagne truffles down the long, scratched Formica table, one of dozens on the ferryboat's main lounge deck. It was flanked by long vinyl benches, big enough for parties, card games and naps. The box of truffles slid almost to the window and spun once before coming to a rest.

"My apologies to anyone who thought I wasn't coming, or would be late," I said, with the formal intensity of someone ready to pull out a gun and use it. I plunked down at the end of a bench, across from Mark. "I had a horrible, despicable, really bad morning at work. So I apologize in advance for whatever happens from now on."

The seven other men sat in stunned silence. I aimed my eyes at the tabletop and ignored them. A stout little bear with a goatee, who I didn't know, was sitting at the window end of my bench. He waved his fingers gently at me. "I have to go to the men's room …?"

I jumped off the bench as if kicked. The other three guys scooted towards me and off the bench, stepping back away from me.

"Why don't you …" Mark began. "Go down to my car," I finished for him. "Yes, I think I will. I think I'll just go have a temper tantrum. Sorry. See you all later."

I had barely made it onto the ferry at the arranged time, one of the last to board. Thus my car was parked nose-up, ass-down on the portside ramp to the upper parking deck. It was conveniently close to the chain-gate that guarded the ferry's stern. The steel lip of the stern hung over a trail of churning water that pointed back to the dock.

"You stupid sonofabitch!" I stood at the chain-gate and screamed at that churning water. *Chugchugchugchugchugchug-chugchug*, the ferry rumbled serenely. "You stupid fucking sono-fabitch, it was too good to be true, you slick idiot! You couldn't wait for me, you couldn't check with me, you just *let him take it*

… you …" My jaw locked. Never in any screaming fit had I said that word. But my rage surged like a flooding river and the lock disintegrated. "You *patsy nigger*," I shrieked into the throbbing engine roar.

That did it; the whole dam broke. I regressed to a full-blown three-year-old's tantrum, flailing my arms, stamping my feet and wailing from a broken heart. I was beating the bulkhead with an orange rubber traffic cone when a deckhand walked up to me, talking into his radio.

"Apparently your friend had a really bad day at work," the security officer said to Mark. I sat on an ugly chair in the tiny office while the officer rested his blue-clad butt on the desk, and Mark stood in the doorway. Just like visiting the principal.

"Oh, yes, awful, he told us all about it. You don't want to hear," Mark replied.

"Even so, we'd rather he didn't take it out on state property." The security officer had a soft face and hard colorless eyes. He kept his arms crossed, as if that held the whole world in a sane shape.

"He's got seven friends on board who'll make sure he doesn't do it any more," Mark said.

The officer grunted. "He's all yours, then." He sounded relieved.

Ten minutes later I stood at the outside rail with Mark and Scottie, the wind whipping us as the ferry plowed its way out from under the cloud cover towards the sunny islands. I had poured out as much as possible about the day's disaster, trying not to sound like a complete lunatic. Closing down the gallery to come be with them, they could admire. Losing my grip on a fabulously valuable antique gem, they could understand.

"Sixty thousand dollars," Scottie breathed. "Shit, I'd whack state property, too."

"Sixty is an estimate," I said. "A guess. Based on recent auctions and … oh, Christ, I don't want to talk about it." I leaned heavily on the rail like I was about to puke or throw myself over.

"Well, now, wait a minute," Mark said. He and Scottie quickly flanked me on the rail and settled their backs against it, surrounding me. "This isn't about losing an appraisal fee or a commission. I don't care if your boss is the most respected

Asian art dealer on Jupiter, he just acted like a prime shit. To his only assistant, no less! Seriously, if this is how he treats you after four years of you working your ass off for him, then it's time to get the hell out."

"I second that," Scottie said. "You've got all this experience and ability, you should be more than just this dude's showroom guy. What does he think you are, a Wal-Mart greeter?"

"I know, I know." Shame filled me. It was so plain. "I know I've always been the Great Exotic, the show dog. It's just … well, where else could I hold such incredible pieces of art? Do you know I once held an original Hokusai? One of his small paintings, but I got to touch a Hokusai!"

Scottie looked baffled. "Japanese Rembrandt," Mark murmured to him.

"Oh," Scottie nodded. "I should come down and see it."

"Wrong. It wasn't for display. It …" No, I couldn't tell them *that*, either. "No, the real masterpieces, the … the *greatness*, those just pass through. Moving between owners. Albert has … connections. Albert *is* a connection. He's a beauty pusher. It's the biggest drug there is, you know? And guess what, I'm his number one junkie. I've tried to think about quitting, but I just can't, I just …"

"Then think of this as an intervention," Scottie said firmly. "Your boss was a shit to you. He stole from you."

"Technically …"

"He stole your *client*," Scottie went on, "and your job, and your commission. Knowing that he did this, you have the opportunity to do something about the situation. What that is, I don't know. But you do."

"Yes. Maybe. Maybe I will know, later."

"Let yourself settle down," Mark said. "Relax. You've got the whole weekend to think it over."

"I will. I will … think it over. And I will know what to do."

"As long as it doesn't involve destroying traffic cones," Scottie said. "Property taxes pay for those." Scottie took a tissue pack out of his pocket and put it in my hand.

I blew my nose and blotted my tears. "Thanks, you guys. It would've been a million times worse today without you." Scottie pulled me into a bear hug and Mark enfolded both of us. A manfriend hug, bringing me to safe ground. They let me go and we started back along the deck back towards the lounge. Mark and Scottie exchanged a look, some kind of agreement.

"If you want to dip your toe in something else," Mark offered, "we've got a string of open houses coming up and I need someone to stage them. Rent furniture, borrow decorative pieces, you know. My usual girl has decided to devote herself to motherhood, God bless her."

"They won't all be magnificent, but they do need something special," Scottie said. "Will you think about it?"

"Yeah. Sure," I said, mostly to cheer them up and change the subject. The wind was getting sharp, and I wanted to return to the table of houseguests with my hosts feeling better about me.

The rest of the 90-minute trip was much less hideous. Scottie and I went to the snack bar to get me some coffee, while Mark went back to the lounge table. I assumed that he would tell everybody I was okay now and the meltdown was over. Sure enough, when Scottie and I returned, the talk was going strong about payroll software for mid-size businesses. I sipped my mocha in blissful ignorance of the subject. My gaze strayed from the clearing sky outside, early afternoon sun glancing off the water and the wings of seagulls sidling the air alongside us, to the faces of my fellow houseguests. Especially the two I was meeting for the first time.

Eric, the stout little bear with the goatee, led the software debate with fierce enthusiasm and an acid wit about help-desk politics. He definitely had his eye on Stuart, a graphic artist and wicked dancer. Mark caught me savoring their mutual cruising, and gave me a wink. That yenta.

The other unknown face added one or two comments to the debate but asked more questions, bravely trying to learn something in the midst of the computer-geek wit and dish. He was sort of how I'd always imagined an astronaut should look: compact, lean, with a dishwater-blond brush cut and eyebrows set low over his eyes (what color were they? I couldn't see), and a jaw that was square when he held his head a certain way. All of that space-age superiority was offset by rose petal lips and baby-doll dimples. And, there was that *thing* that triggered the gaydar. I've decided it's a kind of caution, the caution of a small mammal checking for predators, from deep inside whatever kind of body has settled around the soul. I know there are exceptions to this not-so-sweeping generalization. But it's my generalization and I'll stick with it. For me, that instinct of small-mammal caution is what distinguishes every faggot on Earth from the likes of, say, Del.

I had hoped I wouldn't think of Del.

There! I could blame his confidence, his sureness, his sheer *competence*, for blinding him to the possibility that maybe, just *maybe* he needed to talk to me, not Albert, about that *yü* ...

Danger, Will Robinson. Meltdown approaching, do not proceed. Increase mocha intake. Analyze whipped cream. Scan dimpled astronaut again. What was his name? I hadn't caught it. But if I leaned over to my neighbor, Jerry, and interrupted his whispered conversation with his devoted partner, Mike, to ask the astronaut's name, instantly everyone would believe I was after him. And that would become the story of the weekend— even more so than Eric and Stuart.

I made the mocha last until we reached the island dock and the group had to scatter to their cars. I had not spoken another word, and the astronaut had not looked my way.

Inevitably, while we all cooked a big pasta dinner in the cabin's spacious kitchen (eight gay men cooking together—do not try this casually), I learned that his name was Ash, short for Ashworth, not Ashley. He cooked for a high-end caterer. His patience during the dinner prep was admirable. And inevitably, during dinner, he asked me to pass the bread plate. He looked at me and smiled and said thank you. I smiled back, and saw that his eyes were some kind of deep hazel flecked with blue.

Still, I kept to myself. There was just too damned much to think about. What would I say to Albert on Monday morning? Would I just suck it in and wait for my chance to strike back? I could give notice at the worst possible moment. I could mislead a client or be rude to the Sotheby's rep or "accidentally" let slip some vital information about Albert's dealings. Our little world was built on such delicate relationships and understandings, it would be easy to pull just one critical thread and watch the whole fabric unravel.

But thinking like that tossed me into a red-hot maze, where every path led back to meltdown. Exhausting. During our cleanup, I straightened from loading my plate in the dishwasher and realized how much the effort of holding a pleasant expression made my face hurt. I rubbed my burning cheeks and eyes in what I hoped was a discreet way. In an instant, Mark wrapped his long arm around my shoulders. "Hot tub for you, pal," he said cheerily. "Come on, we're all going."

Climbing into a big hot tub with seven other men, all of us naked, was definitely a pleasant distraction that cooled off my busy thoughts. Eric and Stuart settled on opposite sides of the tub so they could play footsie and eyeball each other. I placed myself between Jerry and Scottie, two bodies away from Ash the Astronaut/Caterer. He seemed nice, but getting acquainted would be just a little *too* much distraction right now. I really wanted to tune out and let the hot water, island breezes and night sky do their work.

Before I knew it, Scottie was shaking my shoulder. "We're all cooked," he said. "Ready to go in?" He had wrapped a big towel around his thick waist and carried a water bottle.

"I just have to give my toes a starbath," I said. I slid under the water and raised my feet up in the air, soles flat to the stars.

Scottie tickled one. I thrashed up, sputtering.

"This is a big improvement, but still," Scottie said. "Wish you were here. It'd be a better party."

"I know. But I'd like to stay out here with the sky for a while. I'll be all right," I assured Scottie. "I'll sit here on the edge, take a breather."

Scottie looked disapproving. However, he handed me his water bottle, ruffled my hair, and went in.

I hauled myself up to perch on the edge of the tub, and sipped water. I groped for my glasses and put them on, to take a look around me. Out there beyond the house's glow, beyond the expansive deck, forests fell in black legions down to the even blacker waters of the straits. Above, the stars hung like fruit in the deep purple sky. A cool night breeze played around my body, swirling the steam that rose from me. It made the trees rustle in secret conversation. I felt still for the first time that day. *Nothing more is possible*, the blackness of the Earth and waters said. *Nothing more is needed.* I was at the end of something. Completely stopped. Yet the world felt porous, a loose place where events and objects and people were simply the straying thoughts of someThing much, much larger, much *more*. Perhaps a cosmic butterfly, who in a moment will dream it is a Chinese philosopher. If a man sitting on the edge of a hot tub is part of a butterfly's dream, what else might be here in this darkness? The pitch-black forest could hold a rebel army of Chinese peasants. Or a prince carrying heads in baskets. A concubine could come flying through the fir branches, followed by an Emperor. They would only be ghosts. If I stayed in this stillness, they would float past me, and disappear. My naked gay body would be just as much a ghost to them.

I shuddered, suddenly cold. I set my glasses back on the edge of the tub and slipped back into the comfort of the hot water, letting it rise up over my chin to my lower lip.

How old is this part of the Earth? I wondered. What was it doing twenty-two hundred years ago? Breeze, trees, water, stars. It was all probably the same—with more deer and foxes. But not dragons. Not the pale green dragons that Chinese artisans saw with ancestral memory and put into jade. How long had it been since dragons flew in Chinese skies? How long had it …

"*Hey!*" Hands slapped my face. I woke and sat up. Mark crouched over the edge of the hot tub, bundled in a holly-green thermal weave bathrobe. He looked worried. "You're not supposed to fall asleep in these things," he chided. "Come in, for God's sake. We've almost finished the truffles." How dumb, I *had* fallen asleep. Well, I did feel different, if not exactly better. So I exited the tub with a show of high spirits, for Mark's sake. He wrapped me in a fluffy towel and paraded me in front of the other men (Eric and Stuart had already gone upstairs for their consummation) to prove that I hadn't drowned. Even Ash looked relieved to see me walking upright. Cracking trivial jokes, he and I split the last truffle. Something about his eyes and cackling laugh made me feel almost human.

Eric and Stuart didn't come down to breakfast, as we knew they would not. I wasn't hungry, but managed to eat a bit of omelette and toast, which made Scottie happy. I seemed to have been somewhere else while asleep. My head still buzzed with dreams of flying through tree branches, chasing a honey-blonde woman carrying shopping bags. She had stolen something from the gallery—no, from me. We came to the edge of a lake and there was a teenage Chinese girl in a black evening gown walking on water, playing the viola. She was followed by a bald man in yellow robes, holding a long Chinese sword upright in his hand.

In the morning, out of bed, the scenery had changed but the sensation was the same. The cabin, the men, the drive to the marina, stepping onto the elegant old wooden sailing yacht, all felt unreal, still a dream. Not even the dock's pungent smell of creosote and brine could quite wake me up.

Ash and I carried the lunch groceries down to the galley. "Do you know anything about boats?" I asked him.

"Not a thing," he replied.

"Same here," I said. "I guess you and I just hang on and stay out of the way."

"Oh," he said. He looked away, shy. *Oh.* I had opened up a toehold. *You and I.* Ash's inner small mammal was alert, checking the terrain.

"What were you thinking about out there in the hot tub?" Ash asked.

"Old things," I answered, with a small laugh. "Very old things." Ash nodded the nod of vague understanding and sympathy. I immediately regretted my coy maneuver. "I think I'm coming down with something," I said lamely.

"All hands on deck!" Mark hollered from above.

Ash groaned long and loud. "You know what they're going to do with *that*," he said. He and I looked at each other. For a moment, I was *awake*. And we burst into giggles.

"All *hands* on *deck!*" Mark repeated, and Ash and I collapsed in real laughter. We spilled up onto the deck absolutely helpless. Of course, ribald variations on the cliché were flying around between the other four men: "Dick who?" "On whose dick?" "Who *is* Dick?" "And is it worth putting my hands on him?" Ash and I fell apart at every tired word-twist. We were supposed to help cast off, perhaps, but there was no hope. Gradually everyone else caught the gigglebug. We pulled out of the marina's cove into the strait's sunny waters, hooting with laughter. "Make way for a cargo of exquisites!" Mark bellowed to the air. He looked more like a fly-fisherman than a sailor in his baseball cap, but he was happy turning the wooden wheel. "You mean a boatload of nellies!" Jerry barked from starboard, where he held a rope that connected to a sail. He looked purposeful. The rest of us whooped as we picked up speed.

It was a gloriously sunny day in an Indian summer, and the waters of the straits reflected the sky in a deep, tourmaline blue. The yacht was a beautiful thing, leaping along the waves, carried by the wind. Mike and Jerry had some sailing experience, so they clambered back and forth on the golden teak decks, following Mark's commands.

Laughter created a surreal energy in me. I seemed to have pumped myself into a higher level of the strange dream-feeling. The yacht's rocking motion plus the bright sun and the whipping wind raised nausea and a headache; yet it was somehow on the other side of a subtle border. Happening in some other lifetime. What was left of me felt like a radio antenna or a super-telescope. No, a spy satellite. Every slap of a wave against the hull shuddered through my feet and up my bones. I could see the sculling wingtips of every seagull, the curls of every wispy cloud. Maybe I *was* coming down with something. I grinned like an idiot; it seemed to hold back the headache from becoming too real.

We rounded the point of the island and entered the wider sound that emptied into the sea beyond this pretty archipelago. Now the air had a powerful stench in it—sea brine, superb with rot. Having witnessed nineteen family summers at the shore, and the birth of my youngest sister (Mom's water broke on her way to the door and Sis fell into Dad's hands over the welcome mat), that briny smell conjured impressions of very wet and uncontrollable transformations. Dead stuff melting into globs that would soon surge and burst with slimy new bodies squirming around. My nausea rose and fell with the deck—not up and down this time, but side to side. I spotted a black shape on the horizon.

"Freighter! Cargo ship, container vessel!" I yelled to Mark. "The wake is hitting us on the side!" Mark nodded and shouted something to Jerry and Mike, which sent them running to grab ropes and pull on the sails. The yacht gracefully began to change course, becoming perpendicular to the determined ribs of moving water.

For some reason it struck me as funny. The ship bobbing, the men running, the uncaring container vessel, the even more uncaring sun and wind, the sails bellying and flapping. All this commotion, on a day and a sea already so heavenly they felt radioactive. My headache, nausea and spy-satellite senses were perfect, and absurd. I had the impulse to sing. A song came into my head, one that had been an oldie when I was a tot. I had loved it because it was about painted ponies. I sang and made my way along the side deck, swaying with the yacht's rolling motion.

"What goes up, must come down
Spinning wheel got to go round
Drop all your troubles by the riverside
Ride a painted pony on the spinning wheel—"

"*DUCK!*" Mike screamed. The force under his voice hit me like a bat between the shoulder blades and I went down … and felt the swinging boom graze the back of my head as I did. My glasses flew off and skidded across the deck; I lost my balance and sprawled on the polished wood.

In moments, Scottie, Jerry and Ash were beside me. They spread my limbs out and made me lie still. The near miss … it was all still just too funny. I grinned up at them in wonder. "All hands on duck," I said. Jerry tipped my head from side to side, looking at my face. Then he undid my polo shirt and looked at my chest.

"Jesus, Ross," he said. "You're covered with hives."

11.
COOL

"I do not want to hear one word about the Princess and the fucking pea," I told Ash. I lay on a bunk in one of the yacht's two staterooms, stripped to the waist. Ash went on laying cucumber slices on my chest. They already covered my brow, eyes and cheeks.

"You're the one who has to shut up, dude," he said lightly. "Don't knock these off, we only brought one cucumber." I could hear him *tsk-tsk*. "Honestly. Chlorine poisoning from a hot tub. You'll get no sympathy from anyone, count on it."

The cucumbers were already a comfort. Cool spots on my burning body. I hadn't realized I was so feverish. And it was so nice not to look at anything. Just lie on the bunk, blanketed in the wood and brass of the yacht. Its rocking motion was muffled down here.

"Ash."

"Yah."

"Thank you."

"No problem."

"Thank everybody. I've been a kind of a shit. I'm not always like this."

"Nobody is."

"Some first impression, huh?"

He chuckled. A soft version of his cackle. "Hey, I've seen worse. A lot worse." A short silence.

"No fair," I said. "You can't just say 'a lot worse,' and not tell me."

"Why not? Use your imagination. People get stupid."

"Oh, c'mon, c'mon. Please!"

"Oh, all right. I was working a wedding reception. Bussing a table. Teenage bridesmaid reels up to me. Actually very pretty but you knew she'd been harassed for years about those extra twenty pounds. Anyway, she leans on the table, all vampy, and drunk as three sailors. She says to me, 'You—under the table. And me, on your big hot cock!' And she opens her mouth like a porn star, turns green and throws up on the floor."

"Oh dear. Oh dear. Oh that poor thing. Oh dear."

"Stop laughing! You'll lose your face cukes."

"Okay. You're right, that is worse. What did you do?"

"What could I do? I handed her a towel and tossed another onto the floor. She ran off, and I finished bussing. Cleaned it up later."

"*Hmf-hmf-hmf,*" I laughed as much as possible without moving my face or chest. Ash finished laying out cucumber slices on my abdomen. I had a flash of embarrassment about that softness around my belly button.

"Just lie there until lunchtime," Ash said. "See how you feel then. That aspirin you took should deal with the headache. I've got a juice detox recipe at home if you want to try it."

"You're really very kind."

"Hey, why not? I've seen the alternative." I think he smiled when he said this.

"Too true." I heard him move out of the stateroom. "Hey," I called.

"Hey."

"Um ... c'mon back whenever you're finished in the kitchen. I mean galley. I've had enough of being antisocial."

"Sure." I could hear things clattering softly in the sink. "Let me just clean up here."

Cucumbers. Somebody cleaning up in the kitchen. A sweetness filled me like a lullaby—a lullaby that woke me up. I was finally out of the weird dream world.

Water ran in the sink, and a moment later Ash was back. "Okay, I'm here." Something cool touched my lips. "Here, try this," Ash said. I opened my mouth, and bit a strawberry. *Oh.* Wet, sweet, tangy.

"Oh, that's wonderful. Thank you. Is that in the dessert?"

"They could go in the salad, now that the cucumber's gone." He pressed more strawberry to my mouth. "Here, go on, take the rest."

"You know, this is really selfish of me. Maybe you'd rather be out enjoying the sun and water. That's why we all came, isn't it?"

"Oh, I don't know, maybe." Ash settled on the foot of the bed. He must've rested his back against the paneled wall and lifted his legs onto the mattress. I was using my imagination. "Me, I'm running away from yet another wedding reception," he continued. "I've been canceling vacation plans all year for these big-deal jobs. Finally told my boss I was going away and that was it. So, sun, monsoon, avalanche, I don't care, as long as it's not a wedding and I'm not cooking. Last night was such a hoot. It was chaos, and I didn't have to make it anything other than that. The dinner turned out pretty good, too."

"I think I see why Mark asked you up. He finds chaos entertaining, too."

A moment's hesitation. Then Ash said, "I don't actually know Mark. I'm sort of a tagalong." Another hesitation, of a certain kind that small mammals in a small-mammal community learn to recognize. "Stuart invited me."

"Oh." There was my own hesitation, with its little communication. "Is he an ex?"

"Mm-hm," Ash replied. "We've stayed in touch. His company does all our menus and place cards."

If there's one thing community forces on you, it's growth through proximity. "Do you think he and Eric are good for each other?" I asked.

I wonder if Ash grimaced at the question. I would have. "I think it's a weekend thing," he said.

"Me too," I admitted. "But, if it's what they came for ...."
I let it hang, regretting the words. Maybe it was what Ash had come for. Maybe he assumed that was Stuart's motivation for bringing him along.

"So I'm curious now," Ash said, abruptly changing the subject, which as much as confirmed my speculation. "What really put you in that hot tub? 'Very old things' makes me think your boss is about a hundred years old. Real Scrooge. How about it? Now *you* be fair."

If there's a God, It is a just God, because how was I going to say No to him? He had covered me in cucumber and fed me a strawberry. Forget that Buddhism says God is only an illusion of the grasping mind. That strawberry had tasted good.

So I told him. Everything. He listened.

Never once said, "You're kidding," only "Whoa."

Just as the concubine was putting on a dead man's clothes, someone thumped down the stairs into the main saloon.

"Hey, Ashworth, what's for lunch?" Scottie's voice banged on the walls. "Ooh, a man salad!" He had stuck his head into the stateroom. Ash jumped up. "I am on my vacation," he shouted, pushing Scottie out, "and I am not cooking!" He slapped the door shut.

God, what a brave man. He didn't care what the guys would do with *that*.

"So what happens to her?" he asked. His voice had changed positions in the room. I think he sat on the floor and leaned against the door. No more interruptions.

"She takes off the Emperor's ring," I told him. "It can't protect her anymore. She puts it on her bed. End of transmission."

He sighed. "Man, you've got to get that last jade back. I can't stand this."

"Why do you think I sat in that hot tub so fucking long?"

"So, can you get it back?"

"It's gone, Ash. Between you and me, I think whatever comes back to Del is going to be a replica so perfect he'll never know the difference. But *I* would know, if I ever touched it." He didn't say anything. I didn't say anything. But we knew: a replica would be empty. No *story*. We were at a dead end.

We?

"Well, I do know what happens to all of them," I said. "They all die. Two thousand, two hundred years ago. That's it. Bottom line."

He kicked the mattress in annoyance, from where he was sitting. "That is not it, you just told me. Everybody comes back. I happen to like the idea of reincarnation, as a matter of fact. It turns all this fear of death into just another cop-out. So don't you go there. You know you can't, anyway."

I smiled under my cucumber slices. "I know. I know. Every time I go into my temple and see that big golden Buddha, I know. But I often wonder, God, how do we ever progress? Human life spans are so short. And we always forget. We have these lives, we achieve and screw up and try to clean things up from *other* lives, how on earth do we ever learn anything?"

Ash paused before answering. "Maybe you're doing it right now."

That made me pause. "You're too smart for me," I said.

"Just let the cucumbers draw out the toxins. You'll get smarter as your system gets clearer. I promise."

"Oh God bless you, Doctor. I think what I'm learning," I said, "is that this is it, bottom line, the end, for *me*. Del got his jade from Valerie. Maybe he understood her message, maybe not, but it's none of my business. I have to assume they're done. Whether or not he possesses the real stone doesn't matter so much anymore. Greg still has his jade, and probably will have it until he finally gets it about all that Emperor-karma."

"Sounds like he'll have it for the next three lifetimes. What about the thumb-ring?"

"Who knows? Valerie never told me if she knows who that is, in this life."

"So it might be you. It might be yours."

"Ash, if I'm going to live like a sane person, I can't hope. I have to face the fact that I may never know who I was in that life. And if I will never know, then it cannot matter. I still have to go to work Monday morning and figure my life out from there." I sounded a lot more resolved and rational than I felt. Ash stayed quiet.

"Careful what you say about hope and sanity," he said at last. "We all lose the beautiful stuff. I mean, Jesus, I cook for a living, you know? And I sculpt wedding cakes. I have a portfolio full of these amazing things I've done, gorgeous designs. All of it turns to sewage within twenty-four hours. And then, hey, let's look at my album of dead friends and lovers."

"I'm sorry. I didn't mean to be harsh."

"Sorry, neither did I. But hope and sanity are important. At least, I've seen that they have to go together to make a life. They need each other. Like I said, I've seen the alternative. You know, you can change your hopes. But don't ditch the whole concept for the sake of sanity. Because I can guarantee you, where there's no hope, sanity will vanish."

A thought had been growing in me. "How long did it take you," I dared to say, "to get your hope back, after you lost something beautiful? The most beautiful thing ever?"

That made him quiet. It was a tense quiet. But not hostile. "A long time," was all he would say, finally. Then he added, "And it's a very different kind of hope. But it works."

"You sound very Buddhist."

"I've been told I should be. But I'm not, I don't think I could do a practice. I did read around in some books this boyfriend shoved at me." He laughed, as an afterthought.

"What, they were funny?"

"No, *he* was. The whole situation. He was the craziest mix of Bible camp counselor and sailor on leave, because he was about to take vows and be a Buddhist monk in a monastery" –

"*What?*" I shouted, and sat bolt upright. Two-thirds of my cucumbers plopped onto the floor. "*Dave?* You're talking about *Dave?*" I brushed the cukes off my eyes. Ash was staring at me wide-eyed, mouth open.

"Oh my God," he whispered. "I wondered if you had met him, when you said Temple and Golden Buddha, but" —

"*Met* him?! I introduced him to Buddhism! In that temple! Handed him Kleenex when he couldn't stop crying during the Heart Sutra! We were together right up to the moment he got out of my car and walked into the temple with nothing to his name but the clothes on his back! He told me … he pledged to me …." I had to stop, because my voice was shaking and a part of me was still just a little bit old-fashioned.

Ash took it in, and then said softly, "He told you, you were the last one for him, the last one of this lifetime. Holy shit. He must have used that line all over town."

I clapped my hands over my face and fell back on the bunk with a long, gut-deep howl.

"Small fecking world," Ash said, when my howl drained away.

"Especially to Dave's penis," I agreed. I looked over at Ash. He had a strange, wild look in his eye. A grin began crawling up one side of his face. I had to grin, too. Suddenly, inevitably, we were laughing again. Helpless. Me rolling on the bed, him rolling on the floor. He threw a cucumber slice at me. I threw it back at him. That did it. We were in a pitched battle of flying cucumber slices when Scottie opened the door.

"May it please your Royal Highnesses, lunch is served on the main deck," he announced in bad British toff-speak. Ash and I pelted him with cucumber slices and he slammed the door in retreat.

Up on deck, it was still a glorious day. Lunch was a platter of sandwiches, potato salad, green salad, and a big bowl of strawberries with three kinds of gelato for dipping. I picked up two strawberries, sliced one into Ash's greens and one into mine. Ash said nothing, just grinned and snickered. I had an appetite again, and easily joined the conversation like my old self. Of course we had to recount my near miss with the boom, and my silly chlorine poisoning, from many different angles and with many jokes at my expense. That was how the day rolled on. By the time we docked at the marina, in the late afternoon, Ash's new nickname was Nursey-poo, and mine was Sicko.

The islands are far enough to the north that even in the last breath of Indian summer, evening light lingers. Jerry suggested a leisurely walk through the town to get our land legs again. We spread out, comfortably aimless, only intending to meet up at a particular restaurant for dinner. Nature did its work and we went off in couples: Mark and Scottie, Mike and Jerry, me and Ash. Me and Ash?

Compact as he was, he stood a half a head taller than me. Rosy as his lips were, there was a solidity to him that had nothing to do with his astronaut's jaw. Smell of cucumber, sting of strawberry, firecracker cackle. No shrinking back at the tale of my Touch, the jade, the gallery, the Chinese lifetimes. He had listened, allowed it to be real, and it was enough. And then we had unearthed the Real Dave. And laughed about it. That alone was ground to stand on, and look at each other. "Where to?" Ash said.

"I always get lost in this place," I admitted. "Something about island time, it all gets fuzzy to me."

He nodded, as if such a thing were not at all unexpected. "Okay. Let's go." And we ambled off.

Did he still feel protective of me? Still being Nursey-poo? I didn't want to ask that question. If *enough* would string us together for an afternoon, an evening, a weekend, I was glad for it. I needed nothing more than to walk beside him on those village streets, chatting about what we saw in the store windows, as the sun slipped underneath the trees and the waters, and the hot blue sky melted to a gold-skinned violet. I wanted him no further, and no nearer. Not yet.

Things were in motion.

I was part of a plot. One that began in the Han Dynasty Imperial Court. The plot was not necessarily about me— whoever I was then—or any one particular player in that mess of love and politics. It was more like a roiling force beneath the Earth's surface, that sought cracks in the tectonic plates, sought a way *out*. It was a force as uncaring as the cargo freighter passing miles from us on the sound, or that freighter's wake playing outward, outward, outward until it dispersed into the quadrillion little motions of the sea.

Now that I was awake to my own memories—however patchy—of that Imperial Palace, I could feel my life rising and turning on the plot's determined wake. Ash stood outside of it—like an island visible beyond the turbulence.

Mulling this notion while window-shopping, I could almost see my temple's head lama adjust his glasses and lace his fingers together. "Karma," he would say in his fractured English, "like riding a big motorcycle. Needs balance. Find *natural* balance. Then riding is easy." Yes, the Middle Way, not grasping and not loose. The gateway to experiencing Emptiness. Did that little Chinese girl hiding on the stairway hear the man in yellow robes speak of all this?

Suddenly I saw something through a store window that made me stop short. I grabbed Ash's arm and pulled him into the store.

It was a spiritual gift shop and bookstore, the kind that Dave archly called "Krystal Kove" before he discovered his inner bodhisattva. I led Ash right past all the wind chimes and silky clothes to the music racks, and found what I'd seen through the window.

Valerie L, walking on water and playing her viola. A somewhat faded copy of the concert poster still hung on the back wall, visible from the street. Well, it *was* a great photo. Her CD in the rack was their last.

"That's her," I told Ash, handing him the CD. "That's the woman with the jades. She was the concubine."

"Whoa," he said, turning it over in his hands. "You've heard it?"

"Sort of. It was pretty late and I fell asleep."

"Must be good. Any more of her?"

"Not here, they're out. But I've got a CD of her with this chamber ensemble, in my bag. We can listen to it later if you want."

"Cool. I think I'll get this. Someday I'll ask her what it was like being an Imperial sex toy."

"Eeeww. You're worse than Dave."

"You can see why I was his last in this lifetime."

I swatted him on the arm and he cackled. Oh, I did feel human again. Then, "Wow!" he exclaimed. "Look at that!" And he made a beeline for the jewelry counter.

The salesgirl brought out for him a large jade pendant, about four inches long. It was a translucent pink jadeite, with white clouds drifting in the stone. "Look at that, look at that," he said over and over, holding it so closely that I couldn't see much of anything. Finally I put out my hand and he gave it to me.

The jade was carved in a looping half-twist, giving it one continuous surface. But the artisan had contrived to make hundreds of tiny hollows in the stone, so that the loop seemed to be a feathering curl of pink tendrils. It could have become a snake or dragon biting its tail, but there was no face. It was an abstract form that suggested a plantlike sea creature or loosely woven rope. "What do you think?" Ash asked.

My inward voice repeated, faintly, the artist murmuring *ooh, baby, so good, baby*. "Good quality jadeite," I said. "Lovely." I laid it back on the counter.

Ash picked it up again. "Come on, this is a contemporary master jeweler working in Maori style," he said. "Don't you ever look at other kinds of jade? Or just the antique stuff with the sex and violence?"

I really didn't want to give a lecture, or tattle on the artist. The afternoon had been so golden. But Ash was staring at me with a kind of challenge. *Go ahead, disappoint me*, his small mammal squeaked from inside his hiding place.

"I do have an opinion about this piece, but what's the point? You think it's beautiful, so the artist has done his job. It's beautiful. Now we should go, we have to meet the guys in fifteen minutes."

Ash stayed put, holding the jade. "No, dammit, you've got me interested," he said, with a tone that was half-annoyed, half-humorous. "I'll bite. What's your opinion? What do you see here?"

I wanted to be kind to the artist, for Ash's sake. Odd, to realize that so clearly. I took the jade from him again and held it up to the store's lights. "Do you know how jade is carved?" I asked.

"Started with a stick and sand, then went to a foot-driven mechanism turning a bamboo wheel and string, or a bamboo drill-point, that ground abrasive sand into the stone," Ash replied with a hint of pride. "'The hardest wood met the hardest stone in a kiss of sand.' My jewelry teacher loved that line. But it was a fecking slow process, a lot of it still needed to be done by hand. So, now there are electric drills, and top of the line are sonic tools that cut with sound waves. Like butter, almost. Probably what this guy used to make this."

"Probably." My agreement came with an ache in my soul. Those sonic cutting tools, handled by craftsmen as skilled as the faux-Maori, soon would be pirouetting over inferior jade to recreate the exquisitely twining dragons on the Han Prince's two-thousand-year-old scabbard slide. Careful dye jobs and some fake age patina would make reproductions that didn't deserve to be called *yü*.

"So, yes, this design is dazzling," I went on. "It's abstract, it's technically difficult, brilliantly engineered. But all of that bypasses the unique qualities of the stone. Like the artist was in a hurry to be a genius. I wish he'd had more patience with the stone, really partnered with it instead of just pushing his idea into it. He might have found something extraordinary." I glanced at the price tag and shrugged at the three-figure cost. I laid the pendant back on the counter and waited. Possibly I had just snapped the threads that had been spinning between me and Ash all day. But possibly not. I couldn't tell. Ash had half-buried his face in his hand, thinking.

"It's still beautiful," he said at last, "but you do have a point." He set the pendant back down on the counter and we headed for the cashier. He was silent, still thinking, while he paid for Valerie L's CD. When he was done and stepped away, I leaned over to the salesgirl and murmured something. Her eyes widened and she nodded vigorously. Quickly, she laid two of the store's business cards on the counter. I wrote my name and number on one for her, and pocketed the other with a smile. She smiled back. I rejoined Ash, and we emerged onto the street.

"You do that again, I'll have to report you," Ash chided. "Giving your number to a pretty girl. *Tsk!*"

"*Tsk* yourself. I'm a salesman, and I think her establishment has a demand for which I can find supply."

"I can report you for talking shop, too. We're on vacation, remember?"

Vacation or not, we were ambling at a more-than-leisurely pace. I looked at my watch. "We're going to be late," I prodded him. He grinned, stopped and stretched his arms wide, rotating his shoulders. "What are *you* in a hurry to be, Grasshopper?" he asked. Mischief in his eye.

I grinned back. "Not a thing," I said. Right then, I could have pretended we were in Greece, or Istanbul, or Mumbai, and wound my arm through his, to walk the evening streets that were dimming to twilight. The contact would have told me things about him, how he liked to be caressed, what scared him, what made him laugh. I kept my hands at my sides. Why hurry?

"Wouldn't you know it," Mark snapped as we got to the table at last. "Here we finally meet to discuss the homosexual agenda for world domination, and you guys miss the appetizers!"

The idyllic vibe ended when we returned to the cabin, where Eric and Stuart had endured a little too much proximity. Their weekend thing was definitely in decline. They bickered and bitched at each other; they were mad because no one had called them to invite them to the restaurant. The tale of my chlorine poisoning and near-miss with the boom (and the man-salad Scottie glimpsed) lightened the atmosphere considerably, but the two weekend lovebirds quickly split off with their closest friends in the group—which meant Stuart latched onto Ash and monopolized him for the rest of the evening. And Sunday breakfast. And the ferry ride back to the mainland. I never got to play Valerie L's chamber ensemble CD for him.

About twenty minutes before our approach to the mainland dock, I announced rather loudly to the group (again gathered in a big vinyl booth around a scarred Formica table) that I was going to take a walk on the outside deck. I figured, if Ash could disengage from Stuart, he would find me. If he didn't, well, I had a lot to think about. Specifically, how to deal with Albert Jarro tomorrow, and the next day, and the next. It was the same question I had tortured myself with on Friday night, before getting into the hot tub. But something had changed in the meantime. The world was still that loose, porous place where anything could happen. This time, though, there were paths leading outward, paths that I could feel under my metaphorical feet when I tested the idea of *this* choice, *that* choice. No red-hot maze, no meltdown ahead. Only life, continuing.

Ash came up on my blind side. "Hey," he said, making me jump.

"Hey back. Your ears look pretty bent."

"Bent, stretched, tied in knots. I now know all about Eric, to the subatomic level. Whatever you do when you step off this ferry, dude, don't go near Eric. At least, don't tell *me* about it. Please." He shivered in the wind and looked up at the encroaching cloud cover. "I hope that's not an omen."

"Doesn't have to be. Could just be clouds."

"I'll go for that." The ferry's PA horn crackled and bleated the call for us to return to our cars, we would be docking in ten minutes. Ash groaned. "Damn. I thought I had more time. Now I'm going to have to spend the next hundred miles giving my analysis of everything I've learned about Eric. How Stuart can process and drive at the same time is beyond me."

"Ride back with me," I said suddenly. Ash looked shocked. "Seriously. Get your bag out of Stuart's car and ride back with me."

Ash thought for a few beats. Something was in the way. "Wow," he said finally, "thank you. I wish I could. I'd *rather.* But … it's this fecking work relationship. My boss has to extend our contract with Stuart's business, and he's been giving us a discount, which we need, and …." Ash looked so deeply embarrassed, I would have jumped over the rail with him right there, into the churning water under the ferry. I would have died with the word "fecking" on my lips.

"Well then, would you like to have dinner sometime?" I asked. Making *this* choice, rather than *that.* "I'll cook," I added.

Ash stared at me, hugging himself against the wind. That grin started up one side of his face. Not at the edge of wild laughter this time. Softer. "Sure," he said. The PA horn bleated that the ferry would dock in five minutes, drivers must now return to their cars. I dug a grocery receipt and a pen from my pockets, and handed them to Ash.

"Write your phone number there," I said. "I'll call. We'll set up a time." He did, grinning all the while. Yet I did not have that triumphant feeling I got after making a sale. It felt more like *I* was the one who had just accepted a deal.

Ash gave me a swift hug, and then pushed me away. "Get to your car!" he laughed. "Go on, git!" We ran, down our different staircases, for our cars.

I cranked the radio loud on the drive home and sang along with every stupid song, even the commercials. The highway was full of wonders and opportunities, not traffic. The soaring sense of possibility lasted through the evening, into the night, and into my dreams, which I immediately forgot upon awakening, but retained the echoes of joyously courageous scenes enacted by me and Ash.

I was so energized, I arrived at the gallery well before 8 am. I ran through my morning routine, checking the vitals of the security, temperature and ventilation systems, humming a silly hello song to all the artworks and antiquities. Albert wasn't due back before eight-thirty, so I had plenty of time to myself. Or so I thought. At five minutes to eight the quiet shattered when a furious pounding exploded against the back door.

I must have teleported to the security camera monitor. Heart racing and hands shaking, I clicked through to the view of the back door.

It was Del.

I may have looked like a spooked rabbit when I opened the door, but Del looked worse. His breathing was ragged and his composure was gone. Despite the crisp black trousers and impeccable blue shirt under his brown leather flight jacket, I wondered if he had slept at all in the past two days. He stepped into the gallery's office without my invitation, past me, without seeing me.

"Del?"

He turned around sharply. "I changed my mind, man," he said, with a rasping dry throat. "I want it back. Can you help me? I've got to get it back."

The Dragon Throne

Whosoever knows how to lead well
is not warlike.
Whosoever knows how to fight well
is not angry.
Whosoever knows how to conquer enemies
does not fight them.
Whosoever knows how to use men well
keeps himself below.
This is the Life that does not quarrel;
this is the power of using men;
this is the pole that reaches up to Heaven.

—Lao Tzu,
Tao Te Ching

German tr. Richard Wilhelm,
English tr. H. G. Ostwald

12.
DUEL

For a nanosecond I thought Del had gone mad. *Get it back?*

"I'll do everything I can," I heard myself say. Maybe I was the one who had gone mad. Or was it shame for what I had called him on the back of the ferry? I steered him into a chair in the middle room and ran back into the office. I dialed the appraiser with the glossy card.

He answered. His voice had an odd little accent darkened by years of cigarettes. I told him I was calling on behalf of Albert Jarro's new client. *"Hien?"* he growled, skeptical.

"A jade was delivered to you on Friday, a scabbard slide— "

"No! Not to us!" he snapped, too quickly.

"The client wants it back as soon as possible"—

"We have no jade!" Another blink and he would hang up, and not answer his phone again. I plunged ahead before he reached the "d" in *jade*.

"The last two jobs you did for our clients were so successful and so precise, that of course we wanted you to do this job, too, *especially* this one. But the owner, all he wants is the best price for a basic job. Somebody named Hudson in Michigan is asking a lower fee, so he wants to go there with it, and I've never *heard* of this guy! I'm pleading with this client! He's crazy, I tell him, you're the best, Albert knows you, has *used* you" -I hoped that word's other meaning would reach him—"but now he's going on about lawyers and the *police*, can you imagine?" I allowed myself a semi-hysterical laugh, choked off quickly.

Perhaps I *had* learned something from Albert Jarro about subterfuge. Dealers all play Blame the Client when something goes wrong. But a persistent, angry client could take Albert to court and blow the gallery right out of the water if he didn't get his item back. Publicity would attract the attention of the Chinese government to an undocumented Han jade. In that scenario, this guy's ass was in as much trouble as mine, and he'd better be motivated to pull the scabbard slide back from wherever he had sent it. I prayed that my babble and my choked-off laugh would hint-hint-hint at something more: that I had uncovered a sting operation, and the jade had been the bait.

Whatever he believed about my story, it worked. "I don't know how you fucked this up, you little" —and he called me a name in a language I didn't recognize—"but I don't talk to you. I deal with Jarro, only Jarro. You I never see." And he hung up.

I set my phone down quietly. This was a good beginning. The guy was off balance, and definitely had received the jade. Probably he had not *seen* it; likely he simply had taken the package from Albert and sent it off to the duplicating house— connected through yet another broker, somewhere overseas, someone known only by phone, e-mail, fax, and direct bank deposit.

Embarrassingly, the adrenaline of it all made me need the toilet. Shut in the small closet, holding my Precious, I could close my eyes and relax. Sort of. I had set things in motion. Now everything depended on Albert—and whether Del believed in him, or me.

That pee break was the only reprieve. When I opened the washroom door, Del was in the office, talking to Albert—just back from Toronto.

"The man is a professional, and very much in demand," Albert was saying. His voice was smooth as a lullaby, but his fingertips touching, making a cathedral arch at his heart, told me he was near panic. "For me to barge in on his work and demand the piece back would be, well, the gravest insult. I want to protect my relationship with him, you understand."

"There's no man on Earth won't stop work when asked," Del retorted. His imperial poise was back, enflamed by a smoldering rage. "You gave your word that my jade was safe. You looked me in the eye and said I would get it back. I want to see that happen. Today."

Albert sighed, looked away and cleared his throat. Patient in the face of impossible crudeness. Del's eyes narrowed.

"The request is already in, Albert," I interjected, stepping fully into the room. They both swung around and stared at me—neither one exactly pleased. Oh, well. "I just talked with him a few minutes ago," I continued. "He does want to speak with you. But since our client has not committed any part of the fee yet, there should be no contractual problem."

Del shifted with satisfaction and threw an expectant glance at Albert ... whose aura turned to ice. "I'll call him right now,"

Albert said softly, casually, and stepped to his desk. I caught Del's eye, and nodded at the door. Del took the cue and we exited all the way to the front showroom. I let out a huge sigh.

"Am I looking at a dead man?" Del asked, with a glint of mischief.

"Very dead. Feels good," I replied.

Del glanced back at the door. "Okay. Before he gets off the phone, tell me as much as you can what I almost stepped in," he said.

Oh, sure. Ask me to explain in twenty-five easy words how a spider spins its web. But all Del needed was a nudge in the right direction. I glanced up at a security camera. Del's eye followed mine. He raised an eyebrow, understanding. I stepped close to him. "Vern paid a lot of money for that sword," I said softly, "*because he thought it was the real thing*—not a copy. Not a fake." Del straightened and studied me. Then he swung his gaze around the room, covering the ceramics, sculptures and scrolls with a cold assessment.

"Nothing in this room is fake," I said quickly. "Nothing that *leaves* this room is fake. And we certainly don't *sell* fakes. Not in this room." All of this was true. I spread my hands in a show of supplication. "You have my hand on that," I added. I was standing beside a stone Buddha head displayed on a Qing Dynasty shrine table. I turned and cupped my hands around its face, as if examining it, or asking it to vet my sincerity ... but really throwing Del a strategic suggestion.

Albert swept back the curtain and stepped in from the middle room. He brushed past me as though I were a cobweb. "We're not entirely screwed," he announced to Del. "The jade can't be returned today, but will be ready for pickup tomorrow evening. I hope that will be satisfactory, because it's the best we can do for you."

"It will be satisfactory when I have the jade back in my hands," Del replied. "But I'm not going to wait for it here. I'm going to meet you at the appraiser's office tomorrow, and the man himself will hand it to me. If he doesn't have it, the police *will* be involved."

Oops. I hadn't meant to be psychic. Really, I hadn't. Back-stabbed or not, I could not allow Del to destroy the gallery. I opened my mouth, but Albert spoke what we were both thinking. "Don't waste your time with them!" he said, with a shrill edge and a fixed smile. "This is beyond their understanding, transactions like this are much too complicated for the law enforcement mind. It's all personal, you see, art deals are subjective and passionate, just look at your own passion here! A perfect example! The law wants nothing to do with that. You're much better off letting us get your jade back ourselves. I can assure you, the police have no interest in the business of antiquities. It's just not worth their time."

Del was as cold as black marble. I have never seen a person so angry, or so quiet. It was like Death waiting at the threshold. One breath, two, as he stared unblinking at Albert.

"Mr. Jarro," he said finally, in a tightly controlled voice, "I can assure you, in this case the police understand art dealing perfectly. And it *is* worth their time."

He pulled the left lapel of his leather flight jacket aside … and revealed the city Police Department badge pinned to his crisp blue uniform shirt.

Albert seemed to have lost his voice. His mouth opened and closed, his hands fluttered, he shrugged and turned away. "What time tomorrow do I meet you, Mr. Jarro?" Del asked, in a steely tone that the Archangel Michael himself would have answered in a hurry. Albert gestured lightly and said nothing. He headed for the middle room.

"Six o'clock should be about right, shouldn't it, Albert?" I called to him. Albert shook his head and held up his index finger, before disappearing through the curtain. "Seven," I said to Del, "but be there at six anyway."

"You'll be there?" Del asked. I nodded. "Dead man will be walking," I said.

"Good," Del replied, "I'll need you, dead or alive. Peace." He offered his hand. I shook it. This time my hand was as strong as his. The Prince needed me. I unlocked the front door and let him out.

I watched him walk away, and then locked the door again. I removed the set of gallery keys from my key ring. Dead man had just a little farther to walk, just a little. First, through the middle room. My room. My deep aubergine womb, where clients could dream of faraway luxuries coming into their hands. I retrieved my case of lenses and loupes from their drawer under the counter. I stepped over the next threshold into the back office and let the curtain drop softly behind me. I stopped, surprised.

The great iron vault door stood open. Wide open. Wider than it had ever been allowed to stand open before. Albert was not at his desk. I averted my eyes from that side of the room, and went to my desk. I pulled a flattened packing box from behind the file cabinet, opened it out and carefully lowered my case of loupes and lenses into it. After it came my framed appraiser's certificate. Other little photographs. Reference books. A *millefiori* glass paperweight, made in 19th-century Hong Kong for English tourists in Italy. Albert's phone rang. And rang again. I looked up; Albert hadn't appeared from anywhere. The phone still rang. I went back to packing the box. After six rings the phone bumped to voice mail and went silent.

I opened my file drawer and pulled out what was pertinent to my work and not the gallery's. It was a very slim stack of folders. Four years, so much learned and so much spoken, and all I had on paper was correspondence about my certificate studies. Copies of the appraisals I had done. There was my original contract with Albert. I would need that. My throat tightened. What had I really accomplished here? Objects had moved through my hands, into and out of the showroom. I had been a charming image, a voice, an impression. A persuasion, a dream. Nothing more than that? Nothing more? Outrage built in my stomach, emotion piling up. I shoved the file folders into the box and they bent.

"What's most telling," Albert's voice suddenly threaded out from inside the vault, in a soft, casual tone, as if we had been in a friendly conversation all along, "is that I always believed you. It was never a conscious choice. I simply, naturally believed you."

I swallowed, and slowly straightened. Oh, how I did not want to do this. I did not want to turn, and walk to the vault's open door. I did not want to. But of course I must. *Breathe.* My left hand's fingertips stroked the mala's tassel. One foot in front of the other. Until I stood in front of the open door.

The vault was a room about ten feet by twelve feet, with moon-globe lamps hanging from the ceiling. The walls were lined with deep steel shelving units. The shelves were packed with crates and boxes of all sizes and shapes. Cubes, flats, rectangles, tubes. Just looking at them, my inward voice became a softly rumbling choir that blended with my vision, trembling the lamplight around the boxes. *We are here, the ultimate, the true history, the greatness,* the choir whispered.

There was just enough room for a wide center aisle. Albert sat in the aisle on a little folding chair, facing the door, his head turned aside to direct his gaze somewhere over my right shoulder. His legs were crossed at the ankle and his fingers knitted together, resting on his paunch. The picture of a prosperous man peacefully lost in thought. He was silent, patient, waiting for me to take the picture in.

"Tell me what you believed," I said.

"First, you tell me how much the police paid you for this."

"That's not what's happening, Albert."

"Oh, please." He turned his head to look directly at me, provoked. "A woman walks in here with Han jades that would fetch more than a hundred thousand at auction. No history to them, no provenance, nothing. I have the sense to walk away, but you stay. You insist that I look at them and see that they're real. I should never have looked at them. But it was you, you see." He shifted, unlocking his ankles and fingers, leaning forward in the chair with his hands on his knees. "It was you I believed in. You have been so committed to … to the way of things in this business. You are so deft with people, especially the unsophisticated. This man, then, arrives with the scabbard jade. He agrees to everything. Your work, I assumed. You have been brilliant, I thought, you have made everything so easy." He paused, then went on in an even softer voice: "Now tell me how much they paid you. And, was it me they wanted, or were you all using me to get to my associate?"

"I am being paid nothing, Albert," I said. "It's not about you or your associate. It's the jade. That man is the rightful owner and I want him to get his jade back."

"Pah!" Albert exploded in an ugly laugh. "That jade was *stolen* from its rightful owner, the man it was buried with! Are you and this policeman going to re-bury it?" I said nothing. Albert looked disgusted. "No, he's going to pop it on top of a new scabbard, tuck in a cheap sword, and hang it on his wall," he sneered. "No doubt in some moldy studio apartment. Is that really what you want to see happen to that masterpiece? My God, you might as well re-bury it."

I bit back the words I wanted to spit at him. *And you would re-bury it in some collector's secret vault!* I held my hand still, the hand that wanted to grab the vault door and fling it shut on him and all his treasures. I swallowed again, and breathed. "Albert, there have been aspects of … of the way of things that have bothered me for a long while," I said. "But I've hung in there and kept quiet."

"And profited handsomely," Albert added bitterly.

"I told you, I am not being paid to betray you or anyone you know. I only want to get the man his jade back."

"He would have had it!"

"*His* jade, Albert. The true one."

"He would have had a unique work of art no different from what he put in my hands. No less exquisite, no less beautiful. Not one atom less of a masterpiece."

That was the truth. What could I say to outweigh it?

"He asked me to help him get it back."

Albert stared at me. Disbelief levitated his eyebrows. He understood something. He *thought* he understood, believed he understood, although he was wrong. The assumption blew another laugh out of his face, less ugly this time, but wet with rage. "And for *that* you would destroy me?!"

There was no point trying to counter his assumption. It didn't matter, anyway. "Your appraiser, or whatever he is, thinks he's dodged a bullet, so if Del gets his jade back your association doesn't change," I said. "When Del gets his jade, he will do nothing more about this. It's not a sting. That I can promise you."

Albert studied me, with a look that could carve meat, a look that I had not seen often. I kept breathing. "And what more will *you* do about it, Ross? I think that is the important question," Albert purred.

I took the gallery keys from my pocket and laid them on Albert's desk.

"I need to think. I've had a lot of illusions die in a very short time."

Albert sat back in the little chair with a sigh and a dismissive wave. "All right, go, then. Think. Acquaint yourself with realities. What I do is nothing, you'll come to see that soon enough."

"Nothing? Albert --!" I couldn't help thinking of poor Hokusai, hoping to pay his landlord. "You find treasures, this so-called appraiser arranges for someone to make a copy, the copy comes back to the owner, the original goes out to bring in big money, your cut comes home. The proper owner never knows the difference." Just talking about it made my stomach churn. "Elegant, yes, and of course the original artists are all dead, so they don't care. But why do you of all people need that kind of operation? Why take the risk?"

"Oh, for God's sake, don't be so naïve."

"Money? Is that all?"

"Oh, you really have failed the test. Fail, fail, fail. *Money.* What does money mean to anyone, when holding a beautiful piece of history in one's hands and passing it on to the kids gives such meaning to stunted lives? It's not money—it's *hunger.* You've seen it. One copy alone won't do for hunger like that, so our trade should not be stingy with what comes to us. The rewards are so great."

One copy alone won't do …. What he was describing made me shake. Outrage, or nausea, or both, I didn't know. Yes, there are ordinary people everywhere with a bit of money, who yearn to own a splinter of history, a fragment of a distant culture. Even if that object is secretly a fake, and secretly there are dozens, hundreds, thousands of masterful copies treasured with as much tenderness.

"…with money," Albert was saying. "What else feeds the beauty, Ross? What keeps it flowing?" His eyes flashed like brilliant glass; he looked drunk. "Artists need it, collectors have it—and my God, once you see how much money is actually out there, and all the half-wits who are willing to throw it at you --"

"This isn't what I'm here for, Albert. This isn't why I wanted to work for you." My throat actually filled with tears.

"Fool." Albert's eyes were slits in their plump pouches, and his smile was just a show of teeth. "You unreachable fool. I thought I was polishing a great diamond from rough stone, bringing you in, so close. But all I find now is a fool."

"Think whatever you want," I said. "I'm sure you were in my position at one time."

"Of course, of course I was!" Albert said impatiently. "But I saw things clearly. What *is.*" He stood up. Emotion made his wisps of hair stand up, too. "I'm trying to tell you the truth about that jade. And about your policeman. Listen, fool. You think you've achieved something by ... by ... *helping him*. But that jade is *beauty*. And beauty doesn't care," he went on, swaying slightly, still glassy-eyed, "about anything. It is complete, and needs no one. Your policeman may want his jade, but the jade does not want *him*. It has no need for him. The *greatness* in that jade—God, how I wish you had never made me look at it! Who's going to touch that greatness? No one! It was not meant to be touched, or possessed. It simply *is*. And tribute must be paid." Passion blazed through him and made the vault's air throb. It was a moment that artists have tried to carve into stone for millennia.

"Wherever that jade was sent," I said softly, finally, "surely they've photographed it enough by now to make one good copy. Just one, for you to keep."

"*NO!*" Albert howled. He fell back into his chair and broke into sobs. "I couldn't *keep* it. I couldn't *sell* it. I couldn't *show* it. Oh God, you should not have made me *look* at it!"

I had never seen Albert cry before. I had seen my father cry, and my Filipino grandfather and three Filipino uncles, at funerals or when drunk and remembering the past. Always it seemed to be a wedge of history rushing out from the man, a past too large and confusing to be borne by anything but tears.

"I'll give you my letter of resignation tomorrow evening, Albert," I said quietly. "Thank you for all you've done for me." *I refuse to stay in your palace, I refuse to be your concubine,* was right there on my tongue, ready to be said. Maybe I missed a chance, not saying it. But I kept my mouth shut.

A faint desire for the gemology microscope, sitting hooded in the corner, tweaked at my gut. But no, Albert and the gallery were its owners, even though I had been the only person to use it. So I picked up the last thing on my desk that had any meaning for me—my Rolodex. I put it in the box, hefted the load, and walked out the back door. No one's concubine. Not anymore.

The ten-minute walk home was hard, being mostly uphill and with a heavy box to haul. I got over the threshold thinking only of a hot shower pounding my shoulders. Once that need was met and I was wrapped in my robe with a mug of tea in hand, I sat down and started to be afraid of the future. And then exhilarated. And then afraid. And then tired. In bed, at least, I could put the pillow over my head and wail into the mattress. But it was still well before noon, so I put on my sweats and went to the gym. By the end of my workout and my third shower that day, I saw three steps to take.

Number one was to call Mark and set dates to see the houses he needed staged. I made the call in the car. Number two was a visit to a copy shop, to make up a new business card for myself. Number three, which I plunged into as soon as I got home, was to gather all my financial information and begin the process of getting a small business license. As an afterthought, I went through my wardrobe of neckties and dress shirts, and put most of them in a bag to be given away. There was something very satisfying about that.

In the midst of that hectic afternoon, I rediscovered the grocery receipt with Ash's phone number on it. His voicemail greeting was crisp and minimal, but just the sound of his voice was like a cheerleader's kick. I suggested we think about some night next week for dinner, and left my phone number, e-mail and cell. I hung up hoping I hadn't overdone it.

I spent the next day looking at houses with Mark and planning their showings. "New problems are more fun than old ones," my mother liked to say, and I had to agree with her there. The sheer novelty of the day rejuvenated my attitude, in fact seemed to elevate me to a different planet. I found myself full of inspiration about how to re-jigger my Rolodex of gallery contacts into resources for this niche of interior decorating.

"Well, aren't you a new man!" Scottie exclaimed as Mark and I returned to their office to discuss the finer points of doing business together. "Amazing, isn't it?" I agreed. "It must be the tee-shirt. Something about wearing a nice tee-shirt with a blazer helps a guy move on with his life so much faster."

Moving on. Letting go. Reincarnating. It felt so easy, so light, up to a point. The fun of it was in getting to that point. As the time moved closer to six o'clock, I grew jumpy, irritable, as if I'd had too much coffee. I checked my phone messages; Ash had not returned my call. I lunged at any excuse to dither away the minutes: balancing my checkbook, re-organizing my wallet. Both Habit and Reality were mute. My feet did not want to get into the car. My hands did not want to turn the steering wheel. I wasn't late, but as I walked up to Del where he waited on the sidewalk outside the mystery appraiser's office building at six o'clock precisely, my stomach seemed to be trying to escape through my ribs. Stopped, perhaps, by the resignation letter addressed to Albert that rode in my jacket's inner pocket.

The building was one of those low-rise complexes where small businesses could tack up a sign and put an office in front of their warehouse. Black smudges of mildew crept out from the seams of the stucco-board exterior panels.

Del had tossed the leather jacket on over his uniform again. I put a smile on my face, and handed him my new business card. "'Connoisseur At Large,'" he read from it, and looked at me curiously. "Yeah, that would be you." He pocketed the card and jutted his chin at the office door. "Shall we do this?"

"I'm ready," I said, although I didn't feel ready. Del opened the door and let me go in first. Chivalry? Or making me the point man who would take the first bullet? Perhaps he wanted whoever met us in there to think I was the big shot and he was the bodyguard. There was nobody at the cheap-veneer reception desk in any case. There was a buzzer, however, with a handwritten sign in block letters, RING FOR SERVICE. I rang.

After a minute's wait, I rang a second time. Another minute, and the door behind the reception desk clicked several times, unlocking. A weathered, bespectacled little man, brown as a nicotine stain, with a cigarette dangling from his lip, slipped into the reception office. Even before he growled *"Hien?"* in that tobacco-dark voice, I knew it was the mystery appraiser himself.

"This is about the jade from the Albert Jarro Gallery," I said, careful not to identify myself as Albert's assistant, which of course I wasn't anymore. If the appraiser recognized my voice from the phone call, so be it. He squinted at me, then Del. "You're fucking early," he said.

"Mr. Jarro didn't actually say what time we should meet him here," Del replied, "so we thought six o'clock would be good." Quite true, good one, Del. The appraiser turned his squint back and forth between us, trying to make up his mind about something. I turned to Del with a look that I hoped meant, *Now.* Del raised his hands to his hips and gently rotated his shoulders back and his chest out—a move that could be a simple man's stretch for comfort, but it had the effect of opening his jacket just enough to let the police badge peek through.

"I'm the jade's owner," he said calmly. The appraiser sucked on his cigarette, flipping the end up and down. "Where's Jarro?" he asked, expelling a cloud of smoke around the words.

I wanted to say, "He'll get here when he gets here," in a voice as calm as Del's, but as I took breath to do so the cigarette smoke hit my lungs. I coughed, coughed and could not stop. The appraiser looked at me suspiciously. "He's my private appraiser," Del said quickly. He took my card out of his pocket and held it out to the nicotine man. "Here's his card." The appraiser took it and read it, and squinted viciously at me. "Fucking bullshit," he muttered, and crushed the card in his hand.

"We'll take the jade, if it's ready," Del said, still calm. I nodded agreement, clearing my throat and gulping air. "Motherfucking bullshit," the appraiser said to both of us, and slipped back behind the door. It clicked with several locks as it closed.

I opened the outer door and stepped outside. "Don't disappear, it's your turn in a minute," Del called to me. I nodded and waved assent. I just wanted fresh air.

I couldn't move more than a step from the door. The world was porous again, its solid nature knocked loose, perhaps, by the coughing. An army of Chinese soldiers in ancient armor stood in front of me. As one—and on whose signal?—they all dropped to one knee on the patched and potholed parking lot. Magnificent expectation filled the evening. The army chanted in unison, *Ba na pa tu dai chu lai! Sha le ta de tou wei wu ya! Bring forth the bloody traitor! His head will feed the ravens!* Or was that the roaring of trucks on the nearby highway?

I reached behind me for the door handle and backed into the office. As I turned around, the inner door clicked and the nicotine man slipped in, holding a much-stamped box in one hand. He stretched over the reception desk and shoved it at Del. Del received it. The nicotine man muttered at us in his native tongue, whatever it was. With a last evil look and no receipt for Del to sign, he slipped out the door again.

Del quickly slit the box open with his pocketknife. Box,

padded envelope, another box, more bubble wrap. Finally he held the jade in his hands. There they were, two dragons of pale celery-colored jade, chasing each other, twining tails and meeting each other tooth to tail. Del held it up to the evening sunlight coming in the office windows. He turned it over, and over, and over again, peering into every crevice and cut. His face was full of anguished doubt.

At last he thrust it at me. "Here, you hold it," he said. "Tell me if it's real."

"Just a minute," I said. A quick glance around the small office did not reveal what I needed, so I ventured behind the cheesy reception desk. I dragged a folding chair out to the front. I sat, settled myself securely, and held out my hand. Del placed the pale dragons in my palm.

13.
THE THIRD JADE'S STORY—PART I

Ach'a! She has given me a tremendous sword!

Even clothed in the polished, black wood scabbard, the exquisite object trembles with life.

The jades on the scabbard, the guard and pommel are the most delicate, perfect green—the green of the lotus between blossom and vine, where the white flower fades into the stem, and one becomes the other.

At the scabbard's tip, hanging close to the ground, a single dragon coils, calling up protection from the earth. Two dragons on the slide welcome the blade into its home. On the hilt of the sword itself, the scabbard-dweller's character and purpose are announced: the guard, carved from the same breathless, clear green jade, fashions the spreading branches of a peach tree. The spaces between the leaves and the long-life fruit, a filigree as true as nature, allows this infinitely hard stone to shield my hand while being light to hold. The pommel, capping the hilt, is a phoenix with outstretched wings—the celestial bird of rebirth. So bejeweled, this sword has no fear of any enemy, nor of death itself.

The cords wrapping the hilt warm to my grip instantly. It is as vital as touching the neck of a horse. No matter that it's lovely. A sword, like a horse, has a destiny and must be commanded.

The room is empty—good fortune!—and I take the first stance of combat. I hold the scabbard at my side, left hand embracing the tails of these twining dragons, right hand secure on the hilt. An inner emptiness is essential to the beginning of battle. I let my mind and limbs go quiet. And then, like lightning, without thought, I flash the steel from its hidden home, my body lunging forward.

There I stay, sword poised above my head. The steel's brilliant *sssssssssssssssssss* lingers in the air. It fades into the air of my room; into the wood, the embroidered hangings, the stone of the floor. My flesh prickles with it, my hair rises to attention. I have learned not to smile too easily, but this draws my pleasure directly to my face.

Ach'a! She has given me a tremendous sword!

It is like meeting a friend.

I welcome this friend by dancing the blade through the classic rites of combat: sweep-turn-lunge-draw-pause. The sword is so balanced and easy in my grip that it seems to leap for the ritual movements on its own and my body simply follows.

And as with true friends, the ritual forms are not enough; the sword and I begin to invent where to go and how to move. But this playfulness raises a rage in me—a battle with ghosts. A battle remembered. A battle that should not have happened.

We were surprised in our camp. What spies did this rebel leader employ? The birds themselves? My men were taking their morning meat. Their weapons were close by but the men stood and sat un-armored. The sudden rain of arrows and stones caused shocking harm. I was at the door of my tent and so was able to throw on my helmet and torso armor, even as arrows ripped through the roof and walls. I grabbed my sword from its sheath and ran back into the camp, wheeling the blade about me to deflect arrows, looking for my officers. Stones pinged and battered my helmet—

And there my strange vision stops, for I have slashed a bed-curtain clean through with my birthday gift.

The scar beside my eye throbs. It is enough to remind me that I lived through that attack, and worse. I lived through betrayal, confusion, victory, and the return. If I hold memories that overtake me, it is not this sword's fault. I lay the scabbard aside and examine the bright blade.

Here, too, the workmanship is extraordinary. The steel is a silver river of rippling patterns. This master swordsmith's hammer and forge have drawn the spirit of water into steel!

This thought makes me smile again—freely, for how perfectly this gift mirrors she who gave it. Did she know, in her monastery, that the clear ringing tone steel makes as it moves through air is called its water song?

It is for her, as much as for the great beauty of this sword, that I re-sheath it so gently. It slips between the two twining dragons as sweetly as breath. A red silk tassel tied to the scabbard tripples over my hand like laughter. How I wish I could hear Water Song laugh. How I wish I could make her laugh.

The danger of our affection steals over me again. It is a mixture of melancholy, anger and rainshower longing that has weighed on me ever since I sent her the first silk letter, after the archery contest.

We had looked at each other. In a simple way, at first. She, a new, young face in the concubines' pavilion, had a reserve and sadness and simpler dress than the more familiar characters. She looked back at me, as if she had felt my gaze. The openness of her expression was utterly different from the schooled, calculating faces of the court. I stood as startled by this as by a flash of lightning.

I asked Cookpot her name. He hesitated, then told me. *Water Song.* "From the mountain temple," he added.

Thus the thunder rumbled after the lightning. *The concubine taken from the temple!* My shock must have gone to my face, for her expression changed, too. There could be no doubt that she knew my fame from that incident, with all the subtle jeers that follow losing face to one's own father. Yet she did not seem ashamed or frightened to be sharing her gaze with me. Instead of averting her eyes, she took up her folded fan and touched it to her shoulder, above the heart. Thus she honored me as an honest person.

Waves of heat rolled through me from foot to brow. I had the impulse to bow to her—honor her as a compassionate, selfless young sage. I did not bow. It would have been disastrous. The impulse to preserve dignity and face was stronger than whatever was burning in me. Fortunately, at that moment I was called away to the contest's next round. There I fell into my habit of stubborn concentration and effort when confronted with a blizzard of distraction. Each of my arrows found the target's center and I rose from a waking dream to discover I had won the contest and bested all comers—a fine recovery of face!

Still there was restlessness in my heart, a desire to honor the young concubine. I wanted to make peace with her. After all, had I joined my father at the temple festival, I might have persuaded him to leave her there in her religious life.

It didn't take much questioning to discover that Cookpot was already fast friends with the concubine! I pretended to be very upset by this news, for Cookpot had entered my service in our boyhood and by this time we were solid companions of the heart.

Cookpot bowed and prostrated and pleaded that his sentimental nature was to blame. The young girl was having a very hard time among the Emperor's women on account of her lack of family. To make matters worse, she retained her maidenhead and the Emperor seemed to approve of this!

Waves of heat rolled through me again. "And what do you two discuss?" I asked my *shih*, a bit brutally.

He prostrated again, several times and with flourishing sleeves. That was his way of telling me I was butting into a private situation like a stupid aristocrat, but he forgave me. "Dear Prince, you know my love of poetry is unstoppable, it is like a sweet tooth, perhaps the work of a mischievous pixie, who can say? All I know is, I must tune my poems like a fine instrument, and for that I need but one accomplished reader," he said. "This tiny concubine has become that reader. Her commentary tweaks and twists my poor words until the bamboo curls! If you have found pleasure in my songs at dinner these past months, you can thank her wit, and not my own poor scattered dreams."

I fumed, irked—and not for the first time—that a servant had more freedom than a Prince to talk to pretty women. On any day, it would be difficult for me to exchange greetings with my father's women, excepting my own mother. Now that I was famous for my filial virtue, it would be damned nigh impossible. Any word to the concubine would have to be so formal and public that it would strangle the message growing in my heart.

"You send her your poems?" I asked Cookpot.

He sat up from his prostration, no longer wanting to be funny. His face alone told me I needed to be careful, very careful. "I only want to thank her for holding no grudge," I told him. "One message. That's all. Some lines from Lao Tzu. Nothing personal."

A doubtful look flashed across his face, then dissolved in his customary good humor. He bowed, and it was done.

Yet, when I read the verses Cookpot had chosen and set down in his best hand on a length of silk, it still felt incomplete. How could I put my own heart into the message and have it not be personal? I decided to employ Lao Tzu himself as my servant. I picked up my brush and added my own variation on the Master's most famous verse. *If the Way could be foretold, it would not be the Way.* To that, I put my stamp. And as Cookpot rolled up the silk and tucked it into his belt, the fog of confusion and longing, scented with melancholy and an un-nameable anger, gathered upon me for the first time. This was a step onto a perilous road. Thus, I resolved in my heart that it would be the only step. I sent a silent prayer to all the gods and all the dead that only good would come of this.

Has it truly been just one full year since I sent that first silk? Not long after, it was my birthday, and today it is my birthday again. When I glimpse my own features in a polished mirror, I know I am no longer the youth of a year ago. Instead I see a warrior, leader of an army. A man, a killer of men.

How many times this year did I cherish the thought of Water Song like sunlight after a winter storm, and still I said to myself, *Only this step, no more—No further on this road?*

I should put the sword away. Close up the box and set it someplace secret.

Her silk note still lies in the box. I shuddered when I first read it, as if shaking out of a dream. I shudder to glimpse its characters again.

The sole of your foot, the entire earth.
The palm of your hand, life itself.
All others slip away,
Returned to the stars.

And her stamp, red as new blood.

I kneel by the box, helpless. The gift sword, the poem ... it is all as complete as a word. She not only understands me, she has chosen me.

Sunlight, after a storm ...

I must think. I must move. I must get out of this palace.

Returned, after a hard gallop through the summer dust, my attendants whipping their horses to a froth trying to keep up. I gave them no explanation. I am no longer a boy who needs to tell Ministers and tutors his whereabouts. I am the General of an army. Let them think I miss the battlefield.

Soon I must be ready for my birthday celebration dinner, but I am supposed to be having a bath and a rest after my ride. I remove the box from its hiding place and lift the sheathed sword again. It is the same: full of life, as complete a message as the great sages could deliver in one long swirl of ink. A dragon for the Earth, a phoenix for Heaven, the peach tree for a long and fertile life. In the center, two dragons coil around one another at the doorway to the sword's home. And the poem, with her stamp.

Waves of heat roll through me as if no time has passed at all since she looked at me and touched her fan to her shoulder.

I was a fool to think that I could step off this road at anytime. Perhaps after that first silk I could have done, but now it is far too late. Shallow child! To assume that hiding in a tree to watch her exercise would be a game, and mean nothing! Arrogant, stupid aristocrat, who devised a way to hide love letters, despite the peril to her—and to Cookpot! And now … now … she has taken a terrible step. She has followed me like a bodiless spirit on this road until, as if that spirit had entered a newborn colt, she has taken a step of her own. Her own choice, to give me this gift, before the official hour! Now she stands next to me on this road, solid and willful. Did I know she would? Did I actually want her to?

Certainly, I knew. I knew all about this danger, long before today. And perhaps, yes, perhaps I wanted her to make just such a choice.

Not many months ago, in a cold farmhouse far from the Imperial Palace, I lay in a dark room and considered the entire parade of my actions upon this Earth—from first memories to the sudden, reflexive blocking movement that hit the assassin's arm and turned his knife to the side of my face, rather than into the eye. I was spared, by what god or spirit I don't know. So I resolved to examine this precious garment called a man's life. I asked the dead to send a proper guide for these thought-pictures, but always it was Water Song who took my hand.

Always I withdrew from her thought-touch. I wanted to see her proper place in the parade, not walk with her in more forbidden ways, even if it was only in meditation with five thousand *li* between us.

But no matter where my memories coursed, when they returned to my bed in the farmhouse and I considered the days ahead, Water Song stood at the end of the road, at the Palace Gates.

I was afraid this thought-picture would become an angry spirit if I passed it by. I sought to recall the few notes I had written to her on silk from the field. They had gone out for direct delivery to Cookpot with my other personal correspondence, knotted shut in a code only Cookpot and I knew, to identify the recipient. They were short. In the first place, I had almost no privacy. Officers and attendants were always bursting in upon me. In the second, the experiences of war were parting me forever from the youth I had been, the young man at an archery contest who saw a concubine and thought it would be an adventure to hide in a tree and watch her exercise. Now I was leading an army into strange landscapes, bewildering dialects and sudden mortal dangers. Thoughts of Water Song -- dreams that she held my head in cool hands and offered me water and food—sweetened the tense nights. But what could I actually say to her in a letter?

Her own letters amounted to exactly two. She let the great sages speak for her heart, the same way I let the weather and landscape speak for mine. Still, seeing those precise ink-strokes skitter lightly down the silks, I felt a breeze ripple across my blood, and once again I crouched on a limb with red and gold leaves fluttering around me, watching the little concubine's dance flow like water. I would swear she knew I was in the tree, despite my careful concealment tricks, despite her blindfold. I would swear she knew it was me.

At dinner, three evenings after this adventure, I was certain she knew it was me.

My father's command had changed everything. Suddenly I was the General of an army that would search out and crush the rebellion in the North. It was a test, a challenge, an open door, and the most dangerous forces were the ranks of ministers watching my every move in those first hours. I turned my stubborn sense of focus onto the task: *Show nothing. Display nothing. Reveal nothing.* But I could not yet control the bonfire of heat that leapt through my limbs when Water Song's eyes passed over me. And I could not look away when she let her pale little hand trace her whole form, from hair to breast to lap. The movement was as slow and light as her movements in the garden; filled and guided by Life itself.

She knew, she knew it was me, hidden and watching her private hour.

That night, my first dinner as a General, taxed me as if I were learning a new sport or combat technique: hold up my face like a shield to the Court, while calming the furious emotions inside me.

Although Water Song was the cause of the emotional storm, she also became its cure. The secret we shared, that private hour in the garden, revived, multiplied and spread every time our eyes touched -- until it was a room within the room, a refuge with a well of nourishing waters. Its only inhabitants were Water Song and myself—not even Cookpot could enter this sanctuary, although he had helped make it possible.

Sometime during that dinner, I saw how I might speak to Water Song in this secret room, while still holding that shield-face up to the Court so that it covered her, too.

When that memory rose and faded as I lay in the darkened farmhouse, I dug my fingers under my tunic and touched the dragon belt I wore next to my skin. I wanted to tear it off and throw it into the fire, then send the concubine a message that she should do the same.

But I could not, I could not move lest I disturb the dressing that held my eye inside my face. I wanted my eye. I wanted my face. My flesh-face.

I lay there on the farmer's straw mat and composed one letter after another to Water Song in my mind. In them I begged her, advised, her, commanded her to destroy the letters and free herself from this reckless affection. I laid out the reasons, like a General planning battle. I quoted fragments of the sages' writings that warned against letting passions take hold. Having become a General, fragments were all I could recall of the sages. I also pleaded from those passions, inventing delirious characters of a thousand ink-strokes that would take up the whole silk and convey the danger she was in. In the end I did nothing. In a dawn after fitful sleep, I awoke calmed. Another way was clear.

I could ask my father to release Water Song from concubinage, to marry me.

If she had not yet entered his bed, it would be a simple matter. In fact, my father could command a nobleman to adopt the maiden concubine as his daughter, and then the marriage would be a completely respectable union between two families! The elegance of this solution gave me peace.

I could not divulge this whole plan to Water Song, nor even to Cookpot, but the beginning steps were at hand. First, I had to heal my wound and return to the campaign. Then I had to succeed in the campaign, and bring the rebel leader's corpse to my father. And when I convinced my father to introduce me to his sage-concubine, I had to pretend we had never met.

Yes, it was elegant. And I achieved all three steps ... then nearly destroyed the whole thing, when Water Song entered the room for dinner with the Emperor and myself.

She wore his ring.

How did you get that? I wanted to shout at her. I wanted to slap her, knock my father to the ground, break the table, smash the teacups. *Our victory is only possible if you are still a virgin! How could you betray us, how could you!* would be in every blow.

But I had had my education. Show nothing. Display nothing. Reveal nothing. Not even when my father had the ridiculous impulse to pose another riddle—one that only Water Song could have put in his head, for it was an unanswerable question. Can one be both a deadly warrior and a Master of the Way? *How long has it been since you were a deadly warrior?* I wanted to snap at him. My scar throbbed. I gathered my wit and delivered my reply.

"To master the Way, the Tao, is to disappear into the flow of Life Itself," I said. "In combat, to disappear is impossible. It is desertion. One must accept that one is a target -- every day, every moment, every breath, death surrounds the warrior. Life is only as broad as the sole of one's foot, or the spread of one's hand on the sword-hilt." I looked at the concubine, who sat in silence. My anger was hitting her like blows. I looked at my father. He, too, heard the fury in my voice, and thought it was for him. His composure was taut, ready to strike. Let him receive this, then. He wanted to see war reveal my character. Here it is.

"Therefore the warrior in combat must *become* Life," I said. "He does not disappear into Life; he pulls Life into himself to the point of bursting. The warrior who is most fully and completely alive in combat, he is the one who causes the enemy to slip. Out of life, into death. It is the enemy who disappears."

My father, the Emperor, received the message. In his seat, on the cushion, in the silks, he was no longer the Emperor, and no longer my father. He and I in that moment were truly men, killers of men. He was ready for my challenge. I was ready for his.

And then Water Song spoke. The humility in her soft voice was like sure, cool hands touching the Emperor and me.

"The single error is to assume there is a Master of the Way in this room who can teach the correct answer," she said. "We are each on our own path. The Prince has a task to fulfill at the head of an army, so his is one kind of combat. The Emperor is the Center of the World, the bridge between the Earthly and the Divine. His combat is far different."

Another concubine, trained from childhood in the ways of courtliness, would have cast her eyes downward. Water Song gazed directly into our faces. Her appeal walked naked between us. "The concubine is also a visible target, in her own way," she continued. "She is grateful for her allies, who shield her in grace and kindness, in the midst of those who do not understand why she remains a maiden." She laid her hand, the one wearing the Jade Turtle ring, on her breast. The other hand lightly caressed it as she bowed deeply to the Emperor. She looked directly into his face. And then into mine.

The call to action is hot, but shame is cold. As if falling from a running horse, my anger lost its seat and landed in a snowbank. Water Song knew nothing of my plan to ask for her as a wife. How could she have had any thought of betrayal? Cookpot had told me long ago that she was facing trouble with the Emperor's women. Why shouldn't she seek the Emperor's protection?

My father, too, had eased out of his challenge back into a good humor. "What do you think, Son? Shall I seat this concubine at our councils?" he asked me.

Don't joke about her, Father, I thought. *This small woman just worked a miracle.* "I think if she were beside the Emperor at every dinner, the Ten Kingdoms would know harmony," I said.

The Emperor chuckled into his teacup and drank. Water Song met my gaze and smiled a very small smile, more in her eyes than her lips. She touched her belt—the hidden belt, which surely rode her waist under the Imperial silks. In reply, I touched my belt, too—the one securely hidden under my robes.

That secret room still sheltered us both, and had grown—built on silk.

Today, on my birthday, with this gift sword in my lap, I touch that belt again. Again my fear tells me to tear it off and burn it—destroy the evidence of our affection. No one need know that this magnificent sword came from my father's concubine.

Instead I remove the belt slowly and tuck her silk poem into the false back.

If the Emperor will not have her beside him at his every meal, I will have her beside me at mine. I will ask for her today, at my birthday dinner.

🦎🦎🦎🦎🦎🦎🦎🦎

Furious!

I had no chance to speak to my father privately, not even a whisper in his ear, today. He arrived late to the celebrations. I had been sitting for hours watching gift after extravagant gift be presented and then taken away. Now that I am a famous general, a hero of the Empire, lords and kings and other nobles are willing to bankrupt themselves for my affections. I was frankly bored by the parade.

Then, with a great commotion, my father the Emperor entered the hall. The waves of risings and prostrations made the room look like a stormy lake. The Emperor settled himself and commanded the celebrations to continue. Several of his wives and concubines followed him in and floated to the floor cushions in clouds of perfumed silk. Water Song was among them but I could not afford to send her even the briefest of looks—I was now truly center of attention, the Emperor's attention, even if he wasn't looking at me. Whatever hot spirit had risen up in us, father and son, at the dinner with Water Song, it lay crouched between us, silent and bound but waiting.

After the gifts were all given, the entertainment started. Unfortunately so did the greetings and personal felicitations—delivered to both myself and my father by an unending line of servants and secretaries representing the visiting nobles who filled the room with their entourages. If I interrupted the greetings to send a message across the room to the Emperor (*please, Son of Heaven, grant me the gift of your virgin concubine as legitimate wife*), it would be noticed immediately and remarked upon by everyone in the hall. It would spread around the palace within the hour, around the city overnight, and across the Ten Kingdoms in a fortnight. Such was the glory of being an exemplar of filial piety. What would befall Water Song then, especially if the Emperor said No? No. I have to make the request privately. There is no other way.

❀ ❀ ❀ ❀ ❀ ❀ ❀

Sleepless with this problem. Once again I take the boxed sword from its hiding place, and lift out the long precious form. The wood and jades are cool, but grow warm in my hand. I kneel and cradle it, hilt pressed to my cheek. I stroke the wood as if it is a beloved body. I caress the dragons as if they are a beloved face. I am helpless before her choice. She has disobeyed the Emperor, the Son of Heaven, for my sake.

Obedience. I had time, while healing my eye, to ponder *obedience.* In a large hall full of people, *obedience* may be something comical, just a sea of color bobbing and bowing to one man. But during the campaign against the rebels, I came to see *obedience* as a kind of celestial building material, plentiful yet volatile; the right to use it must be earned by a ruler if he wants to construct anything.

Obedience. For almost a full year I and the rebel general both had ordered thousands of men into vicious battle again and again. Why did they agree to it, I wondered in that dark, cold farmhouse when I lay flat on my back. Our armies gave and took death and destruction, in *obedience.* Surveying the earth littered with corpses and pieces of corpses, I felt the full, horrifying absurdity of *obedience.* That horror had become part of my muscle and bone by the time I looked in the rebel general's eyes, when he knelt, bound and bloodied, at my feet in a sloping, rocky field.

He wore an oversized helmet fashioned in rough manner out of leather and wood that should never have borne the blows that marked it. It sat atop a cloth and leather mask, so that from a distance he looked like a fearsome earth spirit. My legion commander reached for the helmet, ready to strip it off, but I stayed him with a gesture (again, *obedience*). Whatever this rebel dressed like, my father had already sent word of the man's true identity. I meant to deal with him as one nobleman to another.

I pulled his helmet off myself. No wonder it was oversized, and able to take battle; the rough-hewn outsides covered a finely-fashioned cap of steel plate. The mask he wore underneath, up close, was almost laughable—only a child would fear such thick red lips and white-streaked cheeks. I lifted it off his head. His true face was filthy, with sweat and grime, plus the heat of the mask had made him break out in pustules. Still, his features were proud, the shape of noble birth.

I put my fist into the mask and set the helmet on top of it. "Did you never ask yourself, Double Phoenix"—for that was his true name, and upon his capture after such a long chase, he deserved to hear me speak it—"whether they were following you, or the mask?"

I was tempted to shake the mask and make it growl. But humiliation would be the worst thing to do. I had had enough of the brutality of war. It was time to be an Emperor's Son. Double Phoenix said nothing; he only watched me, and held his heart in his face.

I set the helmet and mask on the ground to my left. I then removed my own helmet (and glimpsed my second in command make swift signals to put guards on the alert for enemy archers) and set it on the ground to my right. I let Double Phoenix see the full face of the man who would execute him. I drew my sword, to let him see that, too. Our eyes met and held. His shoulders relaxed, even in his bindings. We recognized each other as equals, men of superior blood. In a different fate, we might have been generals of the Emperor's armies, kings of neighboring realms, allies strengthening each other. Instead, here was our meeting and farewell.

"This is how you answer for you actions," I said to him. "There are those who did not follow you, yet will answer in this same way, only because they are your family. I hope you can pity them. The gods know I do. One of them will be my elder brother, the Emperor's First Son."

The effect on him was subtle, but plain enough. He knew he was being honored; I set before him the chance to accept the enormity of his crime. That spiritual offering from him would ease the passage of his innocent relatives through the realms of the dead.

We were all silent, for there were no more words in Double Phoenix' life, only an action. He slowly leaned forward, and gave me his bare neck.

I moved to his side and raised my sword, seeking the best angle for a clean strike. This moment was different from *obedience*. Rather, we were performing a great ritual. If it was *obedience*, we answered a commanding power beyond even the Emperor's reach. It was a power with no name, one that could not *be* named. I felt that power on my shoulders, waiting for the appropriate end to my pursuit of Double Phoenix.

I ended it.

That day completed my change from youth to man. Until my own death, birthdays will be no more than social occasions.

I kneel with this birthday sword cradled in my arms and lap, and want to weep. She who gave it has no knowledge of this power on my shoulders. Her gift feels light and clean and my hands feel like hot dung. My sword arm aches, remembering the impact of steel upon muscle and neckbone. I should be holding my battle sword, my blood-grimed friend, killer of men, not this delicate bright blade.

Instead of throwing the sword aside, I press my face into the hilt, into the jades, and let the tears fall. During the campaign I retreated so often to that room Water Song and I share in our hearts, I would not give up this sword for the Dynasty's throne itself. The little concubine's impossible act of disobedience has defeated everything.

Done with tears, I wipe my face—and see that several exceptionally valuable birthday gifts have been arranged in a corner of my quarters. I light a small lamp so that I can carefully close the sword back in its box and re-tie the cords. I put the box with the other gifts.

In a moment's panic, I scramble to loosen the dragon belt next to my skin. Did I remove the poem, or only dream I did? Ah. I did. There it is.

Another moment's hesitation, and I take out my writing brush, ink, water, and a length of silk.

I write Water Song a letter.

14.
RESURRECTION

"Yo!"

Sunlight ... a garden ... someone saying ...

"YO! BROTHER!"

A harsh sound ... from another world ... a planet colliding with reality ...

"COME BACK, GODAMMIT! You're gonna come BACK! Come back NOW!"

... pushed back ... out ... into an earthquake ... a world shaking ...

"LISTEN, man, listen to my voice. You're going to follow my voice. Follow my voice home. We will take care of you. You hear my voice, man? Follow it, now. Come back, now. Easy does it. That's right. Just follow my voice home."

Yes, easy to follow that voice. Obey its warm strength. Protected there. Yes. Follow. Easy. Earthquake ends. Heaviness. But the voice is there. Follow it. Darkness.

"That's it, brother, you're coming back. All the way back. We're here for you, man. Just keep following my voice. Good. Gooooooooood."

The darkness is warm ... a rhythmic beat ...

"He's got a pulse now, Officer. Getting stronger."

"Good. Okay, brother, you're on your way home. Come on back, all the way. Breathe, man, breathe. Come on, don't make me do mouth-to-mouth again."

Cold-rushing harsh, wet-relax warm ... obey the voice ...

"He's breathing. Keep talking."

"C'mon, man, come on back, 'cause you've got to give me my jade back. Your fingers so tight around it, I'll have to break 'em to get my jade, and I don't want to do that. You've got to come back and let go of the jade, man. Hear me? Come back and relax your damn fingers, or you'll never play the violin again."

Follow the voice ... familiar things ... warm things ... jade ... fingers ... violin ...

It was tentative; a halting emergence from a dream; but a sense of *I* trickled through me and re-built my nerves. Arms; legs; back; back of the head; hard floor. At the end of one arm was a ball of cold bright nothing. I remembered that speech was a possibility. I gargled and found that my lips—yes, I remembered my lips—were still numb.

"Try again, brother. Say your name. You know your name? What's your name, man? Come on, tell me."

Good question, I thought. Name. I gargled anew, trying to say *Han Yü*. That was the presence all around me, but fading from me on the inside. What did that mean? Why was it thinning there, like fog before a sky of different blue, while shining in such particular warmth beside me?

"Try again, man. Say your name." That voice, so warm and strong and drawing obedience to it like breath. *That* was *Han Yü*. *Han*, Mountain, *Yü* ... jade? Two sounds that meant the same thing? But *Han Yü* was disappearing into the Voice, and another name forming around it. So what was my name?

My body, coalescing, pulled a set of words into focus. It was too long for my numb lips and leaden tongue to manage. But wait, a shorter version played like sunlight through leaves, a single syllable that smelled of love and memory. "Woss," I mumbled at the Voice. "Wamus." Close enough, for *Hector Roosevelt Lamos*, or just *Ross*.

And still, it wasn't complete. After all that work. Some other name was just out of reach. Some other memory. It receded from my grasp almost willfully, running down dark corridors. *I see you, I know you, I've got you*, I shouted after it, amidst the buzz of my returning bones. It left a trail. I could follow it anytime ... anytime I shed the weight of this re-formed body.

"Good, good! You're almost here, Ross, almost home. Try opening your eyes. Can you open your eyes for me?"

"No," I said. "Too bright."

"Okay, no problem. Keep 'em closed. But tell me, man. You going to let me have my jade? Or what?"

"What?" What did the Voice mean? Then I noticed that the cold bright nothing at the end of one arm was dimming. It divided into several parts. One was an extension of my arm; oh, yes, my hand. It was wrapped around something ... something that had once been a door, or a bridge, or a jet plane, or something, but was now just small and hard and warm. The other divisions belonged to *Han Yü* ... or whatever his name was now. They were warm, too, and strong. They connected to bridges crossing to the rest of *Han Yü* … oh, his hands, his arms. His hands cupped around my hand holding the small thing.

"Okay, I can feel you getting warmer. That's good. Get some heat back in your bones. Feels good, doesn't it, Ross?"

"I guess." The cold bright nothing became warm and specific. Like a shift in a musical key, *Han Yü* dispersed and dimmed around a short syllable—the seed of the Voice. "Del?"

"I'm here, man." All right, memories were returning, obediently following the Voice into my nerves. A roomful of weapons and a very large man. Del agitated, sleepless, angry. Del coming towards me smiling, and then angrily speaking to … oh. *That* figure, *that* man, tipped the load and everything clicked into place like an ocean of falling dominoes. Uh-huh. Okay. Ross Lamos, ex-employee; I opened my eyes and let the stained, acoustic-tile ceiling materialize. Then I pulled in a breath and hauled myself upright—groaning, since apparently some large marching band had practiced its halftime show on my ribcage. And sliced my tee-shirt wide open to do it. I looked around the dingy office. It was a blurry place. Del put my glasses into my free hand, and I slid them onto my face. The world came into focus.

Good grief. Del had called 911. Two EMTs were crouched beside me, with defibrillator paddles ready. They apparently had their suspicions about my resurrection. I felt embarrassed, silly and annoyed. Did Del say he had done *mouth-to-mouth?* Just my luck, to be unconscious for that.

"I'm all right," I told Del. "I mean, I'm better. I'll be all right soon. I'll just sit here a while."

"Here," of course, was the under-furnished front office of that so-called antiquities appraiser. And I did not see the domino-tipper. "Wasn't Albert Jarro here?" I asked Del.

"For about two seconds," Del said. "Poked his head in, saw you on the floor and me doing CPR. Then the EMTs got here, so who knows."

The EMTs, in fact, had business to conduct now that I was awake and lucid. They weren't convinced that my swoon was unrelated to my family's medical history. My flat refusal to get in the truck and go to the hospital for observation ticked them off, but Del quietly assured them that he would personally deliver me should I keel over again. After that it was just insurance information and professional goodbyes. In all that time, the little man with the dangling cigarette never once opened his locked door to see what was going on in his front office.

Finally the front door clicked shut and they were gone. Del then looked at me with an eyebrow raised. He held out his hand. I was still clutching the jade scabbard slide.

"Definitely yours," I said, and put it in his hand. My fingers were stiff and had to be willed open. When the *yü* dropped from them, a tingling wind rushed through me and I sighed. Breathe out. Breathe in. But from the expectation in Del's face, I knew we weren't home yet.

"Um, I think I've got another shirt in the car," I said, fingering my ruined tee. "Can we go somewhere? Somewhere with beer?"

15.
THE THIRD JADE'S STORY—PART II

I dreamed a day, a dark day.
My sighs had filled the sky with clouds.

I do not want to sit and hear a new poem from Cookpot, but his simple entreaty is punctuated by a careless flick of his sleeves—which we have agreed means, *This is about the Situation.*

And the musician kneeling humbly behind my *shih* is the blind and mute master who accompanies Water Song at her exercises in the Sunrise Garden. So I send all my other servants away, and listen.

I went to hunt a wild fox,
Thief of my best cock.
Whose heart has turned against me?
Whose word has chased kind spirits from my house?

All right, Cookpot has put the Situation into poetry. After the Spring Plowing, after my father and Emperor, the Son of Heaven, broke the first ground with the sacred plow to call down a good harvest for all Ten Kingdoms, slowly and quietly the whole Palace and Court began to cool towards me, then chill, then freeze. Invitations to dine or sport dried up, where once they gushed. Offers of marriageable daughters were withdrawn. And the "extraordinary lessons"—meetings and lectures, part of this strange search for an heir to the Dynasty outside of the traditional family lineage—have become interrogations, although retaining a veneer of reverence to my station. My father remains beyond it—perhaps oblivious, perhaps not. Tiny niggling obstructions have prevented me from sitting in my father's presence alone for the entire spring. Since he left for a state visit to the East, accompanied by First Son, glances have become whispers, and whispers have become talk. The talk is that I covet the throne—and my father's death.

The musician changes his melody. Cookpot stops to listen. The tune becomes light and feminine, with a surprisingly bitter, downturned note at the end.

A lady, sweet of face,
Opened the gate to that fox.
Beware of making any woman jealous!

Beware a woman's pride!

Cookpot watches me carefully. We already know, from conversations overheard and interrupted, that this talk grows from that old disgrace at the mountain Temple, when my Father took Water Song as a concubine, which caused me to lose face. Supposedly I am still enraged about that. In this mind, my successful campaign against Double Phoenix was undertaken only to deceive my Father about my feelings. What nonsense. But this woman ... Cookpot can't mean Water Song. The verse doesn't fit her. The musician keeps playing, repeating the light, feminine line with the bitter note at the end.

He means First Wife. Jealousy and pride are her special perfumes, and they permeate any room when First Son is discussed. I lay a hand on my belt, to tell Cookpot I understand.

The musician's tune picks up speed and becomes jaunty.

I rode to hunt a wild fox, Cookpot sings.
He laughed at me and licked his fur.
He led me to the high places,
And hid in rocks and shadows.
All the birds chattered,
And told him where I rode.

First Wife opened the gate to the wild fox. And who is this fox, her ally? Someone with a wide net to draw in much news. I turn over possible names in my head — until I hear the tune weave a familiar nursery song, about a king giving orders, underneath the jaunty melody.

That wild fox tried to crow like my best cock,
He tried to make the sun rise.
'Yours is gone, so here am I!
Yours is gone, so here am I!'

Ice in my blood. My scar throbs. I know who the fox is.

A minor minister of finance rose rapidly in status when the collapse of Double Phoenix' rebellion left that region in a shambles. The Minister's reconstruction scheme actually worked, thanks to the locals' utter exhaustion and newfound desire to obey the Son of Heaven's decrees. In less than a year, this Minister has gained a new title, a new wife and house, and elaborate new robes that he flaunts at Court. Best of all, no one jokes any more about the state of his teeth. Somehow, in this season of the Emperor's travels to the East, this Minister has been left behind as the Emperor's voice and hand.

I cough, to stop the song. "Is this a reworked poem, my *shih*?" I ask Cookpot lazily. "I believe there's a deer in the next verse, a young doe who leaps like a sudden breeze and lands like the rain. I seem to remember her in several of your songs."

Cookpot remains silent. He turns his body slightly towards the musician. The blind old man plucks a high, sweet note, followed by a cascade of notes, scattering like a storm of dry leaves. Then another single, high note, followed by that familiar note twisting down into bitterness.

Cookpot turns back to me. "The jealous lady in this poem has sent her lover off to chase the fox," he tells me, "for many reasons, all to be sung later. But it is true, there is a doe in this poem, and the jealous lady now sets herself to hunt down that creature."

"Enough of this poem, then," I say, feigning a yawn. "Cookpot, let's you and I go for a ride. Music Master, here's coin for wasting your skill on a tale we know too well. Wait—here's more, no doubt my *shih* will need your sweet instrument again, soon, to give me another song." I press the second coin into the musician's long, delicate hand, and he does a surprising thing. He refuses it. Presses it back into my hand. Then he gropes for Cookpot's left hand. His tapering nails tap-tap-tap on Cookpot's jade thumb ring, the archer's ring I gave him after a contest long ago. The musician tap-tap-taps it again, then wraps both his hands around it and raises it to touch his brow.

I blush, and swallow a sudden choking. There is at least one other at Court who is faithful to me.

Riding far into the countryside, we enter a vast meadow. The only eyes and ears inside its bounds belong to buzzing flies and a small herd of cattle grazing in a corner. I command my attendants to stay outside the field, by the trees, guarding the perimeter. Cookpot and I ride to the center of the open land. We are visible to all my servants over the short, scrubby grass, but so are they visible to us. We dismount, and stand together between our horses, letting their bodies shield us.

"Is Water Song in danger?" These are my first words.

"No more than usual," Cookpot replies. "But she still wears the Emperor's ring. None can harm her, with that."

"Not even the Emperor's 'voice and hand'?" I ask bitterly. "Damn it, I should simply take her out of here. All three of us, we should flee back to her temple in the mountains! Hide there until I can straighten this out."

"It would seem a milder revenge," Cookpot answers, stroking his horse's neck, "to return what was taken."

I sink onto my heels, tear up a clod of warm earth and crush it in my hand. Yes, it's a clumsy notion. Even in my own ears I sound more like an impetuous boy than a man, let alone a victorious general. "Well, what can I do?" I snap, rising, tossing away the dirt. "My every move is watched, reported, countered. Five days ago I sent my best courier off to catch the Emperor's caravan. I had him memorize the message, so it couldn't be stolen. I asked my Father to send for me, and receive me in private. Dear friend, I intend to ask for Water Song. By way of a plan," I add, when it seems he has stopped breathing. "I will suggest that he choose a nobleman to adopt Water Song, so that she has a family's protection among the other women. My father will be curious about my interest in her well-being. I will say that … that upon meeting her, I spoke my heart in the Emperor's presence. If this woman were at the Emperor's side, the Ten Kingdoms would know peace." Mouth dry, I hope this is what I will actually say. I hope I will get the chance to say *something*.

"Will your father know which Emperor you mean?" Cookpot asks. Sometimes I want to strike my *shih* across the head.

"He'll know perfectly well that *he* needs no family alliance bring her to his table," I reply sharply. Cookpot bows his head, confused. Shame and anger at my thoughtless words swell in my throat. I should have revealed my secret to Cookpot sooner – he would have understood why I placed Water Song at the Emperor's side. But even to my closest *shih* and brother of my heart, I do not reveal everything. This wonder, however, has rested and grown in my breast long enough.

"There is a thing you must know," I begin, softly, heavily. Cookpot looks at me with caution and curiosity. I tell him of an "extraordinary lesson" that took place just after the Spring Plowing. First Son and I sat with three Ministers. They spoke of a grave danger to the Ten Kingdoms—invasion—and asked us what course of action the Son of Heaven should pursue. The particulars of their scenario do not matter. What mattered was that First Son's response was careful, measured and distant. He has intelligence, does my brother, but he is not a natural soldier and spoke of great reliance on spies and generals. My response, therefore, brought one Minister out of what looked like a deep doze. "The defense against an invasion begins long before a barbarian has the first dream of gaining territory," I said. I then spoke of the Son of Heaven's responsibility to see that all the peoples of the Ten Kingdoms—aristocrats and peasants alike—live under just laws, fair taxes, charity in times of famine and drought, and uncorrupted deputies. Such a life makes those who dwell in a Kingdom, by their happiness and loyalty, the first defense against danger. I said more in this vein, having thought much on the mystery of *obedience*.

I came to an end, and the Ministers called for tea. First Son gave his apologies, rose and left. He could do this, being who he is. The Ministers seemed relieved at his departure. Our conversation continued for more than an hour, on the subject of a population's happiness, and grew quite lively. When I left the room at last, First Son's servant was waiting for me in the corridor. His master wished a private audience with me.

The servant led me to a cozy veranda looking onto a garden gone giddy with spring blossoms, so thick and colorful they seemed to be pushing each other off the tree boughs. First Son was there; he did not turn at my approach, but only motioned for me to stand next to him. We were silent together for a while, gazing out at the silly bursting flowers, and then he leaned towards me.

"If our father places his burden upon your shoulders," my brother said softly, close to my ear, "the entire Earth will be fortunate." I glanced aside at him. His long face and broad brow, nodding above me like his tall mother's would, were placid, but his eyes were vividly alight. "I shall serve the Son of Heaven as I always have," he continued. "I am at peace with the turnings of the Way." And with that he left me.

I stood looking out upon the buzzing garden, but saw nothing, heard nothing. A weight, that was yet light, filled my belly and chest, my shoulders and neck. I pressed my lips together, lest it burst from me like a trumpet-call. The weight (yet light) filled my brow and rang in my ears. I knew a thing clearly, as the truth.

I will be the next Son of Heaven.

This is the only reason for the search, the emphasis on virtue, and the extraordinary lessons.

My father is building this visible process to ensure *obedience*—to both his choice and to me. To *me*.

I *want* this. I *do want* this. I felt this destiny flood my hands, and all through my flesh. My feet burned on the veranda's wood floor, hot with truth. *I am the Son of Heaven. When my father dies, all the world will sing this, and it will be so.*

I left the veranda in a burst of movement and strode through the halls and palaces and courtyards to my stables. Only locking my legs around the rocking body of my best horse in a dead run, with the hard pounding of hooves and the taste of dust, could calm me. I rode to this very meadow, and made my attendants wait at the edge. Here, in almost this very spot, I pulled at the reins until my stallion stood on his hind legs and pawed at the air. I howled, a sound I still don't understand, for it was neither triumph nor sorrow nor rage, but still a sound to drive out devils.

When I came to myself (I tell Cookpot), sitting on my horse (now grazing amiably), my first thought was of Water Song. "She is like a quiet room in my heart where the truth abides," I confess to my *shih*, as we stand in the meadow beside our horses. "I will be Emperor, and I must have her beside me as my Empress. That will be what I say to my father, when he receives me."

Cookpot bows his head again, slowly, as if a weight has been laid upon his neck. "It is your destiny," he agrees, with a weary voice. "Like your brother, I serve the Son of Heaven, as best I can." He swallows, and adds, "Therefore I must warn you—be careful how you word this, since such a request could seem to prove you unfilial. The talk is such that --"

"The talk is of my wish for his death!" I exclaim, perhaps too loudly. Quietly again, I finish, "There need be no mention of Water Song to anyone until my father releases her to be my bride."

Cookpot nods. "Then we must be patient, and hear what your messenger brings back," he agrees. "If I may suggest to my Prince, however … extra visits to your ancestral shrine, with offerings to your father's health, might move certain spirits in your favor." And let me be seen doing uncalled-for filial duty, yes. I nod curtly and re-mount, as does Cookpot. We set off for my attendants at a walk.

"Is the music master's language known to anyone else?" I ask, after a pace or two, before we are within earshot of my retinue.

"Unbelievable as it may seem, he works out a private language with each new student," Cookpot replies. "We have had many amazing conversations on some remarkable subjects."

"No doubt. One can wonder whether his afflictions are a curse from the gods, or a blessing."

"Do you truly not know his story, my Lord?" Cookpot asks, his eyebrow rising. My *shih* loves tales that turn an assumption on its head, especially when the tale is true. I remain silent, and he jumps in.

"My master was born as able as any child, but more bright of eye and quick of tongue. He was a prodigy on the lute, and soon mastered every instrument and style. Naturally he was brought to court, where it soon became clear what the family had hidden. This young musician had the spirit sight. He saw what was true in everything around him … and in every person. Much to his sorrow." Cookpot pauses, and I wonder if he will say more. Abrupt endings are not his style. I prod him just a bit, and still he hesitates. "The boy could not help letting some of his truthful sight slip into his songs," Cookpot finally concedes. "This was in the reign of the former Dowager Empress."

"Ah," I sigh, as Cookpot's hesitation becomes reasonable.

"She had him blinded and his tongue cut out."

"Ah," is all I can say, to end it. We rejoin my attendants in silence.

We ride back slowly, still in silence, until a messenger comes galloping up, with the news that my best courier, a virtuous man who would rather play with a child than drink, has been killed in a brawl in a brothel just a half-day's ride from the Emperor's dwelling in the East.

I will go myself. I will go in my full estate as a Prince, I will retrieve my courier's body for his family, and I will visit my father. I thunder my orders and my servants fly about like birds startled from cover. And yet, there are a thousand problems, delays. What happened to the instant *obedience* of my army? It is nearly two days before I am assured, as the mid-day meal is brought in, that we may leave at the next dawn. Now I know why my father was in such a bad temper when we left on that fateful progress around the Kingdoms. We were supposed to start out within a season of his succession, but organizing it took nearly two years.

Cookpot is not at the meal, and does not hear the final arrangements. It occurs to me, I have not seen him for a whole day. No one else has seen him, either. I am about to send a soldier to bring him to me, when a very young servant comes forward and prostrates, red-faced and in tears. The day before, the favored *shih* had given him something to deliver to the great Prince, and in the whirlwind of my preparations he completely forgot about it. He reaches into his sleeve and takes out a tightly knotted piece of silk, and offers it to me on hands stretched over his head as his brow rubs the floor. The knot is from my wartime code. *Be sure you are alone when you read this.*

Very quietly I pick up the silk and put it in my sleeve, as if nothing at all is wrong. Very quietly I dismiss the young servant and thank him for remembering the delivery. I inform my servants I am having a rest. I go into my bedchamber and lock the door. Then I vomit into a bowl.

Picking apart the knot, my hands begin to shake and tears start up in my eyes. Something has happened. My *shih* has vanished and left me a note. I want to throw open the door and howl, *Bring me my shih!* But I know my voice would be a child's hysterical shriek. Instead I address Cookpot in a wet, hissing whisper, crying as I pull at the twisted silk. "Gone, are you? I can't wait to hear why. Sing me a perfumed excuse, flip those rhymes off your tongue, it will be rich. I never had you whipped, never, and this is how you repay me! Gone, when I need you! Gone, when danger is all around! I am so grateful you never came to war with me! Then you would have known whipping! Damn this tight twist, straight to hell. There, I've broken a fingernail, are you satisfied? Come on, silk, let me hear, let me read, what my snickering *shih* has to say!" The silk falls apart limply in my hands.

It is two silks. One is a stream of characters in Cookpot's hand, the other … I catch my breath. The other is written in my own hand. *Forgive me*, it begins. *I heard such stories of your immortality dance at the temple festival, I convinced Cookpot to help me hide in the garden to see you for myself. Please have no anger towards Cookpot. I had to win a bet with him before he would consent to expose his friend in obedience to his lord.* And my stamp. Along the edges of the silk, in small characters, is Water Song's hand: *The Tao that can be spoken of is not the Tao. I am grateful in excess for Cookpot's friendship.* And beside her stamp, like an afterthought, in tiny characters, *And yours.*

I am baffled. Did I write this? I heard no stories of her dancing at the temple festival, only that she debated with the Emperor and made him laugh. I take up the other silk.

My Lord and Prince, it begins.

I have done a great wrong, thinking that it would help two friends.

You asked me to find a way wherein you might observe the Emperor's Concubine more closely, without being known to do so. Having accomplished this, and learning from my Music Master that the incomparable girl not only detected your presence but drew your spirit into her dance, a fear took my heart and I wrote the enclosed note in your hand, basely exonerating myself in the guise of your apology. I expected her to destroy the silk and say nothing. Oh, I am a fool about women, as much as any drunkard!

Somehow the affection between you and Water Song has become known to First Wife and our Wild Fox; thus they have sown and cultivated the Situation for their own ends. But that affection, much as it has nourished both of you with a hope, is a false hope, and I bear the blame of it. The consequences to you and the Concubine are all upon my shoulders, and I am in a hell of ghosts until the truth is known by all the world. It is this truth that I now work to set down, and so am withdrawn from your presence.

For this withdrawal, I can ask your forgiveness. For the rest, I am only —

His red stamp marks the end.

I lower the silk and stare at a square of sunlight that has settled on the floor tiles. Truth? How much of what you write, Cookpot, will be the truth? I noticed Water Song at the archery contest; she met my eyes, with a face so open and clear that I was thunderstruck; she touched her shoulder with her fan, to honor me, when she saw that I knew her name; none of that was your doing. It was my blood that flamed hot. I wrote the first silk myself. You only carried it. I expressed a wish to see her more closely—and you are my most obedient servant. *Obedience*. When we are accustomed to friendship, even love, it is simple to forget the duty within *obedience*. You, Cookpot, are my most obedient servant and in that duty, you are my greatest friend. It is your nature to be so. What is this grief of yours? It's as if a bridge should feel damned because an army crosses it, as well as thieves, murderers, and fleeing lovers. There may be a poem in this, Cookpot, but is it sensible?

I should go to Cookpot, ambush him with forgiveness and reason him out of despair. But first I carefully loosen my robes to remove the secret belt, and I add Cookpot's two silks to the little library. Just as I secure my outer robe again, there is a knock at the door to my outer chamber.

The servant who calls through the door is one who often brings Cookpot to my rooms. Awash with relief, I bid him open the door—but the visitor who steps through is not my *shih*.

It is the Wild Fox. His luxurious robes are so layered and pleated and draped around his slight frame that he throws a shadow as big as an ox.

I do not disgrace myself; my stillness is that of a General unpleasantly interrupted. But he knows he has caught me unawares. He just stands, and smiles, his wide lips mercifully covering his tangled teeth. My wartime strength returns and burns under my skin.

"Have you made a decree excusing yourself from bowing in proper respect to the Emperor's son?" I growl.

"I serve the Son of Heaven, first and last," he says, and lets it hang there. A bold move, claiming the highest ground in the most insolent way. Laughing at me while licking his fur, indeed.

"State the reason for this visit," I say, with danger under my words. I will make my whole body a weapon if I have to. Let him understand how little his robes can protect him.

"I have come, since the Emperor cannot, to expose your crimes. A most foul conspiracy has become known to me, despite your clever attempts to hide it."

"I must be the cleverest man in the world, since it is hidden from me as well."

He actually snickers. "You dress yourself prettily, pretending not to—"

"If you have an accusation, make it!" I roar.

After a pause, he blots a drop of my spittle from his cheek with one fingertip.

"Messages have been intercepted and recorded," he finally continues. "You plot to murder the Son of Heaven, and capture his throne."

"Lay those messages in front of me, and I will expose their lies."

He shakes his hands free of his multiple sleeves, and claps. The door slides open and the servant scoots in on his knees, holding several rolls of wood strips and a cloth-covered bowl. An odor comes in with that bowl that makes my bones tingle and my hair rise. It is the odor of the battlefield—faint and masked by cloying flowers, but a soldier does not forget that smell. Death. The servant doesn't even look at me. He obeys this Wild Fox, and reads aloud from the rolls.

Death to the Emperor.

I think about his death night and day, and see a thousand grisly ways to achieve it, a thousand subtle ways as well.

The servant sets down the roll and opens another.

Yes, my clever darling, appear to grieve at the funeral, wear your mourning clothes for a year, be the paragon of filial sons. The Dragon Throne will be yours.

And another:

I am sick with desire for the Dragon Throne. My ambition knows no bounds, walls, borders. I want to bridle this Heavenly Beast, grip the reins and ride it to exhaustion. Perhaps I will fall from the saddle, but I doubt it. The signs are too auspicious for my ascendancy.

"These were intercepted as they traveled between you and your little slut, the whore who calls herself the Emperor's favored concubine yet betrays him every day," the Wild Fox says mildly. He motions for the servant to continue. The man is sweating, but his voice holds steady. He reads what I am accused of writing, words about Water Song's thighs, hands, mouth, and the moist petals of her lotus. I burn with helpless rage that anyone would write of her in this way, ashamed that I have thought of her just this way many times, and sick to have these thoughts now tainted by the Death-smell of that bowl.

Your beauty will be paraded throughout the Empire, I supposedly wrote to Water Song.

You will be the Love Goddess of all the world and I shall watch joyfully as peasant and aristocrat alike join with your loveliness in pillows of bliss, drinking your –

"ENOUGH," I howl. The servant snaps the roll shut and bows his head.

I stare at the Wild Fox through slitted eyes, breathing silently through my teeth as if I am about to strike. My world, my reputation, my standing, my every hope and thought of the future crumbles to ash and vanishes. Only the Wild Fox remains. He looks off into the distance, as if the place where two walls meet has some fascinating sports event going on. He fans himself with tiny motions.

Under the sole of my foot is the entire world. In the palm of my hand is life itself.

Without taking my eyes from the Wild Fox, I move to the servant's side and kneel beside him. "Who intercepted these messages?" I ask him in a calm voice.

"My Lord, I do not know," he mumbles.

"Then say who you think intercepted them."

"Two eunuchs, my Lord."

"Serving whom?"

"The esteemed First Wife of our Emperor."

"Why do you think these creatures are the ones who intercepted the letters?"

"They speak of letters and this conspiracy constantly, my Lord, as ones who have heard much."

"Well done," I whisper to the servant. I rise and move to the Wild Fox's side, slightly behind him. "Is it truly the Son of Heaven you serve, or the line of succession—and all the ways power will shift among us when the Emperor has his end?"

He seems to shrink into his robes slightly—as if they would hide him. But his gaze stays distant, indifferent. "I do not question the Emperor's decision regarding the succession," he says. "He seeks a man of virtue. What one may question, then, is how much virtue he sees in his son."

"Question all you like, you do not know my father's heart. Nor mine."

He pauses. A hope sparks in me. I may have him. But then he turns his head to gaze at me over his shoulder—tilting his head back, baring part of his throat. A gesture a woman would make in intimacy. Disgust rises in me. His perfumes are strong and I want to crush him like a worm. He smiles slightly. "But I do know something of the Concubine," he murmurs.

I step away. I *must* be careful. I must be as a general besieged, with supplies and munitions running low … and the smell of Death in the room.

"Much news goes into the women's palace," I say, "but some comes out, as well. This orphan Concubine is better suited for cloisters than an Imperial bed. I am certain all of the Emperor's wives and concubines would gladly be rid of her. If she is hated among the women, it is no proof of conspiracy against the Emperor."

The Wild Fox *tsks* and fans himself again. "If only it were that," he sighs. "She was quite forthcoming—quite generous, you might say, in her offers—when I showed her the last letter"—he tilts his fan at the servant, who draws forward a last clutch of wood strips—"and the hand of he who wrote it. She recognized it immediately, of course." The servant pushes the bowl towards me and pulls off the cloth cover.

A severed hand.

The general in me calmly notes that the gray-green color and rigid fingers mean this hand and its owner parted ways about twelve hours earlier. But the general dwindles and recedes like a dream, drowned out by the scream in me—which I cannot let out, I will not let out between my clenched jaws.

It is Cookpot's hand. The archer's ring still graces his thumb.

"The letter he was writing when my soldiers entered his room," the Wild Fox says from somewhere far away, "was most shocking, even after all we already knew." The servant's voice then chimes like a distant bell:

You sassy little mare, if our hopes are not to be destroyed, you must flee with the Prince tomorrow at dawn. Be there in his retinue when he puts the final poison to the Emperor and First Son—you will be at Jade Mountain's side when he claims the Dragon Throne! Come to me tonight by the

most secret way, and I shall disguise you for the journey. Of
course, seeing you undress will arouse my hideous passion,
the one that made you scream into your pillow and bite
through the silk, as I –

"STOP," I cry, and the servant obeys. A sob escapes him as he hangs his head. Somehow, noticing this, noticing the trickle of tears down his face, noticing how much all of this *obedience* has cost him, stills my spirit. This servant loved Cookpot, too. With my gaze on the man's discreet, distraught face, I can feel the earth under my foot again, and the life in my hand.

"Does our Emperor's esteemed First Wife know of this letter?" I ask.

"She knows all," the Wild Fox replies.

"One can surmise that she asked you to investigate the Concubine, and me, when some one thing aroused her suspicions," I say. "It may have been a small thing, but she saw much in it. What was that one thing?"

"A rare gift, one that passed from the Concubine to you on your birthday. With a poem that all but proclaimed you the Emperor of the Universe." I am quiet, and the Wild Fox coughs impatiently behind his fan. "The Great Lady has suggested I arrest you both tonight, and she will call for execution tomorrow. It is well within my power. Since you have exposed no lies in these letters, I may as well proceed." He starts to turn away.

"Hold there!" I say sharply. He stops, with a small sigh. "There is a way for the esteemed Lady to have everything she desires—without calling for executions, without appearing to be involved at all," I tell him. "Her name and reputation will remain pure, no one will glance her way." The thought growing in my mind is appalling, for it is a lie and a blasphemy. But I have failed at the duty I had promised so easily to Water Song— protection. Blasphemy is the only path that shows a way to keep her fate, and mine, in my own hands.

The Wild Fox puts his fan away and tucks his hands in his sleeves, listening. He would rather arrest me.

"My retinue is prepared to ride out at dawn," I say, "towards the East, towards the Emperor and First Son. Let it happen. For here is the first lie in your letters"—I hold up my hand as he starts a retort. "As I said, you do not know my heart. My purpose in this journey is to kneel before the Emperor and give up my chance at the succession. Yes. I will step back from the Dragon Throne in favor of First Son. You may tell First Wife so." The Wild Fox eyes me, weighing this information.

"You wonder how you can trust me to do this," I continue. "Here is how. Let a secret plan proceed as well. I will send the Concubine a letter this hour, asking her to come to me in disguise tonight, and hide within my retinue until we are well outside the city walls. Then—I shall tell her in the letter—she may take a horse and return to her temple in the mountains. For this chance, it is certain she will come. But you must have your men step aside and allow it. For at dawn, when my retinue reaches the city's outer gates"—I stop and swallow; the blasphemy is like a stone in my throat—"At the gates, I will hand her to you. That, sir, is the guarantee that I do not seek the Dragon Throne and only wish for peace in the Ten Kingdoms."

The Wild Fox stares at me in a kind of wonder. I manage a slight smile. "The life of an Emperor is worth more to an Empire than one concubine, or one Prince." I say. "And in truth, if I could not have Water Song beside me, I would be a very bad Emperor indeed. That is the second and greatest of your lies, sir. You know well there is no conspiracy, no plot for the Throne. The Concubine and I loved each other, in letters. That is all. Now I will write to the girl. You may wait here in my outer rooms." I turn my back on the Wild Fox and the servant, and enter my bedchamber, locking the door behind me with a firm click of the bolt.

My legs cannot hold me any longer. I fall to the floor. He wants to hear my howl. I know he's waiting for it. I won't give it to him. I crawl across the tiles to the far corner. Cushions and a discarded robe are piled there. I plunge my face into the mass of fabric and scream until my throat is ragged.

When the great force of the scream has passed, I notice that my head has been beating against something rigid and sharp-edged under the cushions. I paw the cloth aside to see.

It is the box holding Water Song's beautiful sword.

Hiding it so diligently, then, was a waste of time. But it revives the General in my nature. He holds the box, and sees the possibilities. Praise all the gods, he finds a length of silk and brings out my writing table, brush, inkstone and water. He knows what to write to Water Song, telling her just enough of all that has transpired. Nothing of having seen Cookpot's hand—only that he is slain, and this Wild Fox means to do the same to us. *If you can find the means, disguise yourself in some way and go to the gate of the concubines' compound,* the General writes. Nothing of the blasphemous lie. She should not have to bear such knowledge of my ways.

And the General knows—as my heart reels and cowers in my chest—to remove the sword from the box, and place my secret belt there instead, carrying only the final letter. Tied back up in its fine silk cords, the box looks untouched, as on the day it was given to me. I wrap the sheathed sword in the other silk letters, and slide it under my bed pillows.

It takes all of the General's strength to make me stand, lift the box and carry it to the bedchamber door.

The Wild Fox hasn't moved from his spot; he fans himself lazily. The servant still kneels, head bowed. With relief I note that the letters and the ghoulish bowl have been taken away. I turn the box in my hands to show it to the Wild Fox. "This is the gift I received from the Concubine," I tell him in the General's well-controlled voice. "When she sees it, she will know all is lost." Then I glide past the Wild Fox, straight to the servant, and kneel beside him again. I place the box into his hands.

"For the sake of a poet's laughter," I whisper to him, "take this to the Favored Concubine Water Song as fast as you can! When that is done, find the blind music master and send him to me." He does not look at me—wise and well-trained servant that he is—but his body fills with life again. He bows slightly, grabs the box and is swiftly gone.

I rise immediately to block the door, and the Wild Fox nearly runs into me in his haste to follow the box. "Would you be gone without farewell?" I ask him. With fury tightening his features, he steps back and bows stiffly. He tries to step around me but I block his way to the door again.

"There is one last thing to be said," I tell him. "Something you would do well to remember." His eyes narrow, scowling. "It is only this," I continue. "That the Emperor's esteemed First Wife, that great Lady, also serves the Son of Heaven as best she can. She has learned, in recent times, that she must do this first, above all else."

His eyes widen and his fury blazes, but he says nothing. He pushes past me and flies out the door after the servant and the box.

I slide the door shut and lean against the wall. The General has vanished from my blood and my legs want to give way again. I stagger into my bedchamber and fall onto the bed, immediately in oblivion.

16.
THE THIRD JADE'S STORY—PART III

It is dark when a knocking awakens me. By instinct I grip something familiar under the pillows: the hilt of a sword. Then I realize I am in my own bedchamber, alone. No servant announces a visitor through the outer chamber's door. The knocking comes again—calm, quiet.

The truth returns to me swiftly—the vile Minister, the letter to Water Song, Cookpot dead. How long have I been in this foolish swoon? My General's nature is outraged. I pull the sword from its sheath as I roll out of bed. Its hissing song surrounds me as I slide open the bedchamber door. "Who knocks?" I call through the outer chamber.

There is a pause, then a rapid, rhythmic tattoo of light taps. For a moment I gape, then realize that it's a familiar dance rhythm. Oh, for all the sages' wisdom! I light a lamp, open the outer door, and kneeling there is the blind music master.

"Master, I have need of you," I say when he is settled inside and I have locked the door. He bows and holds his fists to his brow. Faithful, *obedient* man. He opens his lute case, but I lay my hand on his. "No music tonight, Master. There is a thing to be done that I can place in no one's hands but yours." He closes his case and listens, still as a tree. "First, can you tell me how many hours since sunset?" He holds up two fingers. I sigh with relief. Water Song might not have attempted her disguised escape yet. "Quickly, then, Master," I say, "Go to the gate of the women's compound. Tonight, but I do not know the hour, someone will come through that gate and touch your arm. Bring her to my rooms here as swiftly as you can." I grimace inwardly at letting *her* slip out, but since the Master gave Cookpot so much news of Water Song's place in First Wife's trap, he must know whom I mean.

The old man touches his fists to his brow again. I try to press money into his hands, but he throws it on the floor. He presses his fists tightly to his brow and bows to the floor—once, twice, three times.

"Go, then," I say, choking back sudden tears. "And Master—I wish I had been more of a musician, that we might have spoken together in our own way." He pauses, then turns to me, as if his scarred sockets still had sight, as if he were not a servant, and I not a prince. He looks at me with his full face. And nods, with a slight smile.

I unlock the door and open it for him, and like a perfect servant he scoots out backwards, on his knees. Yet as I close the door I feel I have been blessed by a saint.

Now I am truly alone. All I can do is wait. First I sit here, then there, with the sword on my lap. I re-sheath it, take it out again, put it back. The lamp burns down; hours are passing. I plant the sheathed sword's point on the floor, between my knees, and press my head against the jade dragons twining around the slide. If that vile Minister, the Wild Fox, lets Water Song come to me, what then? Is escape possible? The sword seems to vibrate in my hands and whisper, *"Try!"* But if I were the Wild Fox, with eyes on my prey, I would have soldiers set to slaughter whoever emerged from the Prince's quarters, by whatever door. Still, I am not this Minister. I can only guess at what he is willing to do to elevate himself in the Emperor's Government. Would he in fact allow my retinue—with the Concubine in disguise—begin our departure at dawn? Might there be a chance for escape then? It might be allowed, so that his soldiers could capture us, and thus seem to prove the Wild Fox's lie.

There is no reason to trust this Wild Fox. Has he said one word to me that has not been a lie?

Gods of life! *What if he actually allows us to reach the city gates, just to see what I will do with the Concubine?*

I grip the sheathed sword and raise it. "By my life," I swear to the night, and the lamp, and Heaven, "it shall not be so. Not one soldier will touch Water Song. I promised to protect her, and her life is now in my hands. So be it." I lift the sword higher. "So be it—*forever.*"

I slowly set the sword down. The air and darkness seem thick as honey around me. The carved jade dragons are hot under my hands, like flesh. And there is a knock at the door.

I wait. The second knock is the quick tattoo, the dance rhythm. Now I rise. I draw the sword, approach the door and touch the sword to it. Another breath—and I slide the door open suddenly, with the sword's point.

If the Music Master is there, he has scooted to the side, for I don't see him. All I see in the dim corridor is a small, very young *shih*, carrying a roll of wood strips and wearing robes that are too big for him.

Wearing Cookpot's robes.

I swallow a cry, drop the sword and fall to my knees. The little *shih*, Water Song, drops the roll of wood strips and flies into my arms. She smells just as I have imagined: flowers, delicate spices, fresh water. Her arms are strong and she grips me as if pulling us together into one person. I oblige with my own broad arms crushing her into my chest. Somewhere behind us, there is the sound of the door sliding shut. Faithful Music Master. We weep into each other's hair, and each whisper the other's precious name. When at last we pull apart to look at each other, I have to laugh—her tears have ruined her ink mustache and mine have smeared her ink eyebrows and hairline. She smiles too, and touches my face. Her fingertips come away black. My face must be just as foul as hers.

Without a word I move away to fill a bowl with water and gather cloths and cleansing oils. When I turn back to her, she has slipped out of Cookpot's robes. I catch a glimpse of bloodstains around the neck of the garment, just as she folds it under, discreet. I concentrate on Water Song: her under-robe is a simple pink cotton, with tiny embroidered flowers and birds. It is the only garment covering her skin, and clings to her in patches, where she has perspired from wearing a man's robes in the warmth of an early-summer night. Seeing me with the bowl, she lowers herself to a cushion and sets the folded robes to one side. The clashing sight of that woman's form, and the ink-smeared face crowned by the man's top-knot, sends a shock to my knees.

I kneel beside her, and gently put my arm around her. I dip my fingers in the cleansing oils, and slowly rub them over her face. She closes her eyes and sinks back against my supporting arm. Now I can feel the exhaustion in her. I wet a cloth in water and clean off the oils and ink. Her silent tears rejoin the water I stroke onto her face. As the ink comes off, I can see she is ashen, her eyes and cheeks sunken with trauma. If she has Cookpot's robes, she knew he was dead before reading my letter. I kiss her brow. What have you been through, little Concubine? She turns her face into my shoulder and sobs, without sound, just a shaking of her whole body. I touch her ears, her cheeks, and murmur nonsense sounds—really, what comfort can I give? That secret room we shared in our hearts is now all we have in the universe. Beyond it our enemies wait with swords drawn. She must sense the uselessness of words, for she touches my hand, grips it and kneads the muscle around my thumb, as she sobs. She quiets, and sighs. She lets go of my hand and reaches behind her head, to undo her knotted hair. Loose, it unwinds and falls open across my arm like an embrace. She closes her eyes again, surrendered to me. This awakens my manhood, but now is not the time for that dragon to stretch. Intent and slow, I finish washing her face and throat, then her hands, and finally dry her carefully.

She sighs, and turns, and collapses against my chest, all strength gone, as if we have just climaxed the most joyous love. "Jade Mountain," she whispers my name. "Jade Mountain."

I kiss her brow again. "I wanted"—I begin. *I wanted this moment to happen when you were my wife.* But she places her fingertips on my mouth. "Not yet, no words," she says. She rises and takes up the bowl. She freshens the water, and returns, kneeling beside me. "Now it is your turn."

I sit very still, and she tenderly cleans my face and hands of ink stains, as reverently as if she were polishing a statue of some great deity. She concentrates on the shapes of my hands and fingers, learning me, learning how the muscles and veins of my hand become the sinews of my wrist and arm. Perhaps she does not see how the shape of my robe has changed, but she must notice that my hands are trembling.

"I wanted to make you my wife," I croak, to turn my mind towards anything but what roils in my flesh. "I meant to have my father send you to be adopted by a noble family, for your protection, and then I would have asked him … to release you … to be my bride." She stops stroking my arm, which is a sort of relief. I open my eyes. She is staring at me, waiting. Waiting for an explanation, why this lucid scheme did not come to pass.

"Forgive me if you can, Bright Lady," I whisper miserably. Shame fills my throat. "The chance to speak to my father never came … or I dared not take hold of it. There are times when I am more chained and bound in this place than any slave." She simply sits, absorbed in listening. I open my hands. "And so here we are."

A heartbeat passes. Two. Then she rises, and gathers up the magnificent sword from where I dropped it. She seeks and finds its scabbard. She brings them to me, kneels and holds them, the scabbard in one hand, the sword in the other. With finality, she slides the sword into the scabbard, between the two coiling dragons. The *hissssssssss-click* of its homecoming is her word.

"This was my choice," she says. "*You* were my choice." She sets the sheathed sword on my lap. Serenity has returned to her features. "Does the sword please you, my friend?"

"Beyond any thing I have ever received," I reply, stunned. She nods. "Then it is enough," she says, simply. She begins picking up and folding the drying cloths, as calm as a serving-maid. I can only watch her, mute. Can she really be so accepting? I grab the sword and stand. "If we go now," I say, "both of us on one horse, this sword could win us a chance" -- She holds up her hands. Stop.

"It is enough," she says again, with firmness. "Do not run off to battle, Jade Mountain. Stay in this room, please. Stay with me."

Shamefaced, I turn and lay the sheathed sword on my ancestors' altar. My ancestors, so newly become a line of Emperors. I have failed them, too, losing my destiny this way. I light fresh incense, since it seems I will soon join them in their realm. Water Song takes my hand. I didn't hear her approach, her step is so light.

"I would have died young here in any case," she says. Is this to comfort me? "I do not belong in a palace. Sickness, or poison, by my own hand or another's … I would have fled, finally."

"Would you have fled from me? My father means to give me the Dragon Throne. Even First Son sees this—he will step aside from family tradition to uphold it. Then you would be Empress. I would have you beside me at every dinner. Sun and moon together. Peace in every Kingdom."

She casts her eyes down, silent for a moment. "You have

run off to battle again, Jade Mountain," is all she says.

The next sound is a birdcall, from somewhere in the garden outside my bedchamber. The first announcement of dawn.

Water Song's hand tightens around mine. "Stay in this room with me, my friend!" she cries. I sweep her into my arms and lift her off the floor. I kiss her ears and throat, and she offers me, at last, her mouth. For a moment I forget, forget, and only know bliss.

When her feet touch the ground again, she parts from me, and looks at me, alight with her own bliss. "Do you see, Jade Mountain, I do not hold the Prince! I do not touch his face. It is not the Prince I kiss!" She caresses my cheek, and brushes her lips across mine. Then she steps back, smiling, with a fiery light in her eyes.

I stare at her, afraid to think the thought that waits in her face, afraid to feel the emotion that is so ready in her. She smiles, still, from a room that is not this room, rather a room we share alone … and I, in that room alone with her, feel laughter burst from me. I am not the Prince. I have no need for the Prince, next to Water Song. I am myself, and it is myself that Water Song loves.

And Water Song laughs. *Water Song laughs!* For me! It is a wild and brilliant laugh; surely the light of her eyes has turned to sound in her belly and throat. The joy that fills me at that moment could shatter the palace walls. We laugh. I catch her up in my arms and spin around again. For this moment, which could be eternity, we are only ourselves, without name or family—we are only ourselves, and we are free.

Suddenly a sob breaks from me, and I am in tears. I drop her and stumble away. *Grief.* Water Song is quickly beside me and touches my face, a question.

"Cookpot," I answer. "My true brother" —I sob again. She clasps my hand and sinks to the floor. She presses my hand to her brow and weeps with me. Cookpot. Sacrificed, for us.

A second birdcall sounds from the garden, and another bird, far-off, answers it.

My head snaps up from where I have collapsed against a wall. The Palace has closed around us again, and dawn is nearly here. Abruptly I stride over to the ancestors' altar and snatch the sword from it. I grab Water Song by the wrist and pull her into my bedchamber. I hand her the sword, so I can lock the door, and for good measure I drag a large cabinet in front of it. Water Song stares at me wide-eyed.

"The letters should still be under my pillows," I tell her, breathing heavily. "There are two I have to show you." She gropes under the cushions and pulls out the handful of silk strips. They flutter like little banners in the pre-dawn breeze from my garden. Water Song lays them across the bed. I sort through them and find the forged letter, and Cookpot's confession.

Water Song reads the letters with her mouth slowly dropping open. Done, she sits with them on her lap, gazing off away from me. At length she says, "I already loved you. At the dinner, I would have guessed you were the one in the tree. His remorse was useless. Completely useless." She crushes the silks in her hand.

"Are you angry with him?"

"What good is anger? Cookpot had a lightning-bolt imagination; this burden was his own invention. Oh, Jade Mountain, this horror ... how I wish your father had never seen me!" Her head bows and her shoulders shake.

A flurry of birdcalls sound across the Palace gardens. I can see how the air in my bedchamber has lightened. This would be the hour my attendants would come prepare me for our departure. It is time for me to perform my last duty as Prince Jade Mountain, son of the Son of Heaven.

I gather up the silks and slide onto the bed, beside Water Song. "Shall we burn them?"

"Does it matter? The Minister has turned the whole Palace against us. When we're arrested, people will think as he and First Wife want them to think."

With a laugh, I toss the letters into the air. They curl and slip down in a rain around us, covering the bed. I reach behind Water Song and find the sword. I draw it out of its scabbard, slowly, so that its *sssssssssssssnnnnnngggggg* is soft, gentle. "We're not going to be arrested, my love," I tell her. She looks at me in alarm, probably thinking I mean to fight our way out of here. "Hush, we will not leave this room. This gift you have given me is working a spell." I wrap my arms around Water Song and lay the sword flat across her hands. Gently I turn her palms up to raise the sword. Together we balance the light, ready steel flat on our palms, an offering to some god. "By this magic, we will not be arrested," I tell her. "No soldier will touch you. And neither of us will have sight of that vile Minister, or First Wife, or this vast prison, ever again. We will be free, Water Song."

And then my General gives the command.

Like lightning my hand and arm are *obedient*. Before Water Song can take breath, I have caught up the hilt, turned the blade, and swept the lethal edge down our left arms and sliced them open from elbow to thumb. Our blood showers us, beats on the bed-curtains, rains on the floor.

Her mouth, spattered with scarlet, is wide, her eyes horrified. "Jade Mountain—" No scream, no shriek. I let the sword drop and dangle from my thumb. I embrace Water Song again with my able arm and pull her to my breast, bringing her down to the bed with me. The sword is cradled with us. "We are free, Water Song," I say, but my voice sounds far away. From another distance I can hear Water Song say weakly, "Free? This is not … not … ."

"It was all I had left to give you, Bright Lady," I say, or try to, but the room is growing less and less real. I am waking from a dream. In the dream, I would have been Emperor, but I robbed my father of his love. Or did my father rob me of mine? Justice is promised as the dream fades. It pales into morning light, as dreams do. And I remember no more. But I approach a sunlit garden; my love stands at the gate. Her name? Has floated away from her like a veil. It is only her smiling face, her brilliant eyes, and the sunlight. Or is she no different from the sunlight? I move towards her; she steps aside to let me pass into the garden, and she, or the sunlight, says this poem:

May the gods you choose
give you strength in empty places
and whisper
for the echo
Moon on snow.

I pass through the gate, and she is before me still, no different from the sunlight. She is tall, ancient, her face as pale as water, her hair gold as honey. She wears strange garments and comes towards me with graceful steps across the garden lawn, to bring me tea.

Moon on Snow

Tsu Lai fell ill. He lay gasping for life while his wife and children gathered around crying. Tsu Li came to see him and said, "Shhh! Get away from him! Do not disturb the transformation!" Leaning against the door, he said to Tsu Lai, "Great is the Maker! What will He use you for now? Where will He send you? Will He make you into a rat's gizzard or a snake's leg?"

Tsu Lai replied, "A son must go wherever his parents tell him to go! East, west, south, or north. Yin and Yang are no other than one's parents. If they brought me to the verge of death and I do not obey them, then I am only being stubborn. They are not to be blamed. The great earth burdens me with a body, causes me to toil in life, eases me in old age, and rests me in death. That which makes my life good makes my death good also. If a skilled smith were casting metal and the metal should leap up and say, 'Make me into a famous sword like Mo Yeh!' the smith would surely consider it an ill omen. Now, if by chance I were being cast into a human form and I were to say, 'Make me a man! Make me a man!' the Maker of Things would certainly consider me an ill omen. Now, if I regard heaven and earth as a great melting pot and creation and transformation as a master smith, then where can I be sent and not find it fitting? Thus, calmly I sleep and freshly I waken."

—Chuang Tzu,
Inner Chapters, "The Great Master,"
trans. Gia-Fu Feng and Jane English.

17.
FRUIT

"So, you want to know what's in there?" I waved my beer glass in a general way, but Del knew what I was pointing at. It was in the inside pocket of his leather aviator jacket, nestled between his badge and his shoulder pistol.

"No."

"After what you saw it do to me? Are you sure?"

Del grunted. A deep, tectonic sound. He got up and headed for the men's room.

"Jeez, Officer, you could at least say thank you," I muttered into the India pale ale. I polished off that glass—my second - and poured myself another from our pitcher. I considered pouring beer into Del's chaste glass of Coke. We were in a sports bar, just down the block from the appraiser's stained office. Baseball playoff highlights reeled out on the big-screen TV over the after-work drinkers' heads. Isn't that the kind of pranks guys in sports bars pulled on each other, spiking the sodas? We did it in queer bars all the time. Especially when "we" were feeling a mite *used*.

I reminded myself that Valerie L and I were the weirdos here. Just because we were rocked and rolled by these *yü*, didn't mean Del would be, or should be. It was a big step, wasn't it, that he asked for, and then stood by, my appraisal of that cheap Hong Kong sword? Let it the fuck go, I scolded myself, just let it the fuck go. But not even hearty swigs of pale ale could dampen the humming *need* present. The wake was still traveling outward from that ancient murder-suicide, and we had to navigate it.

I put my empty glass down and belched decisively. I pulled a few napkins out of the table's dispenser and fumbled in my pockets for a pen. I could at least write down what I remembered of the dragon jade's story, before time and beer obscured it. I would start at the end and work backwards. The end, the last bit, closest to memory. Beer, so helpful in separating me from the Prince, cloaking me in my own body again, proved to be an ambiguous friend, when I wanted to lift up the folds of that cloak. I shut my eyes and concentrated.

Light, and a voice whose words were felt more than heard. *A garden.* I wrote with my eyes shut, using the edge of a finger to guide my pen. Three lines of words, four ... *and a sweet melting emotion dissolves the flimsy barrier between the Light and not-Light* ... my pen stopped moving. My jaw relaxed. Maybe I drooled.

"YO!" Del thumped me firmly on the arm and I jerked awake. "You passin' out, man?"

I stretched and shook myself, blinking. "No, I feel great." Which might have been the wrong thing to say, the way Del looked at me before sliding back into the booth. But it was true. My head was clear, and my body felt positively sparkly. I turned my empty glass upside-down, and swept my pen and the scribbled-on napkin into my pocket. Hoping he'd take the hint. He didn't.

"I owe you an apology," Del said. "I see some incredible shit in my job, but this is not the kind of thing I'm used to. Look, I've never been a churchin' man, so I put no judgment on what Valerie has taught me about spirit, the Infinite Mind. But up to now it's been intellectual. I've never really seen ... well, after I let that jade go, it was like a big hand clamped down on the back of my neck. I'd never felt so shitty in my life. And then you ... Ross, that jade *took* you. You were *gone.* So I'm a little bit ... ." He made wobbly motions with his hands.

"Think of it like the first time you ever saw a Christmas tree. I always do." I was past caring whether he thought I was mad.

Apparently he was past caring whether I *was* mad, for he went on: "Just tell me what the *point* of all this is." There was desperation in his voice, and moments when he couldn't look me in the eye. "Lives. China. Murder. Empire. What was done or not done. What is the point of *knowing* it? Because if ..." He looked around for possible eavesdroppers, and lowered his voice. "If I could have been an Emperor, if I have that in me, why am I *here?* Why am I *this?*" He spread his hands to show me, not only his working man's uniform, but the coffee-darkness of his skin. On the giant TV screen behind him, a couchful of big-bellied men crammed brand-name frozen pizza into their mouths.

"All my life, I wanted to be Emperor—I mean, President." Del winced at the slip. "It's so easy for me to see clearly, I mean *clearly*, in de*tail*, what to do, how to change things practically, and peacefully. Always has been. But the Infinite Mind keeps saying, 'No.' I never finished college. Never been considered for management jobs. This is my third career." He plucked at his crisp blue collar. "So all these memories Valerie has, and you have, what good do they do? What fruit can they possibly bear?"

I had wondered, hadn't I, what Del would show me, that would tell me how deep in the fight he was. I turned over the thought that had occurred to me, and decided to go for it. "When did you start following Valerie around?" I asked softly. I had remembered Valerie L telling me about taking tea out to Del, to invite him in the house, when he knew her son at the University, and they first met. *She glided, in strange garments, across a garden to bring him tea.*

A cloud of confused fury passed over his face. It vanished, and he stared down at the table with the look of a man trying to bury delicate things. "No fruit there, either," he mumbled. I waited, gave him time. Finally he rubbed his face with those powerful hands. "I wanted to know she was all right," Del said. He gazed off over my head. Maybe he was conjuring, without my help, the memory of a sword that slashed open two arms with a single motion. "I *had* to know she was all right."

I allowed a brief silence. "So maybe the fruit," I said, "is whatever you decide to do next."

He didn't look down from whatever was over my head. Thoughts roamed over his face and through his fingers, tapping each other. I just kept my mouth shut, and my hands still.

At last he stopped, and looked at his watch. That decided it. Wonderful invention, watches. "My dinner break's almost up, I have to get back for the night shift," he explained.

"Ah, sure."

He stood and jerked his thumb at the pitcher of IPA. "Are you going to be okay driving?"

I stood up. My legs were steady under me, and my head was still clear. The bar's sound system burped to life with thundering drums and guitar chords. A stupid impulse gripped me. "I do believe I'm fine, Del," I assured him. The heavy-metal anthem kicked in, and I clicked my heels and danced across the room. I flitted among the tables and chairs, bowed to the waitress and pirouetted out the door, all the way to the parking lot. Doing so, I realized my spy satellite senses were back, minus the fever or chlorine. Del was behind me, at a distance from my dance, trying to look less like a companion and more like event security. The evening was tinged with an early fall crispness. An eighteen-wheeler roared past on the nearby highway, sending a wake of fumed air rippling through the parking lot. I spread my arms to catch its waves and walked heel-toe, heel-toe down a painted line. At my car I spun around on the ball of my foot and struck a pose against the fender.

Del stopped about twelve feet away, watching me—and to his everlasting credit, he started to laugh. He threw his hands up in surrender, and turned towards his own car. As he opened the driver's door, he shouted, "You want to appraise it?"

"Please forget you ever met me," I shouted back. "It's safer if you don't know a damn thing. Tell people it's a gorgeous fake." He waved farewell. I slid into my own driver's seat.

And when I slammed the door, the windshield cracked.

Shit, I thought. What have I done *now?*

I just wanted to go home. Leave it for tomorrow. So I did. My answering machine was blinking when I came in, but I ignored that, too, and muted the ring. Valerie L's solo viola CD, set to repeat on the player, would be my background music.

I plunged into my favorite chair, the one with its own reading lamp, snuggled in a corner by the gas fireplace (ugly fake logs still taunting me, I had never gotten around to replacing them), with a battered notebook in one hand and the bar napkin in the other. I peered at what I had written with eyes closed, along the line of my finger, and laboriously pieced together what one spirit had said to the other at the gate of Heaven.

May the gods you choose
give you strength in empty places
and whisper
for the echo
Moon on snow.

Something was off. Han Dynasty poetry is as pure as the blues. It's earthy, particular, passionately attentive to connections between the senses and the heart. Maybe my translation was bad, maybe I was misremembering the moment. Hell, maybe I was overestimating my ear for literature. But this did not ring like Han poetry.

Or ... maybe it wasn't a poem at all.

It didn't have to be. A spirit leaving the body behind, my Tibetan study maintained, entered into a realm of existence called *bardo*—where the phantoms of one's Earthly desires, fears and prejudices would approach as if they were real, and trick you into a knee-jerk dive into somebody's womb for another rebirth. So the Prince, entering this state, was approached by a mind-phantom that looked like the Concubine, and *whammo!* Dive, womb, birth, and the lines of karma re-activated when she—as in, Valerie L—walked across a pretty lawn with a cup of tea.

Neat.

Awfully neat.

Kind of depressingly neat, when I thought about it.

Because the words I held in my hand were more alive than that. Open-ended. Strange as a dream. My eyes wouldn't leave them; I read the lines over and over. *Moon on snow.*

There was something familiar about this feeling. Something that made the walls, and the piece of paper, seem to breathe along with me. Something Big.

The same Something Big present in the gallery, when Valerie L shook my hand.

No, wait, now it was clearer, it had outlines and a scent of character. What breathed here was that *Other*, the what/who that had receded from me as the dragon jade left my hand—a name (forgotten), a presence (felt), that made *my memories* shimmer in parallel to the Prince, the Concubine, the Emperor, the Poet.

It seemed impossible, but the thought was there ... that this verse had been spoken to *me*—piggybacked on the Prince. Or to that *Other* I had been, whom the Concubine knew. Or *through* me/*Other*, to someone else.

May the gods you choose
give you strength in empty places
and whisper
for the echo
Moon on snow.

Moon on snow. It echoed, certainly, in very personal spaces I hadn't paid attention to lately. Those echoes traced the shape of some fierce longing that moved through my deeps like a whale. But I couldn't be certain yet of its full nature; I could only feel the rippling wake of its movement.

Like that night in the hot tub, like this evening in that parking lot, the world felt loose, like netting, full of holes. Strange things were washing through. I looked up from the notebook paper and saw that it was morning.

Apparently time washed through, too.

My body, however, fully felt the hours I'd been in my chair, whether I had been asleep or, um, *elsewhere*. I struggled up and grabbed my keys. It was time for a long, long walk. I snapped off the CD player, which was beginning its 250th repetition, and said to Valerie L's picture on the cover, "This is all *your* fault."

The sunlight hurt. I shook my head and stretched my face, trying to clear it, searching for that sense of reality I'd been so chummy with yesterday. God damn that woman, why did she have to bring in those jades and make me *look at them?*

I stopped with a jolt, hearing Albert Jarro's anguished voice echo behind my own in my head. I looked around, finally. Habit had brought me within a block of the gallery. I spun around and headed back uphill. I still had my resignation letter in my inner jacket pocket, but the last thing I wanted was to run into Albert today. Or any day. Ever again. My wallet had a couple of stamps in it, so I dropped the letter in a mailbox.

This time I walked with my eyes open and my head up. I took deep breaths as I walked. Lo and behold, it was a pretty day. How long had it been since I had taken a simple walk around my neighborhood, and looked things over? As a free agent, I could take in the trees, the sound of the autumn breeze in their branches, the homes and their gardens, the gently buckling sidewalks, all without my reflex of appraisal.

After a while, the streets led me to a park, folded in between the hills of my neighborhood. Had I ever known it was there? It's so easy to forget the shape of the immediate world when you're building a career on the distant past. This pleasant little spot had mature trees spreading their arms around a broad playground of the old type, with a big swing set and a tall slide. I walked past them to a huge old log that had been stripped of bark and laid down as a bench under the sheltering trees. It was early enough that the log was still cool. A breeze gusted through the park, agitating the trees, chilling my face. Autumn really had arrived. Dry leaves blew past me with a fragrant rustling to prove it. There was a ridge of gray cloud just visible above the treetops. The downhill side of another year, beginning today.

Moon on snow. The recollection of another season turned my mind to where I'd been, and who I'd been, the previous autumn. The gallery and Albert were merely backdrops to the memory of Dave leaning back into the car and giving me one last kiss. Affectionate, then hungry, then gentle, then barely touching, our lips and tongues became spiritual, feathery, pulses of energy. And then we were parted, but it seemed not really parted, as Dave turned away and let the car door fall shut. His shoulders hunched and he thrust his fists into his jeans as he walked up the path to the monastery entrance. At the door he was met by an assistant lama, a scholar with a strict mouth. Dave relaxed as he spoke to the monk; something dropped from his shoulders. He shed something, some unnecessary self, as the monastery door swung shut and cut the current that joined us. Beyond the monastery door, he was absorbed into the river of Dharma, tradition, and vows. Sitting in the car, I felt that the unnecessary thing he had dropped was me. I knew nothing of the betrayals and lies he had fed me as he floundered towards his pure effort. I only knew that I had wanted to share a vital treasure of my life with him. And what did that mean to me, that "treasure?" Was it a thing to present, display, show off? To Dave, it was more; it was life. He had claimed it, it had accepted him, he belonged to it.

A year later, finally, I knew how human he had been behind the great romance of his discovered vocation. How human I had been, suffering the romance, blind to all else. The energy of that gut-deep howl echoed through me, as if I had just finished bellowing it on the yacht. This was followed by the memory of Ash, that grin crawling up the side of his face and the wild, hilarious look in his eye just before he burst out laughing. It would have been so easy to slide into the well-worn drama of betrayal, outrage. But Ash, although no less snookered in love than I, saw comedy. And so, hardly conscious of his action, he laughed, and rescued me.

A high-pitched squeal of delight popped my reverie. On the park's morning-washed hillside, a broad-chested young Latino father played with his toddler son. They sat in the grass and tossed the first dry leaves of the season into the air, over and over. For the son, it was the first time this game had ever been played in all the world, and he was fit to burst with ecstasy. The father, enchanted with his child's joy, lay down in the leaves and slowly rolled down the hill, thus carefully instructing his son. The little child watched him, then dove forward on the grass and rolled down to his father's waiting hands. Father scooped up Son, and ran back up the hill with him, so they could roll down together. Father scooped him up again, ran up the hill, and they rolled down again, yelling, "*Wheeeee!*" Perhaps the fourth time down, Father lay panting in the grass instead of scooping up Son, so Son climbed up and down the hill of his belly for a while. Eventually Father hauled himself up, took his Son's hand and they walked over to the swings, where Father pushed Son gently, not too high. I watched them until they tired of that, too, and ambled off towards home, hand in hand.

Moon on snow. The breeze had stilled, like the park was holding its breath. I stood and walked up to the top of the hill, and stretched out on the ground. It wasn't a steep slope, I had to push myself through the downhill roll, but the smell of the crushed dry leaves was smoky and sweet. The slope petered out and I came to a stop. I lay there looking at the sky, as gray clouds calmly took possession of the blue. Cool sleepiness drifted up from the earth and grass, and a bearded old Chinese man bent over me, smiling. Fresh red blood stained the crotch of his robe.

I shot upright, flooded with adrenaline, gulped air, my head pounding. Of course there was no Chinese man anywhere in sight. My secret inward voice seemed to have become a buzzing chorus. It hummed a profound irritation with that old Chinese man: *That poor castrated bastard, he never got it right*, was the gist. Oh, my God. Had Sima Qian, the Grand Historian himself, stepped through the netting of the world and poked me with his toe?

I stood up and hastily brushed off leaf crumbs. The buzzing irritation had a distant quality, like a fizz rising up around me; part of me, but not really me. The *Other*. Someone whom the Grand Historian had misread, or ignored. Too bad, Whoever You Are, I silently rebuked the *Other*, as I left the park for home

at a brisk walk. Bitch all you want. Sima Qian is all we have
anymore. He's *it* for Han.

I stopped, right there on the sidewalk.

Of course.

I set off again, at a trot. Now that I had the whole story of
the *yü* — *my* story of the *yü*, the one they told *me* -- it was time,
at last, to check in with Sima Qian. Maybe he didn't always get
it right, but he had to have *something* that sounded like the tale
of these jades.

I slipped the book off its shelf and carried it into the living
room. The phone was blinking but I decided to let the messages
wait just a little longer. Lodged again in my favorite chair, I ran
my fingers over the text, scanning for illicit love and peasant
rebellions.

The first Han Emperor, Liu Pang, had nothing for me. But,
as always happened, I could not resist devouring every word
about his wife, the Dowager Empress Lü. Her reign after Liu
Pang's death, behind a series of incapable boy-Emperors, was as
riveting as a horrific highway pileup, stacked with murders and
mutilations. There was no mention of a too-prescient young
musician losing his eyes and tongue, but that would have been
small potatoes. Then she died, and there came the familiar,
comforting words, "… and all members of her family clan were
executed, down to the last child." Sighs of relief were heard for
generations after.

It was in the reign of the next Emperor, Wen, that my
scanning fingers stopped; the living room hummed and fizzed;
not once, but three times. Each time, I slipped a scrap of paper
between the pages to mark the place. After Wen's eldest son,
Jing, ascended to the dynastic throne, I went back and re-read
the marked pages.

No one would say the information was an exact match. No
one would say it *proved* anything. *Poor castrated bastard, he never
got it right*, my inward voice/chorus buzzed in frustration.

I closed the book and gazed thoughtfully at nothing, while
the early afternoon's cloud-filtered light meandered through
my living room. How *could* he have gotten it right? I wondered.
His own life was testimony—awful pun there!—to the disaster
of one offense, one wrong word spoken at the wrong time to
the Emperor, about the wrong man. Nevertheless, the Grand

Historian had had the balls (oh Mind, will you never stop?!) to bear the pain and humiliation of castration rather than commit a socially acceptable suicide, because he had a job to finish: the history of his country. He had made a promise to his father, the previous Grand Historian, at the man's deathbed. The son would resurrect the history of China, out of the oblivion that was the Qin Dynasty's legacy.

But how could he have gotten it right? In that time, the legends that lived longest were accepted as fact. Shihuang-ti, the First Emperor of China, the one and only ruler of the Qin Dynasty, had ordered all the books burned and the historians murdered; he was determined that all history and culture would begin with *him* (establishing an unfortunate pattern in his nation's psyche, sad to say). Roughly two hundred years later, as the next Dynasty, the Han, looked like it was wobbling towards its downfall, Sima Qian must have known that scholarly sources would gloss events to make themselves, and the powerful ones they served, look good. All he had, really, was his own gut judgment. There must have been days when he just sat and stared at his roomful of notes. There was no way he could foresee that the Han would pick up again, after a brief interruption, and his work would be considered a history of the *"Former* Han." He was looking at the past, not the future. In awful reality he was cut off from the future. His political position was destroyed. All he had was a title, boxes of notes, a mission, and incessant pain between his legs.

I ran my fingertips around the edges of the book, the pages worn soft and oily as flesh. This was the fruit of the Grand Historian's courage. I opened it again, to the index, to see how much more I could learn about the reign of Emperor Wen.

Not ten minutes later, I slipped another scrap of paper into the book, and closed it. Emperor Wen and the Grand Historian held out to me what could be an answer to Del's question.

My message machine held nine messages, including Ash, who had returned my call more than twenty-four hours ago, suggesting the next Monday night for our dinner together. I immediately called him back to leave a message on *his* voice mail, that Monday was fine, and I would try calling again. Tag, Mr. Astronaut, you're it.

There was also a chirpy-voiced woman who identified herself as a volunteer at the Buddhist temple. "Just to remind you?! That tonight is our talent show?! In the Lower Hall?! And our monk Trinley will be emcee?!" Trinley—that would be Dave.

Six months ago I had come across a key ring of his in a drawer, the last artifact of our two-year liaison. I threw it in the trash with great force. At that moment, his only crime had been to prefer a celibate spiritual discipline to life with me. Now that I knew what the run-up to his ordination had really been like, it all seemed to have happened in a weird dream. No point in getting upset over any of it. I wondered how that feeling would hold up to the sight of him animated as he used to be, entertaining a roomful of people as he used to do.

Well, not entirely as he used to do, I discovered. No green tights and tunic this time, topped with a motorcycle jacket, announcing him as the Elf of Bad Attitude. No slouch, or hand on hip with one knee flexed, cigarette clipped delicately between two fingers, smoke curling languidly past his thick-lashed eyes. No, none of that. Dave had learned to stand up straight. I couldn't help noticing how this allowed his maroon and gold robes to hang beautifully on his frame—and that he'd put on a bit of weight, which became him. But the open freshness of his freckled face (sculpted cheekbones notwithstanding) suggested that he had recovered his natural state, as the best little boy his mother ever saw. As he wielded the microphone like that long-lost cigarette, it was evident that he was on his way to becoming the world's first fully ordained, Tibetan Buddhist stand-up comedian. I noticed people in the audience glancing over at the temple's head lama to see if this was quite what he'd had in mind when he arrived from Kathmandu to anchor the Dharma in American culture. But our Rinpoche, our elderly Precious One, our root guru, was giggling and slapping his knees, so everybody loosened up. I chuckled quietly under the guffaws as Dave/Trinley made fun of himself, a gay American transitioning to life as a monk. But as the room's laughter built, Rinpoche fell quiet. I realized he was watching me.

My heart lurched. The old lama knew what nobody else had registered: Trinley had not yet mentioned me. As if I had had no role in his becoming a monk.

The lama's eyes were soft and bright behind his glasses. His gaze touched me like a kind hand. His understanding made it all right to feel all the un-named things I was feeling. His kindness stretched wide the net of the world. All of my hurt washed through. There was no catch in my throat, only the amplified sound of my own breathing and heartbeat.

Trinley's spiel intervened. He was into a long story about the big yard sale when he sold all of his possessions—which happened to be on the parking strip outside my building. "So this guy, single guy, comes walking past, and he does the look, you know, the yard sale look." Trinley demonstrated, and Trinley can do yard sale shoppers like Richard Pryor did junkies. He caught impeccably the slowed pace, the head turn, that lean to the side to study the merchandise while keeping the rest of the body pointing down the sidewalk. The audience was in stitches. They'd known this guy, they'd seen this guy, they'd been this guy. Trinley stretched it out like the pro he could have been, if only. He then mimicked the fellow's scan of the CD collection, and his knowing, "'Aaaaaaahh! You're *over* Barbra.'" The audience fell apart.

My jaw dropped. I remembered this guy. His remark had been loud enough to carry, and Dave had laughed. Then I got busy with a few customers, and forgot about it … until I noticed that the guy was still there, chatting with Dave; and again, later, he stood with a handful of CDs and greenbacks, ready to pay. What was odd was, he turned away from Dave and wrote something on the money before handing it over. I glimpsed all this in passing as I dealt with a sudden visit by the building manager, and forgot about it once more.

Now it came rumbling back. That had to have been his phone number on the money. Dave had disappeared for a couple of hours that evening, and when he came back we had a fight because he had left me alone in an apartment full of boxes.

A sound escaped me that wasn't a laugh, although it was high-pitched. Fortunately Trinley was delivering his final punchline, and my sound was quickly masked by the audience's laughter and applause. I clamped both hands over my mouth and squeezed my eyes shut. I wanted to laugh and applaud, too, but not at his standup routine. My sounds were meant for his performance a year ago—as "Dave" went down kicking and screaming on the way to rebirth as "Trinley."

Life, of course, went on while I covered my eyes and whimpered or whatever into my hands. I could hear, beyond the waves of emotion washing through me, Trinley's voice introducing someone, and the spatter of applause. I rubbed my eyes, checking for tears and snot. When I opened them, I saw Betsy positioning herself behind an electric keyboard.

Run! said Habit. *Wait, look at her*, said Reality.

Somewhere, she had found a pantsuit of midnight-blue velvet. A new mala made of large rosewood beads, turquoise and silver hung around her neck, vibrant against the blue velvet. Her coarse black hair still resisted combing, but her face was pink with excitement. "These are some Dharma songs I wrote," she said, smiling down at the keyboards. "I'm sorry if they're boring." (*What did I tell you?* said Habit. *Shut up*, said Reality.)

And she sang. Good God. Betsy, my poor nemesis, baffled by everything normal, had a magnificent voice. Her first song was about a duck watching the former prince Shakyamuni starve himself on a riverbank; the duck wondered why that man didn't just float and fly. Her second song was about sitting at a bus stop and imagining the rather awful people there as a painting in a museum. The audience applauded that one loudly. Betsy glanced up shyly, then quickly looked back down at the keyboard. "This next one isn't finished, I think," she said in her flat speaking voice. "I don't think I have all the words yet, but here goes. Oh. It's called 'The Noble Avalokiteshvara's Invitation to the Venerable Shariputra.'" People edged forward on their folding chairs. I was gratified to realize that everyone else was as gobsmacked as I at this new, unimagined Betsy. She lifted her head, eyes closed, and sang:

Moon on snow
A treasure-house
That will not outlast your skin
Nor even one foot's tread.

I went rigid, all thought frozen. *Moon on snow?!* My inner chorus buzzed and fizzed ferociously: *Again, again! Something has been stolen from me!* But there was no stopping the music, or her powerful voice.

Gold on water
Scattered daily by the Sun
Spent in an hour
No more, no more.

Look again
at those who surround you –
we are laughing
mouths open to the sky
delighting in you.
Join us when you can!

Shake loose of victory
And her sister, defeat.
They are burdens chaining your legs.
Join us when you can!

Her melody purled and trailed away, leaving an awkward silence. Betsy's face flushed scarlet. "I'm sorry," she squeaked, near tears. "I said it wasn't finished."

For a split second the room was utterly silent. Then a man cried out, "Bravo!" And the crowd exploded in applause, rising to their feet, stomping and cheering. Betsy's eyes opened wide in shock. She stared at the crowd's eruption, then bolted into the chairs, down the central aisle. She went right past me, where I sat on the aisle, still too fried to stand up and applaud. I turned to watch her pass … and what I saw hanging down her back turned my buzzing inner outrage to a rushing of winds passing through the net of the world.

Betsy's mala had a large ornament tied between the guru bead and the gold silk tassel. It was a jade thumb ring, a white stone with red markings like spattered blood. One edge of the ring was pulled outward, making it an archer's ring, not a scholar's. If I looked at it under a microscope, I would probably see that it was more than two thousand years old.

When I could raise my eyes from the thumb ring, the crowd had not yet ended its ovation. I had to stand to see whom she had run to in the crowd. She had her fat arms wrapped around, and her face buried in the bosom, of Valerie L. The tall woman hugged Betsy tight, and kissed her on the top of her head. Her fingers caressed the thumb ring, held it lightly, then let it go; it swung gently against Betsy's back.

18.
BACK

Two days later, I handed Valerie L three envelopes. One was addressed to Del, one to Greg, and the third to Betsy.

"Well, now you *know!*" she had cried, with a big grin, as she swept into the café and plopped herself down. Her happy clamor stopped with the envelopes.

Back in the crush of astonished Buddhists after the talent show, Betsy would not let go of Valerie L's arm. "This is my music teacher," she told everyone proudly, and frequently. Rather than let Betsy overhear me asking her music teacher for a coffee date, I put a note in Valerie L's hand. It wasn't until I was driving home that I knew exactly what I needed that meeting for.

Valerie L held the envelopes in her hands and looked at them, with a listening tilt to her head, like a bird. She was letting her Touch work.

"You're not going to tell them what you saw?" she asked, surprised.

"I'm filling in holes," I replied. "I think you'd agree that the story itself is just for us—you and me. It's pushed us, hasn't it? Set us in motion. Maybe Greg will benefit from knowing his part, but Del isn't interested, and Betsy ..." I shrugged. "You'd know best about her."

Valerie L kept that birdlike listening look, this time looking at me. "You're dropping the provenance too, aren't you?"

"That only mattered to Albert and the gallery. Oh, I didn't tell you—I'm done with the Albert Jarro Gallery, and with Albert. Frankly, the jades kicked me out. They made me see what I hadn't wanted to see, what was happening to me in that world."

"Del told me what you did for him. That was marvelous."

I was glad somebody thought so, but I restrained myself from saying it. "He asked me a question, afterwards, that I addressed as best I could," I said instead, "but I don't know if he fully understood me. There's a passage from Sima Qian in that envelope, that might help."

She turned the envelope over. "Can you tell me what it is?" she asked with a mischievous glint in her eye.

"Use the Force, Princess." I returned. "Sima Qian, *Records of the Grand Historian.*"

"Oh, my God. You found the Emperor!"

"You and I would love to think so, but don't make a dissertation of it. I suggest you let Del read it first, then he can read it aloud to you. Take it for what it's worth."

She turned the envelope again, studying it. "I think it will be worth a lot." She tucked it into her cloth shoulder bag.

"Speaking of worth," I said, "the business card I put in with in Greg's letter is for a bookstore that can buy out his stock of CDs, and he can get back to building guitars. I laid out a rather broad hint, and I hope he takes it. I'm waiving the usual broker's fee, by the way."

A slow smile spread like butter over Valerie L's face. I realized, with no small welling of satisfaction, that I had surprised her. We took another moment of silence to sip coffee. I dandled my mala's jade, hidden in my palm.

"When did you find out about Betsy?" I asked.

"It's funny—she's one of my music therapy clients. We've been slogging away for years now, and her progress has been erratic. But the same week I came in to you with the jades, she had a major breakthrough. Something just lifted. On a hunch, I showed her the thumb ring. She immediately put it on her left thumb, before I'd said a word. And music started pouring out of her. The Poet was there, right there in front of me. I could see the Chinese man superimposed on her, right down to the dimples. He was very happy. Well, you could see the change in Betsy - a week later she's singing in public!"

I shifted uncomfortably. There was something I was supposed to remember, something that fit in right here, but I couldn't think what it was. "Well, the envelope has the final verse to her song," I said. *I heard it when I held the dragon jade,* I wanted to say, but my throat closed up and my face suddenly felt hot. The now-familiar fizzing of the *Other* started up again, but at a distance. Its foot-stamping fury was weak and faded, like a child nearing the end of its tantrum. *I want what is mine, I want what is mine.*

Valerie L was looking at me again, like she could hear that spectral ruckus. "You wrote it?" she asked. I smiled wanly, lightly massaging my tight throat. "You can let Betsy think so," I managed. That seemed to pacify the *Other*. My throat relaxed and the heat left my face.

Valerie L was still looking at me. "Tell me the words," she pleaded quietly. I couldn't help meeting her eyes; her regal stillness, containing a hunger, compelled me. In our gaze, the net of the world stretched open again, and the fizz of those *Other* lives rose around us. I recited:

May the gods you choose
give you strength in empty places
and whisper
for the echo
Moon on snow.

The fizz around us receded, calmed. The wake of ancient, horrible events had finally played out into a limitless ocean.

Her face was raw emotion, bottomless in its reality. "Thank you," she said softly.

The silence built under our locked gaze until I thought I would fly to pieces. "So, have you been to China, this time?" I asked, in a brittle voice.

"No."

"Good. Don't. Don't go back. It will break your heart." My voice cracked. I felt tears brim my eyes. Valerie L grabbed my hand. I squeezed it and bolted from the café.

Yes, I stiffed her for the check. But I think she didn't mind.

I strode briskly down the sidewalk, blind to my direction, chest heaving in dry little sobs. I had chosen a café in the city's 19th-century pioneer neighborhood, which now seemed a picture of the net of the world: a stone and iron latticework of arches, walls, railings, alleyways, with the blurred wash of Human history rushing through in a torrent of colors and lights. Not even Sima Qian could make these rapids stand still long enough to become legend, fit for memory.

I stopped at a crosswalk to wait for the light. In that pause, surrounded by human bodies, the *Other*'s memories fizzed up and exuded one more misty scene. I half-closed my eyes to let it coalesce and gather light. It was the Emperor, that old warrior, collapsed in grief on his floor, robes in disarray, following the funeral for his son, his noble Prince and victorious General, the choice of his heart to inherit an Empire. The man's wails struck me through. A thought welled up in my heart, so fiercely that it burst out in a silent cry to him: *But they only loved each other. There was no plot. It was only love.* Whereupon the Emperor raised his head and looked at me. At that *Other.* And faded away.

The street light changed, and the circle of human bodies around me moved forward. I was a few steps late.

Safely on the other side of the street, I sidled into a bus shelter and sat down. I gripped my mala's jade, letting the carved edges cut into my palms. Deep breaths cleared my head of the mist and fizz, and caused two neighboring young women to edge away, leaving me a pleasant amount of space.

Breathing, it suddenly dawned on me what could have triggered Betsy's breakthrough: my crazy demand that she set the shopping bags down. Quit shoplifting the guilt. I didn't blame her for the tragedy and nobody else did, either. It made me laugh out loud, in the bus stop. The laugh cleared my head. I was out of tissues, so I wiped my eyes on my sleeve. The two young women glanced at me and left the shelter altogether.

I no longer had any doubts about the passage from Sima Qian. It was indeed the only answer Del could have to his question about what fruit these memories could bear.

Emperor Wen promulgated the imperial decree that the punishment of the families of a criminal be invalidated, the Grand Historian wrote, *corporal punishment abolished, and other criminal punishments made more lenient. The legal reforms reaped favorable social effects.*

Sima Qian then summarized: *"personal profits not sought, criminals not punished corporally, the innocent spared." People of the posterity extracted the phrase "the innocent spared" to refer to a sound law … .* Yes, a sound law. For four hundred years, the entire length of the Han Dynasty, Emperor Wen's legal reforms shaped his Empire's idea of justice. For two millennia, Sima Qian's history book made it stay in memory.

Could it be, Del, you Prince of a man, could it be possible that you are here as you are to somehow demonstrate true justice to the world? And that hidden inside a despot's ruling was a shout of love across Heaven to a lost son?

The innocent spared. Remember this if you can.

I stood up, wondering where I was. It was not many blocks to the waterfront, so I headed there. I avoided the tourist docks with their gaudy gift shops. Further down, where the sidewalks became older and cracked, were the working docks, redolent with engine fumes, creosote, and male sweat. At the end of each long, broad pier a huge orange crane lifted containers off of ships. They wore their fealty painted on their sides: Hanjin. Yang Ming. China Shipping Co. Clan names of the new empire, which still can't help erasing its own history upon decree. The containers anchored me in the here and now, told that *Other* exactly what day it was.

Oh, yes, I saw my role in the tragedy. I was definitely there, playing my part.

I had the *shih* assassinated and his thumb-ring brought to me, still on his severed hand. Of course I read the story begun on his wood-strips, before I burned them. Then, I had the first knowledge of the still, cold bodies on the bed that had become a lake of blood. I ordered the Prince's sword and scabbard brought to me. I had the Concubine's quarters searched, and the Jade Turtle ring taken from her bed. I had it broken, so no one would ever wear it again. By my command, Water Song was not buried beside Prince Jade Mountain. Instead she was carried back to her precious temple, to be entombed in an obscure, unguarded corner of their burial field. She was erased from the Imperial History, and from every tongue.

The thumb-ring, broken turtle and the sword were buried with her. If rumor persisted that an Imperial Concubine lay in the temple's field, her grave would be easily robbed. All evidence of her existence would disappear.

Except it didn't. And she didn't. And the story didn't, caught as it was inside *yü*. Instead, my own life as Dowager Empress, kept at a distance from the reign of my First Son, was long and eventful, but has utterly vanished from human memory.

That is, unless I continue to remember. I'm not sure I want to. This world does not need an Empress. In truth it never did. The sea tells me that, and the evening air, leaning towards sunset. It's enough that I can stand here on this dock, facing west past the port's cranes, out over the water, towards China, as a man of smallish frame who looks much older than his years. I know what I was and what I did. I have forgiven, without knowing what it was I was forgiving. I have been forgiven, without a full accounting of my crimes. Still humming in the air around me is the remembered sight of my husband's desolate grief, the echoes of his weeping; I remember how it turned my success to bitter ashes in my mouth, and my glory to despair, even before my First Son was enthroned. What transcendent resolve was born in me out of that darkness has been fulfilled, on this day; in this place and time, in my life as a man pursuing beauty, and it is enough. Beyond this moment, everything is possible, including a luminous gratitude. Gratitude that being a man in my own way this time was, at last, enough. The world is new, greatly changed, yet still much the same, still exquisite and cruel, full of beauty, wonders and love.

Oh, yes. I must call Ash to confirm our dinner date.

I am ready to touch the greatness.

ACKNOWLEDGEMENTS

A first novel is too frequently called a first child, and getting it published is too easily compared to childbirth. I would rather say that being at this point, seeing my first novel come into the world, is more like a not-unexpected tumble over the edge of the nest—and the sudden discovery of wings.

I have needed great help putting this book together, and it has arrived in abundance. Interdependence is the marrow of our lives on this little Earth. My gratitude is enormous to the following people, and I hope that what returns to each of them for their generosity brings them as much or more happiness as I feel now.

Roland Crawford, for reports from deep inside an art dealer's world; everyone who read and critiqued early drafts; William, for the gift of a laptop; Marguerite Kearns and the Owl Mountain Retreat Center, for awarding me a week's solitude in the New Mexico high desert; all the friends who donated support to get me out there; the desert itself, for its profound silence and rigor; all of my housesitting clients from 2004-2006, for sheltering me while the book got written; Rondi Lightmark and Ken Goodall, for fine editorial eyes; David Clayton-Thomas, for permission to use a bit of "Spinning Wheel," his 1968 hit with Blood, Sweat & Tears; Dr. Jeffrey Schoening, scholar, for the hymnlike translations of Dharma texts in use at Sakya Monastery of Tibetan Buddhism in Seattle, Washington; Arch Brown and the Arch and Bruce Brown Foundation, for honoring *Yü* with Second Place in the 2006 Arch and Bruce Brown Foundation Fiction Contest; the Pacific Northwest Writers Association, for naming *Yü* a Finalist, Adult Novel, in the 2006 Literary Contest; all the people I glimpsed and overheard, all the books that fell into my hands and images that made me stop and gaze, all of the subtle messages that yes, I was doing the right thing; and of course, first and finally, Monica, Humble Concubine, without whom the story never would have happened.

CPSIA information can be obtained at www.ICGtesting.com
Printed in the USA
LVOW06s1731010813

345833LV00006B/782/P